NANSHE CHRONICLES 3

CURSED SAINT CAPER

JESSIE KWAK

First edition August 2022

Cover elements by Shad.off, CGPitbull, and Daniel Zadorozny

Cover design by Jessie Kwak and Robert Kittilson

Edited by Kyra Freestar

www.jessiekwak.com

THERE'S MORE TO THE STORY!

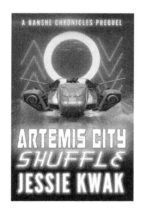

... in *Artemis City Shuffle*.

Raj and Lasadi may both be down on their luck. But as a series of near misses and close calls spin their futures into a collision course, that's about to change.

Get the free Nanshe Chronicles prequel novella!
jessiekwak.com/nanshe

CURSED SAINT CAPER

NANSHE CHRONICLES 3

What do you remember?

CHAPTER 1
RUBY

EVERY TIME RUBY QUIÑONES LIFTS HER HAND TO KNOCK on this door, she's twelve years old again and terrified: of what's on the other side, of who might open it, of the baby strapped to her back who won't stop crying. Of the blank spots in her memory where her past used to be.

No one passes this door without noticing. It's almost twice the height of any other door in this quiet residential neighborhood, and set into the solid stone of Artemis City's outer wall, the convent behind it dug into the core of the dwarf planet itself. It's painted a warm blue, the color of the Indiran sky, Ruby has always been told. As a child, Ruby hadn't believed anything natural could be so blue. Now that she's been to Indira, she knows the color is perfect. The blue sweeps upwards to a gorgeous circular stained glass window done in abstract shades of amber and gold that glows from within, a quiet beauty that instills reverence in passersby even if they aren't devout.

Ruby doesn't remember if anyone paused that day to watch her twelve-year-old self raise a shaking fist to knock. That terrified girl knew three things. Her name. Her baby brother's name. And that whoever lived behind the door were the only ones who could help her.

Now she's here to help them.

"You don't see many people building into the wall," Lasadi says behind her, and Ruby shakes off the memories.

She's not alone this time. The captain is here, along with Ruby's little brother, Alex — and Jay and Raj. Ruby's stomach flutters at the thought of introducing one little family to the other, although that's not exactly right, is it? Aside from Alex, these people are just crew. The people behind the door are simply those who raised her. Ruby's family vanished in the black hole of her memory.

And this isn't a happy reunion. They're here on business; Ayalasi Kateri is waiting for them, and the rest of the ayas are pinning their hopes on Ruby.

"Wait until you see why," Alex says to Lasadi, grinning. If he's worried about returning to the convent, he's not showing it. "It's a bit more common in Shīn Sector, though — there are more natural caves here."

Artemis City is bored deep into the core of Artemis, the largest in the chain of dwarf planets in Durga's Belt. The city's entrance is the enormous ring of the port, built on the planet's surface. A glass bubble nearly two kilometers across protects the actual city below, which consists of two parts. The Bell, one hundred stories of open well bristling with spiraling walkways, inter-linking webs of bridges and passageways, overlapping layers of commerce and housing and business that bleed into each other. And the Vault, the deep core levels of housing, office complexes, and industry head-quarters.

Shīn Sector is about two-thirds of the way down the Bell, one of the many residential swaths at the edge of the commercial hub. It's not a fashionable neighbor-hood, nor is it poor. It's simply unassuming, and not the sort of place most residents of Artemis City would acci-dentally find themselves unless they were visiting someone who lived there.

Or looking for a safe place to abandon their children.

But she's stalling. Ruby knocks.

The door opens quickly — as it always does, as it did that first day. Today an old man in a robe the same sky blue as the door stands before her. He breaks into a grin. "Sweet Ruby," he says, holding out his arms; she steps into them and breathes in strong black tea, incense, a whiff of tobacco.

"Aya Julio," she says with a smile when she steps back, her hands still on the old man's arms. "You look well."

Julio laughs. "Lies are a sin, my girl." He pulls Alex into a hug, then turns cheerfully to greet the rest.

"Aya Julio, these are my friends. Captain Lasadi Cazinho, Raj Demetriou, and Jay Kamiya."

Julio grasps each of their hands in turn, then holds out an arm to welcome them through the door. "The ayalasi is waiting for you."

Ruby lets the others walk ahead, watching their reactions. Walking into the convent is like walking through a veil. On this side, the bustle of the city and everyday life presses down like an invisible hand. On that side, pressures you didn't even realize you were carrying simply melt away. She can tell the others feel it. Jay takes a deep, calming breath. Raj's smile broadens. Even Lasadi's tense shoulders seem to relax — if a touch, only.

And they're still just in the entry corridor: simple carved stone, painstakingly and lovingly excavated from the heart of Artemis itself. Warm recessed lights cast a faintly golden glow over the pillars and the murals between them.

Aya Julio leans in as Ruby closes the door behind her. "I'd hoped to see the lovely Kitty today," he murmurs. "Are you two . . . ?"

"We are not," Ruby says firmly. Saints in hell, she hopes she won't be fielding that question this entire trip; her ex-girlfriend charmed the entire convent last time Ruby visited with her.

Julio squeezes Ruby's elbow, then turns to the rest of the group. "Your first time visiting?" he asks. When he gets nods from everyone — including a cheeky one from Alex — his eyes brighten. "Let me give you the tour." Julio brushes a reverent hand over the nearest stone column. "The convent's founders chose to dig deeper into Artemis rather than build out in the Bell. You'll see why in a second. But it was all a labor of love, an entire generation's work to create this space. The entry corridor is nearly fifty meters long, and as we continue in, you'll notice . . ."

Ruby tunes him out as they walk — she's heard the tour a hundred times, and Aya Julio never tires of new visitors to give it to. After a moment, Raj falls back beside her.

"Now I know where you and Alex get your gift of gab," he murmurs. "I thought convents were supposed to be quiet."

"You can imagine me taking a vow of silence, can you?" Ruby says. "No, this is a teaching convent. Most days it's filled with rowdy local young ones, but there are areas reserved for silent contemplation." She smiles at their guide's back. "I've never seen Aya Julio there, for sure."

Raj laughs, but his smile is shaded with concern. "You good?"

"Course I am."

Of course she is. She's in the closest place she's ever had to a home, which means the uneasiness gnawing at her gut is entirely about why they've been asked here. She motions for him to join the rest of the group.

"Come on, then," she says. "We're almost to the good bit."

Ruby loves watching newcomers' faces when they see why the convent's founders tunneled out through hard rock rather than building in the already-excavated Bell.

It was to reach the Chasm.

Aya Julio winks at her, then turns to watch the rest as they step out of the entry corridor and onto the fifth-floor landing. The Chasm is a natural cavern, nearly one hundred and fifty meters long, and thirty meters at its widest point. Twelve levels of balconies line the walls, scalloped with the natural contours of the stone, nearly kissing where they come together in the upper levels.

Warm, natural-looking light streams down from the ceiling and undersides of balconies, almost mimicking the most pleasant aspects of sunlight. Below, the ground floor is a garden, lush yet tidy, with winding paths, benches for meditation, and a few tables.

The Chasm isn't busy — it's outside of school hours, and most of the ayas and boarders are probably doing chores or preparing for evening prayers. A few figures in sky-blue robes are weeding the garden, and there, in the central meditation ring, Ayalasi Kateri sits in instruction with a pair of students in apprentice robes.

Ruby's heart lurches. Kateri had been the one to open the door to Ruby and her baby brother seventeen years ago, serving on door duty long before she took the mantle of ayalasi. Ruby still remembers the way Kateri's eyebrows drew together in worry, the way she'd glanced right and left down the passageway as though looking for the origin of the children on her doorstep. She still remembers the reassuring warmth of Kateri's hand in hers when Ruby finally got up the courage to say what she'd been instructed to: "I'm supposed to ask you for help."

Aya Julio touches her arm, shaking her free from the memories. The others are squeezing into the lift. "I'm not one for stairs anymore," Julio says as he guides Ruby in. "Though I don't know if young Alex here even knows we have stairs in the convent." Julio shakes his head as the lift begins its gentle descent. "I can't tell you the number of times I caught him climbing up and down the balconies, flashing lights at his friends and causing mayhem."

"Imagine how many times you didn't catch me," Alex says.

Julio's laugh is warm and rich and infectious. "I try not to imagine what you get up to when I'm not around, child. Worry isn't good for old hearts."

Ruby can imagine it, but she hadn't seen much of it. She left when Alex was seven, herself a young woman who either needed to take an aya's vows, or find her own way in the world. Alex had cried for her to take him with her, but what could she have done? She was eighteen. She didn't know how she was going to care for herself, let alone a little boy.

He was better off staying here. He kept his schooling up, he always had enough to eat, and she came back to see him once a week — at least at first. He was lost in his gaggle of friends soon enough, and if he ever resented her, he's never said it. She studies him now, that grin as he teases Aya Julio.

Does he remember begging her to stay? Does he remember crying every time a visit finished? Does he remember the absurd dots-and-dash code he insisted they write their letters in those first few years? Probably not.

The lift opens into the garden, and Aya Julio leads them down the meandering path, past the small trickling fountain, the flowering shrubs carefully manicured and bursting with the scents of cardamom and cinnamon and honeyed nectar. Alex greets the two ayas who are weeding by name; Ruby doesn't recognize them.

Ayalasi Kateri excuses herself from the young apprentices when she sees Ruby and the rest coming, rising easily to greet them. She's younger than Julio, but still it seems she's aged a decade since Ruby's last visit, her light brown hands faintly spotted, new lines around her deep gold eyes. How much of her once-dark hair beneath the ayalasi's veil is pure silver?

Ruby bows her head, and Kateri brushes the warm backs of her fingers down Ruby's cheek.

"Heya, Ayalasi," Alex says, with a grin that flashes dimples and a bow too perfunctory to be properly respectful; Kateri shakes her head at him, but can't quite hide her smile. The ayas could never throw up a shield against the little charmer, could they. He got away with three times what Ruby ever did — and things she never would have dared attempt.

"Please tell me you're not bringing him back to us," Kateri says wryly to Ruby, then turns to the others. "I hope Alexander Abdul is not causing you a fraction of the trouble he's brought to me."

"He's more than earned his place on our crew," Lasadi says, stepping forward to mimic Ruby's bow. "Thank you for having us. I'm Lasadi Cazinho, captain of the *Nanshe*."

"Come," says Kateri when Lasadi has finished introductions. "It's quiet now, but soon everyone will be heading to the chapel for prayer. Let's speak in my chambers."

Ruby's never seen the ayalasi's chambers, probably because she was a good child and never got called in to have her sins read out. She crosses the threshold with a strange veneration; beside her, her brother enters nonchalantly. He'd probably been called here a dozen times in the last year alone.

Turns out the ayalasi's chambers are similar to those of the rest of the ayas — simple, practical. But the head aya also gets the benefit of a small, cheerfully lit meeting room, which Kateri has decorated with plants. A ring of cushions on the ground are the only furniture; tea is waiting on the low table in between them. Ruby almost reaches to serve before she stops herself. She's about to catch Alex's eye, but he's already moving, the youngest one in the room doing the honors. He may have gotten himself kicked out of the convent multiple times over the years, but at least he still remembers his manners when he's here.

Kateri sips her tea, then cups it in her hands. "How much has Ruby told you?"

"That an aya has gone missing," Lasadi says. "And — " The captain glances at Ruby as though worried this might be delicate. "And she cleaned out your funds."

Kateri nods. "That's the long and short of it. I would like to say the money is the least of our worries, but Aya Marga managed our finances for decades. She had access to every account, and the truth of the matter is if we can't recover that money, we could lose the convent within months."

"We'll find her, Ayalasi," Alex says, and Ruby winces. She'd love to make that promise, but if it was going to be easy, she'd have done it already. Marga disappeared without leaving a trace in any of the usual places on the network. Maybe now that Ruby's back in Artemis City she can tap her various contacts to do better work on the ground than she could virtually — but Ruby's got a terrible feeling about this.

What could make a loyal aya suddenly steal everything in the convent's treasury and vanish?

"Did you have any sign she was in trouble?" Raj asks.

Kateri's face crumbles. "I didn't notice anything, and it's my job to understand if any of us here are in trouble. But to me she seemed happy."

"Was *that* usual for her?" Lasadi asks. "To seem happy?"

Raj and Lasadi have chosen cushions next to each other, and seem to have taken charge of the conversation together without any prior discussion. It feels natural, comfortable. The awkward formality between the pair has vanished since they returned to the *Nanshe* from New Manila — along with the previous sexual tension. They're definitely not sleeping together — the *Nanshe*'s not a big ship — but Ruby can't tell if they simply decided to be friends. Raj didn't rise to her bait when she'd tried to pry.

Kateri purses her lips, gaze to the ceiling as she thinks about Lasadi's question. Distant laughter drifts through the meeting room's open door, echoing chatter as the Chasm begins to fill with ayas and resident students on the way to prayer.

"I suppose Marga did seem a bit different lately," Kateri finally says. "She's always been very practical, but she became especially focused in the last few months. Almost to the distraction of everything else."

"What was she focused on?" Lasadi asks.

"Her study of Saint Alixhi. She was working on — well. Not a biography in the traditional sense. I'll admit I didn't quite grasp it."

"A study of Saint Alixhi's religious journey as seen through the framework of her individual paintings," says a familiar voice, and Ruby turns to the door with a smile. The woman standing there is stocky and dark-skinned, with kind eyes and a mouth more accustomed to smiling than to the worried downturn it's currently holding.

"Hello, Aya Teresa." Ruby stands, greets the woman with a warm hug, then pulls another cushion into the circle. Teresa settles onto it and takes a deep breath, accepts the cup of tea Alex pours her.

"Teresa and Marga have been paired for more than a decade," Kateri says to the others. "I thought she could help."

Ruby clears her throat. "When you contacted me, you thought Aya Marga had become obsessed with finding the relics of Saint Alixhi, not just writing about her. Why?"

"Marga always had a fascination with mystics," says Teresa. "Alixhi in particular; she'd traveled to New Manila as a child and visited her shrine, and it caught her imagination."

Ruby nods; the shrine of Saint Alixhi draws hundreds of thousands of faithful pilgrims and curious tourists every year, even though her remains have been absent from it for over a century.

"She'd been working on her book for years," Teresa continues. "But recently her focus changed: Marga wanted to *find* Saint Alixhi's missing relics. She thought the publicity could save the convent."

"Save the convent?" Ruby asks, an ugly stab of

worry in her gut at those words. "I thought she cleaned out the accounts a week ago, only."

"Finances have been tight for some time," Kateri says, matter-of-fact, like she's long accepted a potentially fatal diagnosis. "We've made it by, but there aren't as many students these days, and even fewer pilgrims. Our cushion has been slowly shrinking. Even if Marga hadn't disappeared with all our funds, we would be in this same position next year, or the year after."

Lasadi nods slowly. "Aya Marga thought finding the relics of Saint Alixhi would spark the tourist trade for you?"

"I didn't realize she was serious at first," Teresa says. "Every few years someone says they've solved the mystery of who stole them from the shrine, or they're quote-unquote 'discovered' in someone's estate. But the relics are always fakes."

"Plus they're cursed," Alex says. "There was that collector in Arquelle whose entire family died when — "

"Alexander Abdul," Kateri says wryly; Alex gives her a chagrined look.

"When did you realize she was serious?" Ruby asks.

"The day she disappeared," says Teresa. "I found this in our room." She pulls a scrap of paper from her pocket and hands it to Ruby. In tidy letters, it reads, *Went to talk to A. Leb. about St. A relics, be back soon. Love you.*

"You don't know who 'A. Leb.' is?" Ruby asks; Teresa shakes her head. She hands the paper to Lasadi, who turns it over, frowning.

"'Reach your potential,'" Lasadi reads from the fragment of text on the back. "This looks like some sort of brochure."

Teresa shrugs. "Marga handled much of our correspondence as well as the finances. People would sometimes leave brochures at the door, this may have been one of them."

Lasadi slips the scrap of paper into her pocket.

"Will you find her?" Teresa asks, eyes wide with worry. Kateri gives her a sad look, lays a hand over hers.

"Of course we will," Ruby says. She can't allow herself to believe they won't.

CHAPTER 2
RAJ

"IT'S AN ADVERTISEMENT FOR SOME SORT OF SELF-HELP seminar," Ruby says. She sets down her fruity cocktail, ice clinking in the glass as she turns the screen of her tablet to face the others.

They're in a bar called Segafredo's, which claims to have the coldest beer in Artemis City and a view of the docks, neither of which seem to be true. But it is right next door to the hostel Raj, Ruby, and Alex are all staying at while the *Nanshe* is in dock for repairs, and the food isn't half-bad if your expectations are already low. There's even some vegetables in the curry. And the neighborhood's not terrible either — close enough to the dockyards at the top of Artemis City's Bell to be cheap, far enough down that the rumble of departing ships doesn't wake you up at night. Much.

It's a good place for a private conversation; there are maybe a dozen other patrons in the bar, mostly dock-workers or belt drifters amusing themselves with the gambling tables or the screen behind the bar, which is showing an Indiran sweeps match between two teams Raj has never heard of. The bartender's blasting the soundtrack of Raj's misspent youth, songs that used to be popular on Indira about a decade ago — long enough to go out of fashion, but not quite long enough to have come back around. Alex has already made some choice comments about the constant twang of guitar strings over rumbling bass and electronic beats.

Raj leans over Ruby's tablet, holding out the note Aya Marga had left for her partner. The branding on the screen matches the fragment of flyer, and the rest of the missing phrase is made clear. "'Unlock the power of Spirit within you, and reach your true potential,'" he reads.

"It's a three-day event," Ruby says, scrolling. "Starting tomorrow. Lectures on diet, meditation, goal setting . . . What's color personality science?"

"I don't know." Jay leans forward to spear one of the curried potatoes Ruby ordered but hasn't been eating. "But Las is all sugary pink."

Lasadi flips him a rude gesture, then frowns at Ruby's screen. "Ice bath therapy? No thank you. Do you think Marga was supposed to meet 'A. Leb.' at this event?"

"Anything about saints on the conference schedule?" Raj asks. "Ruby?"

Ruby glances up, blinking, then shakes her head. Something's been bothering her since they left the convent, and he would bet it's more than Aya Marga's disappearance.

"Nothing about saints," she says. "And no A. Leb. Here you go." She hands over her tablet and picks up her curry, shooing Jay away as he tries to steal another potato. "Get your own, you."

Raj takes the tablet and settles back against the well-worn couch, scrolling through the speakers list for the conference. It's a wild mix of people with science-sounding degrees and job titles that have to be made up. "Here's your color therapy," he says. "This person's the founder — sorry, chief mixologist — of a place called Color University. She fixes the color of your aura with some sort of proprietary tech her company developed."

He recognizes a few names from the pulp talk shows that are often on in the background at the less-than-classy bars he frequents. A lot of the anti-tech movement types who sell ways to protect yourself from modern life — things like anti-nanite packs that are basically herb blends to induce vomiting, or sleeping halos to realign your mind after a day of being washed by electronic waves.

"What is wrong with *her*?" Las points to the screen, where a woman is attempting her best flirty smile with lips that look like they've been pressed against a pane of glass.

Alex cranes his neck to see. "I saw a commercial for it once. It's like a spray that covers your entire body in a transparent film to protect your skin from all the nanites and toxins in the environment or whatever."

"'Invisible protection,'" reads Lasadi. "Right, invisible. Can't even tell she's encased in plastic."

"Here's one for you, Alex," says Raj. "Grow muscle mass while you sleep to stay fit in zero G."

Jay frowns at the ad. "I'm suspicious."

"Yeah," says Alex. "Definitely not a replacement for getting your reps in."

Jay gives the kid a satisfied nod, and Raj hides his smile. Since they left Indira, Alex has been joining Jay in the *Nanshe*'s cargo hold gym. Raj had worried the taciturn mechanic might be getting annoyed with Alex, but Jay seems to have taken him under his wing, and Alex obviously adores him.

Their little crew is coming together nicely.

Raj gets to the end of the speakers list and shakes his head. "There's no A. Leb. here. Maybe Aya Marga did just need a piece of scrap paper." He tabs over to the conference schedule, scanning sessions with names like "Inner Peace at Modern Tempos" and "Divining From Within." The marquee talk seems to be with someone called the Voice of Power, and individual "memory therapy and dream stimulation" sessions are available with that person for a month's worth of Raj's rent in Ironfall.

"What's this symbol?" Lasadi asks, pointing to a crescent moon lying on its back so the horns pointed up, balanced on the point of a single teardrop. Raj ignores the way her braid brushes his arm as she leans in. Ignores the faint hint of smoky vetiver and sweet caramel that he catches sometimes when she's this close; it must be some cream she uses, Lasadi doesn't strike him as the kind of woman who splashes on cologne.

Lasadi touches the symbol on the screen and Raj shakes away the thoughts as the tablet flashes to an "Access denied" screen.

"It's some sort of link," she says. "But we need to be logged in to access it."

Ruby holds out a hand. "Give us a look." She pops another curried potato in her mouth, then begins to type. She frowns. "A lot more security than I would have thought."

"Can you get in?"

"Course I can." She turns back to her typing. "How flash are your privilege protections, loves?"

Raj glances around the bar, but no one's paying attention to them. The best part about Segafredo's is it mostly seems to cater to drifters, which means Raj isn't likely to run into someone he's scammed. Artemis City is one of those places where it feels like he's running out of room to stretch his wings. He was starting to get recognized, and he's stepped on a few too many toes. Even when he thought he was paying well enough to warrant some sort of loyalty, he'd gotten burned.

Of course, if he hadn't gotten burned stealing an artifact from the tech giant Parr Sumilang, he never would have needed Lasadi to save him from ending up in an Artemis City jail, or — more likely — out an airlock. It had been one more knot in a string of bad luck, but look where it landed him.

Sitting next to — but definitely not *too* next to — Lasadi Cazinho. His captain, yes. But more than that, a woman he respects, admires, and has absolutely not fallen head over heels for.

Five days ago, he bared her soul to her in a rush of post-near-death honesty. He told her he wanted more than friendship and camaraderie, and said he'd be willing to accept any decision she made. Five days ago, he'd been telling the truth. But she hasn't said a word since, and despite how nice it feels to be sitting next to her, despite how natural and comfortable this little crew has become, he's falling more in love with Lasadi every day.

Which isn't wise, not at all. Wrecking things with Lasadi means wrecking this new crew, and it's awfully nice to be here with people he trusts. He's still got the urge to look over his shoulder, but it's not making him itch out of his skin like it used to. Jay's sitting directly across from him with an eye on the door. Las is beside him with a good view of the bar, and Raj can keep watch on the hallway leading to the bathrooms. Ruby and Alex don't have the same constant vigilance the others do, but that's fine. He and Lasadi and Jay are trained for this.

Raj can wait years for a yes; he doesn't know how he'll possibly live with a no.

"Ah, heya," Ruby says, and Raj shakes himself from his thoughts. "Apparently there's a special programming track for the Children of Saint Alixhi."

"Who are they?" Raj asks.

"Haven't the slightest. But this could be our link to Aya Marga."

"Then we have to go."

Ruby whistles low. "It costs almost ten thousand credits to attend, only." She purses her lips at the screen. "Sorry, I mean it's an 'investment sacrifice' of ten thousand credits to attend. Saints in hell, the way they write: 'Is your need to cling tight to the money you have holding you back from achieving your true potential — and the exponential riches that come with it? Take the first step towards releasing your full potential in life, love, and wealth. Pour your intentions into yourself and demonstrate your commitment to finally achieving your goals with the Voice of Power.'" She shakes her head. "The brass on them."

"What does that even mean?" Lasadi asks.

"It means they're aiming for a pretty exclusive audience," says Raj. "One who won't think twice about the cost."

"Do you suppose that's what Aya Marga spent the convent's money on?" Jay asks. "Or did she run off with it."

"Neither," Alex says, sounding certain. Ruby gives him a second look. "Aya Marga cared about the convent more than anything. And she loved Aya Teresa. If she left without saying why, it's because she thought she'd be coming right back. She wouldn't have blown the money on a bunch of fad diets and auras, and she wouldn't have run off. Something happened to her."

"We'll find her," Raj says. "And this conference is our best lead. We need to get in there and learn more about the Children of Saint Alixhi."

"And then what?" asks Lasadi.

"Then we improvise."

Las frowns. "That doesn't sound like a *plan*, plan."

"Some plans are more fun that way."

For a moment Raj thinks she'll shut him down, but Lasadi finally nods. "I'm not a good enough actor to pretend to care about fad diets," she says. "I nominate you and Ruby."

"I'll need something nicer than this to wear." Ruby

cocks her head at Raj. "Hope you picked up a suit when we stopped in Ironfall?"

"I did." He'd hoped to wear it to impress Lasadi on a date, but at least it'll come in handy for the job.

"In that case, we've got a plan," Lasadi says. "Sort of. I think it's time for me to head back to the ship. Jay?"

Jay drains the rest of his beer and stands.

"You two sure you don't want to stay here tonight?" Ruby asks. "Beds aren't too bad."

Lasadi shakes her head. "I'm always more comfortable on the *Nanshe*," she says. "We'll catch you all in the morning."

The smile she turns on Raj isn't any brighter than the one she gives Alex and Ruby, but it does linger a second longer. Or maybe that's his imagination. But if imagination's all he's got to go on, he'll let it curl warm as sunlight around his heart as long as he can.

CHAPTER 3
LASADI

THE *NANSHE* FEELS WRONG.

No — Lasadi stops herself. Not *wrong*. Lived-in.

Alive. That's the only way to describe what's happened to this ship over the last few weeks: It's come alive.

Lasadi's always felt more comfortable sleeping on the *Nanshe*. She could have gotten her own apartment in Ironfall, like Jay had. But for the last three years her ultimate goal was to earn enough to buy the *Nanshe* from their old employer, Nico Garnet — and every credit spent on housing put that goal further out. The *Nanshe* hadn't been the most comfortable place to live, but that wasn't any fault of the ship. It simply hadn't belonged to her, so she hadn't let herself be comfortable here. She'd kept it spotless, kept all traces of herself tidied up in the unlikely event that Nico might demand the ship back at any moment.

Now, though? The *Nanshe* has gone from one

woman's hermit cell to the home of five people, and the energy is . . . pleasant?

There's another woman's beauty products left in the shower — Ruby's hair care regimen is far more involved than Lasadi's let-it-dry-in-a-braid routine. Alex's jacket is draped over one of the chairs in the galley. A novelty magnet-backed holo of the *Figment of the North*, the famous racing ship she'd been thrilled to fly in the Liluri Star Run, is stuck to the refrigerator. Lasadi suspects Raj bought it.

Of course, the biggest difference is in the rooms. The *Nanshe*'s a Starward-class Mapalad Lowboy, which is advertised to support ten crew and passengers — though that would be tight. The passenger deck has the galley, medbay, and four crew cabins positioned around the forward ladder to the flight deck. Ruby claimed the one that mirrors Lasadi's in the bow of the ship, leaving the two bunk bed rooms off the galley to Raj and Alex. Jay has always slept in one of the two cabins on the lower cargo deck, closer to the engine in case anything goes wrong.

Everyone left their doors open for the maintenance crew to access if they need to, and Lasadi can't help but be curious. None of the other crew members had brought personal items on the job to Auburn Station, or when they flew to Indira chasing after Lasadi. But they stopped by Ironfall on the way here to pick up everyone's things, and now each cabin is showing off its inhabitant's personality.

Raj's cittern is strapped to the wall, sporting the new strings she bought him, though she still hasn't heard him play it. His room is military tidy, in contrast to

Alex's wreck and Ruby's tumble of colorful clothes. Alex has slapped up some decorations, though — Lasadi's heart twinges as she spots a cheap wall display rotating through a stream of stills of Qacha Batbayar, the New Manila Liberation Front soldier Alex left his heart with on Indira.

Even Lasadi's room has a lot more personality now than it did when Nico Garnet owned the *Nanshe*. Jay had once accused her of not even leaving her toothbrush out, and he was right. But now she's put up a few wall displays of her own, though they're just cycling through landscape images that seemed nice and generic. The idea of putting her personal memories on display like Alex makes her break out in a cold sweat.

"Are you done snooping?"

Lasadi whirls, heart pounding like a teenager caught in her sibling's bedroom. Jay's got a shoulder propped against the hallway to the galley; she'd been so lost in thought she hadn't heard him come up from the cargo deck.

"I wasn't snooping. Are you done criticizing the progress in the engine room?"

"It's completely moxed," he says. "I don't know why the hell they had to take apart the drive to fix the fuel flow. I'm going over that invoice with a fine-toothed comb when they're done to make sure we're not getting any 'service upsells' we didn't want."

"If you want to do it yourself, we can fire them."

"I don't want to do it, I just want to complain about it."

"Are they ripping us off or not?"

Jay shrugs one shoulder. "No, they're fine. But they're mucking with my ship and I don't like it."

"They're making her faster and stronger, and we have the credits to pay them to do it," Lasadi says. "So let them work unless you see something wrong." She tilts her head, catching a glimpse of new grease on his fingers. "You were messing with stuff down there, weren't you."

"They haven't replaced the filtration pump."

"Jay, that's on their schedule, too. I'll make you sleep at the hostel with the others if you can't leave the engine alone."

"I'd love to," he says, grumpy. "*Some*body insisted on sleeping on the *Nanshe*, though."

"So you're guarding me." Lasadi laughs. "I can't go zipping off without telling you again, my ship is in pieces. Or are you protecting me from space pirates?"

"Space pirates can try you and see what a mess they got themselves into," Jay says. "I'm just not going to shoot the shit with the others in the hostel while you're back here brooding alone."

"I'm not brooding."

"Then why won't you stay at the hostel?"

"I like it better here."

"Sure you do." Jay jerks his chin at the galley table, and she follows him in, sinking into a chair as he grabs a bottle of whiskey and a pair of glasses out of a cabinet. She takes the glass he hands her, clinks it with his.

"Actually," Jay says, "I think you're avoiding Raj."

Lasadi's cheeks flare with color; she pretends it's the burn of whiskey. "I'm not," she says, though there's no way Jay missed the blush on her fair skin.

"Look. I'm glad you two cleared the air after we left New Manila. But it's been almost a week. How much longer are you going to make him wait?"

"I don't know," she says, and mortification hits as she realizes what Jay's implying. "Wait. Have you and Raj been talking?"

"Relax," Jay says. "No one's gossiping. But Raj asked me once if we were together, and I told him no."

"Okay."

"And I said if he breaks your heart I'll kill him."

"Jay. I'm a grown woman."

"Who's like a sister to me."

Lasadi rolls her eyes. "Then how do you know we talked after New Manila?"

"It was all over your body language, Las. He looked about a million pounds lighter when he came down from the bridge, and you looked like somebody besides me told you he cared for the first time in years and you were completely blindsided even though the rest of us saw it coming a mile away."

"That's not fair," she says, though he's 100 percent correct. She and Jay had started their friendship as pilot and mechanic during the Coruscan war for independence, and after all those hours of flying together, Jay can read her as easily as he can read the diagnostics of the ship. And ship or pilot, he also knows which levers to pull to get them out of trouble.

She sighs. Jay's still watching her, expectant. "I don't know what to do."

"Well, there's a first," Jay says. "What do you want?"

"What's best. For everyone. You remember how

easily people hooked up in the CLA — you're young and in danger and suddenly someone starts feeling like your soulmate. And then the next morning you realize it was just that you both survived a firefight and they're funny and a good listener, but you're actually terrible for each other."

"Are you talking about me and Ana Mara? Because I've already admitted sleeping with her was a huge mistake."

"I'm talking about wanting to preserve a good thing," Lasadi says. "We've got a solid crew, and as captain, it's my responsibility not to make a hormonal decision that backfires and tears apart everything we've built so far." Lasadi polishes off her whiskey. Jay refills it. "How do I know I really like him, and he's not just hot and also saved my life back at Auburn Station?"

Jay's smile turns sly. "Is that how long you think it's been going on? Because I could have sworn it was since you helped him escape Sumilang's place. Why else would you have dragged an Arquellian back to the *Nanshe*?"

"I couldn't leave him there!" she protests. "I didn't drag an Arquellian back here for a lay."

"Obviously," says Jay. "Either that or your game is *really* rusty."

"My game is fine."

Jay laughs. "Sure it is."

She can't help but smile with him; she's missed this. Missed the unguarded moments of her and Jay sitting at the galley table, missed the way laughter dimples his cheek and makes him toss his shaggy black hair out of his dark eyes. But even this is different. The others have left marks in the galley to make their presence known: the new bottle of hot sauce Alex bought in Moie, Ruby's impatient handwriting scrawled on a message board, an impractical ceramic mug Raj insisted on bringing from Ironfall.

Most importantly, the others have left their mark on Jay, unwinding him in ways Lasadi hadn't realized he was bound up.

It's nice. It's really nice.

And Lasadi can't even guess how many ways she could snarl this up if she's not careful. "What would you do?"

"I'd be happy." Jay tilts his head at her. "You remember that, right? That it's okay for you to be happy?"

"But this crew — "

"Also wants you to be happy."

"Sure." The way he says it sounds so ludicrously simple. "If being happy is more important than this crew, why'd you leave Chiara back on Ironfall?"

Jay searches his whiskey glass a long time before finally lifting it to his lips. "You know she was always insanely jealous of you," he says. "Not in the traditional sense. But us being close, traveling together. It was hard for her."

"I know." Lasadi had tried to reassure Chiara — she wanted her and Jay to be happy, but she'd stopped short of giving Jay up. "I always liked Chiara."

"And she liked you, which I think made it even harder for her. But when she asked me to move in with her, she wasn't only asking that. She wanted me to stop working with you. Stop traveling. Settle down. Have kids."

Jay drinks, sets the glass back empty. "Point is, she's never left Ironfall — she didn't even want to take a trip to Artemis City with me. If I stayed with her, I'd never leave Ironfall again, either. What was I going to do, Las? Get a job working on mining equipment, doing the same thing every day, saying hello to the same neighbors every night, get up and do it all over again? My dad did that, and he loved every minute of it. It's not the life for me, though."

"You'd prefer to get shot at in jungle temples and eaten alive by mosquitoes?"

Jay's smile quirks to the side. "Keeps it interesting."

"Well, I'll do my best to make sure we don't fall into a routine. At least we're not likely to get shot at tomorrow while we're gathering intel."

"I wouldn't rest too easy. You done?"

Las hands him her glass. "Yeah, I'm ready for bed."

"Me, too. Sweet dreams." Jay sets both glasses on the counter, then gives her a salute and a smile before disappearing past the medbay to the aft ladder.

Lasadi heads to her cabin and shuts the door behind her with a hiss, enjoying the stillness of the ship around her. She lies on her bed and swipes open her messages once more to make sure she doesn't miss anything before calling it a night. There's a status update from the maintenance crew, a few promotional messages she deletes unread.

And there's a name — a name Lasadi has secretly been dreading to see again, though it doesn't give her as much of a panic attack as the last time she found it in her inbox.

Evora Faye Cazinho.

Lasadi hasn't yet replied to her sister's last message. She still isn't sure whether — or how — to break the news that she's not actually dead, like Anton let her family continue to believe. But Evvi Faye was always a master of one-sided conversations, so Lasadi isn't surprised to find her continuing this one.

HEY, SIS. SORRY FOR WRITING AGAIN SO SOON, BUT I NEED TO TALK AND I DON'T KNOW WHO ELSE TO GO TO. YOU KNOW HOW GRANDMA IS, AND AMIT. THEY DON'T WANT TO KEEP TALKING ABOUT THINGS, THEY WANT TO MAKE DECISIONS. "JUST GET OVER HIM," AMIT TOLD ME YESTERDAY, LIKE THAT'S SO EASY TO DO, HIM AND BELLA HAVE BEEN MARRIED EIGHTY YEARS OR WHATEVER, AMIT DOESN'T KNOW THE FIRST THING ABOUT DATING. AND BELIEVE ME, I'M TRYING TO GET OVER THIS GUY, BUT FOR SOME REASON I CAN'T LET HIM GO.

EVERYONE ELSE MAY BE TIRED OF HEARING ABOUT IT, BUT I HAVEN'T HASHED THIS OUT WITH YOU YET, AND YOU'RE DEAD ANYWAY, SO YOU CAN'T TELL ME I'M BEING TOO SENTI-MENTAL. PLUS, IT'S LIKE I CAN HEAR WHAT ADVICE YOU'D TELL ME EVEN AS I'M TYPING THIS OUT, SO THIS IS ALREADY HELPING.

("GET TO THE POINT," YOU'RE THINKING, HAHA. AND "IF GRANDMA SAYS HE'S TRASH HE PROBABLY IS, SO WHY ARE WE STILL TALKING ABOUT THIS?" SEE, I KNOW YOU.)

STRAP IN, SIS, I'VE GOT A STORY ABOUT THE BOY I CAN'T STOP OBSESSING OVER. I ALREADY KNOW YOU'RE GOING TO

HATE HIM — GMA DOES — BUT THIS IS YOUR PUNISHMENT FOR GETTING YOURSELF KILLED. I CAN TALK AND TALK AT YOU AND YOU HAVE TO LISTEN, HA!

"Holy shit, Evvi," Lasadi mutters as she scrolls to see dozens of paragraphs, each denser than the last. "I'm not your diary."

But Evvi is right. If Lasadi's going to stay dead, she doesn't have a choice but to listen to her sister's rambling thoughts — thoughts she would definitely be able to cut off in person.

Lasadi sighs and settles back to read the Saga of Evvi Faye's (Latest) Heartbreak.

CHAPTER 4
RAJ

RAJ HAD FELT OVERDRESSED STANDING ON THE PLATFORM outside their rundown hostel, until Ruby showed up, strolling out the front door in a stunning chartreuse dress that practically glows against her dark skin. The flattering boat neck covers the gold tattoos on her collarbones, cap sleeves showing off her arms. The skirt flares out over her hips, ending below the knee in a swish of silk. Her look is finished with a pair of strappy white wedges that wrap ribbons around her toned calves and tie at the ankle in a bow.

"You can stop gawking at how well I clean up," she says, and Raj shuts his mouth. She reaches out to adjust his tie. "Though you didn't do half-bad yourself. The captain is going to swoon when she sees you."

"I think you're thinking of a different Captain Cazinho," Raj says. "Pretty sure this one doesn't swoon."

Ruby cocks her head critically, studying him. "Try leaving your hair down. That'll do it."

"Now?"

"Not now." Ruby takes his arm and lifts a hand to one of the stand of shuttlecab drivers who are eyeing them. "If you're playing the part of my date, I don't want to spend all afternoon fending off other women."

Raj opens the door of the shuttlecab and helps Ruby in with a flourish of manners that would make his mother proud, then gives the address to the hotel the conference is being held at — a hotel in Dāl Sector, a much more fashionable part of Artemis City's Bell than where this hostel is located. Dāl Sector is near the middle of the Bell, where "downtown" Artemis City mimics a grand city on Indira or New Sarjun with skyscrapers open to the domed "sky" above, broken up by a web of sky trams and covered walkways. Hotel facades span dozens of stories, busy and glamorous shopping corridors wedged between them. The sky, of course, is an illusion of the glass dome, beyond which the dockyard operates in the vacuum of space

"Where'd you get the dress?" he asks Ruby as their shuttlecab descends into the glitter of Dāl.

"Went on a little shopping spree," she says coyly. "I brought a few things with me, but none of them seemed quite right for a lithium ore heiress to wear as a day dress."

"Given the amount of time I've spent around heiresses, I think you nailed it."

"I know I did. I may not spend time with heiresses, but I've watched enough trash gossip shows to know what labels they're wearing."

"How much does something like that cost?"

"None of your business, love. But it was an 'investment sacrifice to achieve my goals' that I'm happy to make." Ruby winks at him as the shuttlecab docks in front of the Hôtel l'Eza, and hands him an earpiece from her purse. "Shall we go find some wellness?"

The Hôtel l'Eza is a fifteen-story spike in the center of Dāl's glitz. It's outlined in neon pink, the glass windows washed in a mirrored mercury finish that reflects back the scene around it in a moody, liquid blue.

The doors open automatically as they walk up to the hotel, revealing an enormous lobby filled with marble statues: Armless busts of various genders stand artfully around, hips draped with carved stone. It's not real marble, surely — it would have cost a fortune to transport this much rock out to Durga's Belt. But it's an incredibly good facsimile. Each statue stands in its own floating pink neon frame, each frame at a jaunty angle. Low black couches and gleaming black tables, black granite floor tiles set in a honeycomb pattern with blue light playing faintly around the edge of each tile.

It's immediately clear where the conference is being held. At the far end of the lobby, a separate receptionist is checking in some very fancy guests. Each are dressed with the same casual elegance Ruby so nailed — it's not about the clothes, it's about how you wear them. A normal person puts on that chartreuse silk, and every fiber of their being will scream awareness that it probably cost more than a month's worth of Raj's rent back on Ironfall. But Ruby sashays through the lobby like she was born to mingle with this crowd.

"Relax," Ruby says, threading her arm through his. "They're just rich people."

"I'm impressed, is all."

"I don't always take the charity jobs you want to do, Raj. Some of my clients pay pretty well."

"I'll have to make sure they can't hire you away."

Something flickers over her face, and he files it away for later. Maybe it's way too early for him to start thinking things like "years from now," but he can't help it. It's not every day you find a group of misfits in Durga's Belt you can trust. He's been stabbed in the back often enough — he's sure they all have. This little crew is something he's willing to fight for.

Jay's been his corner. Lasadi's coming around. Alex seems committed to something for the first time since Raj has known him, though he worries about the teenage tendency to get bored.

But Ruby? He's worked with her for years, and she keeps her walls strong. He has a guess why she agreed to join him to rescue Lasadi — having Alex back as a permanent fixture in her life has tethered her, given her a reminder she has someone depending on her. But even though he's seen her laughing with Lasadi, joking with Jay — she still almost didn't tell them the ayas had asked for help. She still hasn't shared with him whatever she found out about her family on Auburn Station.

If he can't get her to see she can trust them with anything, he doesn't know how long he can keep her from walking away.

Ruby's accent transforms from gutter Pearls to posh Artemisian when they approach the receptionist. "I love the busts," she says to Raj. "Statuary. That's what's missing from the garden, don't you think, darling? We'll have to talk with Philip when we get back to Arquelle." She turns to the receptionist as though noticing him for the first time. "Do we have to sign in?" Ruby's mouth twists like the receptionist asked her to eat a live slug.

The receptionist's smile remains professionally bright — he's been dealing with this all morning, probably.

"A formality, ma'am." He holds out a pad, and Ruby turns to Raj.

"Not the neon, of course," she says, and it takes Raj a moment to realize she's still talking about the statuary. The screen blinks a name, OLIVIA TAM, and the receptionist proffers it to Raj. "But I love the color contrast. Something bright and floral. A trellis. A statue in a trellis." She turns to the receptionist. "Don't you agree? Or do you think the neon *wouldn't* be too much with the roses?"

The man glances up from the tablet with a puzzled expression, and without examining either Olivia Tam's or Richard Cason Smith's ident cards too closely. Or noticing the transmission chip Ruby slipped into one of the pad's open ports.

"Yes, ma'am," he says automatically. "Roses sound lovely."

"It's perfect," Ruby agrees. "Now where I can freshen up?"

The receptionist gestures to a glossy black and neon blue sitting area partially shielded by a stand of dwarf palms and ficus in faux-marble pots. "You'll find refreshments in the Nebula Room. The opening remarks begin in ten minutes."

Raj steps back to wait while Ruby slips into the bathroom. "Lasadi, are you in?"

"I am," she says in his ear. He scans the lobby they just left, spots her sitting at one of the low black couches. She's wearing a reasonably nice suit, her hair braided and wrapped in a crown — he still hasn't seen her with her hair down, it's always as tightly contained as she is. She's scrolling through her comm like she's waiting for someone to meet her.

"I've got the guest list, the speaker schedule, the whole thing," Lasadi says. "Looks like almost everyone's checked in — you and Ms. Tam are the latecomers."

"There's a couple of hundred people in the Nebula Room already," Alex says, voice also in Raj's ear. He got there hours ago and has been acting as part of the event staff. "Lots of fancy jewelry."

"Leave it," says Raj. He straightens as Ruby returns, holding out his arm for her. "We're not here to pickpocket."

"Wouldn't think of it," Alex says primly, and Raj wonders how many bracelets the kid'll be slipping back onto wrists now he's been called out.

"Jay, I placed the crawler," Ruby murmurs. "Are you linked in?"

"Got it. The whole hotel layout, security codes, everything."

"Excellent," Raj says. "Let's go figure out what an aya needs with a self-help seminar."

The Nebula Room is easy to find — and surprisingly mundane after the lobby's neon and statuary fever dream. The floor is covered by vast swaths of carpeting in an arcane pattern, and a huge, gaudy chandelier is suspended on wires from the four corners of the room.

Instead of a sea of chairs, however, the room is dotted with individual tables. An usher is waiting for them at the door, having apparently been alerted by the receptionist they were on their way.

He smiles brightly after he shows them to their seats. "Can I bring you anything? Water? Coffee?"

"Where's the coffee from?" Ruby asks before Raj can respond.

"Grown here in Artemis City," the usher announces proudly.

"Then I'll have chai. Not too sweet." Ruby turns away, dismissing him.

"Coffee sounds great," Raj says. "Black, thank you."

Ruby ignores the usher when he comes back with their drinks, and Raj has to stop himself from thanking the man again. He's spent years unlearning the upper class habits of his youth; he never thought they'd come in handy on a job.

The usher doesn't leave, though. He clears his throat, waiting patiently for Raj and Ruby to deign to notice him. "And please remember there is no recording of any kind. Any devices will need to stay put away. This material is all proprietary."

"Of course," Raj says, and the man slips back to the door.

Raj sips the coffee as he scans the room. It's filled with people — mostly women. Many are wearing on-trend outfits as expensive as Ruby's dress or more so, though some favor a spiritual aesthetic, with flowing robes and beads. The hotel's event staff are easy to spot — there's Alex delivering coffees at the far end of the room — as are the conference team, who are all wearing some form of white shawl and a name tag. He counts eight.

The buzz of the room shifts; one of the white-shawled conference team has taken the stage. Her smile is broad, her hands held wide as though she would like to bring them all in for a big hug. Her pale skin is flushed pink, her long, glossy black hair reaching almost to her waist.

"Welcome!" Her accent is unlike anything Raj has ever heard; it seems oddly affected. "I'm Evelyn. Right now we are in a special place — a sacred place. A hotel, yes. But a hotel that has been made sacred by your presence. You've all been led to a decision to come here today. You've made intentions. You've made the sacrifice of your time and your money because you believe in yourselves and in the difference you will make in the world. And I want to acknowledge how amazing all that is."

Evelyn smiles brightly and brings her hands together over her heart, then says nothing. About a third of the people in the audience mimic her posture for the brief moment of silence.

It's a nice opening move, Raj thinks. The perfect way to shake out who's familiar with the rituals and who's a newcomer. And to learn which of the newcomers are rule-followers or rebels. Most of those who didn't join Evelyn at first do awkwardly join in as the moment lingers, but Raj spots a few skeptical faces out there — if he had to guess, they're the partners who were dragged here by believers.

He's not the only one scanning the crowd to take its temperature. The other white-shawled conference team members are drinking it all in from the sides of the room. Raj shoots Ruby skeptical side-eye as she eagerly but imperfectly mimics the bow; the conference team will clock them as an eager newcomer and her uninterested but indulgent partner.

"Before we get into today's sessions, we have a treat for you," Evelyn says, absolutely delighted. "You all know our host, the Voice of Power, doesn't often speak in crowds. But today she would like to welcome you all personally."

An excited buzz rises up around the room.

"Ah, right," Lasadi murmurs through the comms. "This is the person I can mortgage the *Nanshe* to have a private session with. Can't wait to hear what pearls of wisdom she dispenses for free."

Raj hides his smile with a sip of coffee.

The audience watches in rapt attention as Evelyn steps to the side of the stage to greet a new woman: She's tall and slender, with glossy blond hair and a simple, flowing blue dress. Dark makeup slashes across her eyes, and gold bangles stack up her wrists. The Voice of Power exchanges a long, warm hug with Evelyn, then steps to the center of the stage.

The room stays breathlessly silent.

Even from a distance, the Voice of Power hums with commanding presence that belies her slim frame and simple dress. She studies the room slowly, as though she intends to make eye contact with every person there. Her hands are clasped gently in front of her; the faint smile on her lips is perfectly warm, welcoming, wise.

When her gaze lands on Raj he *feels* it, electricity

thrumming through him, and for a moment the distractions around him vanish into this single point of focus: her eyes. The room could shatter around them, Artemis tear apart around them, and he wouldn't notice.

Once she's broken her gaze, Raj blinks at Ruby; she looks dazed. *What was that?* she mouths, but she doesn't dare speak even a whisper in the silent room.

Finally, the Voice of Power lifts her hands into a prayer pose above her heart and bows her head slightly. More people mimic her gesture this time.

"Welcome," she says. Her voice is breathy, ethereal. Pitched higher than he'd expect from a woman her height, and tinged with a faint accent he can't place, but which feels true in a way Evelyn's was feigned. "My name is Annika Lebedevya, the Voice of Power. I'm so glad Spirit brought us all together today."

Raj straightens; Lasadi breathes a curse in his ear.

"A. Leb.," Raj murmurs. "We found her."

CHAPTER 5
LASADI

"I'LL SEE WHAT I CAN DIG UP ON LEBEDEVYA," LASADI murmurs, calling up a search on her comm. She's found a seat in the lobby of the Hôtel l'Eza, on one of the low black couches that somehow manage to be even more uncomfortable than they look. No one has paid her any mind; she's dressed like a business traveler and keeps glancing at the door like she's waiting for someone.

Annika Lebedevya has to be the connection, the A. Leb. that Aya Marga left the convent to meet. Lasadi hadn't been able to find Marga on the guest list, but that doesn't mean she couldn't have met Lebedevya outside of the conference.

But why?

Lasadi's quick search for Lebedevya, the Voice of Power, returns reams of gushing profiles that focus on her charm, her wisdom, her closeness to Spirit-with-a-capital-S. Most are fluff profiles; many seem commissioned by a PR firm or copied from a press release, since they have much the same wording.

Lasadi keeps scrolling through the search results until a different type of headline catches her eye. "Bal Vista's Own Saint at Home." This profile goes beyond the flowery praise to feature a visit to the Voice of Power's home in Arquelle. She apparently owns a complex in Bal Vista, on Arquelle's south coast, where Lebedevya's followers stay with her when she's in town.

"Finding any dirt?" Ruby murmurs through the comms.

"Maybe," Lasadi says. "Listen to this: 'Like pilgrims drawn to a miracle worker's cell, the Voice of Power's followers liken her to such influential religious figures from centuries ago as Tesanne of Southton and Saint Alixhi.'"

Lasadi scans further down the article, ignoring the amenities — which seem quite luxe for a supposed saint. "She collects religious memorabilia," Lasadi says. "Sounds like she prides herself on being something of a connoisseur, especially when it comes to mystics."

"Like Saint Alixhi," Ruby says.

"Exactly. Alex? Any luck?"

"I couldn't get close to her, but I did manage to slip a blister mic under her table. Only thing I've overheard so far is that her day's packed with meetings, most of which are going to be in her hotel room."

"Anything about the Children of Saint Alixhi?"

"Nothing yet."

"Okay," Lasadi says, scrolling through the conference schedule again. "If she's holding her private meetings in her room, odds are good any Children of Saint Alixhi stuff might take place there, too."

"And if she's planning on meeting with Aya Marga, that's where she'll do it."

"Exactly." Lasadi unfolds herself from the uncomfortable couch. "I need to get into that room. Alex?"

"On it, Cap." She spots him at the main reception desk, chatting with a young woman; the girl's laugh rings bright. After a minute, Alex winks at her and starts heading back across the lobby. "Got it. Penthouse suite."

"Fancy," Lasadi says.

"Closest to God," says Raj.

"I think you mean Spirit." Lasadi can picture him smiling at her joke; she doesn't need to be picturing that smile, not during a job. She tucks away her comm and starts for the lifts, sensing more than feeling Alex drop the keycard in her pocket as their paths cross. She doesn't react. When she steps into the lift and hits the button for the top floor, the panel glows green to let her know access has been granted by the keycard she's now carrying.

Perfect.

The lifts are set against the hotel's glass facade, giving passengers a dizzying view of the bustle of Dāl Sector as it rises — Lasadi loves the sensation of being swept high into the air above the streets below, but she wonders if it might be a bit much for some of the hotel's other guests. Given how worn the carpet is at the back of the lift, that's where most people spend their time.

"As far as I can tell, no one's in the penthouse suite," Jay says in her ear. "You should be good to go."

"Keep an eye out for me?"

"Always."

The lift door opens into the penthouse suite with a soft chime, and Lasadi steps through, wary, listening for any sound. Jay's intel was right, though; she's alone.

The suite appears to be a giant half circle, with a recessed sitting area to the right, a small round dining table set near a wet bar straight ahead, and the door to the bedrooms to the left. The floor-to-ceiling windows are actually giant screens, currently playing a sweeping view overlooking a vast, peaceful ocean. Maybe it's the view from Lebedevya's compound in Arquelle.

In the sitting room, all the furniture has been removed in favor of a circle of cushions on the floor; the rest of the room seems untouched, except for a large package on the dining table, the wrappings torn open and tossed careless on a nearby chair.

Interesting.

There's nowhere inconspicuous to leave a blister mic in the circle of cushions, so she slips one under the dining table, then turns to the package. A hand-scrawled card sits on the table beside the discarded wrappings: *Lots 46 and 131 sold to A. Lebedevya. Deliver to Hôtel l'Eza.* Lasadi turns the card over to find the words *Thierry et Zhang: Auctions & Private Sales* stamped on the reverse.

Whatever Lebedevya purchased was delivered in a simple wooden crate, which sits in the middle of the table to serve as a display stand for the painting propped on top. A card reading *Lot 46* is propped beside it.

The painting is of a white-capped mountain rising from a sea of rolling red hills, thick swirls of stars smeared into the sky above. A man and a woman in the foreground — both veiled — are dancing back-to-back with their arms raised.

It's unsigned, but Lasadi has spent enough time researching Saint Alixhi over the last few days to recognize the style. And to know the saint never signed any of her work. She snaps a still, then turns to survey the rest of the room.

There were two lots, though, and only one painting on display. What was in the other lot — Lot 131 — that Lebedevya purchased from the auction house?

She doesn't see another artifact, but she does spot a tablet sitting on the wet bar, alongside a few more brochures from the Thierry et Zhang auction house and a handwritten note thanking Lebedevya for her purchase and promising to keep her apprised of any other artifacts relating to Saint Alixhi they might come across.

"She's specifically on the hunt for artifacts related to Saint Alixhi." Lasadi slips the descrambler chip Ruby gave her into the port, waiting for the sequence to run. "She has a painting here she bought from a local auction house."

"We can use that," says Raj. "Good work."

The tablet flashes to let her know she's in, and Lasadi sets the messages to clone to her own comm, scrolling through them as they do.

A few more notes from Thierry et Zhang that she flags to dig into later. And — there.

"I got it," Lasadi breathes. A spike of delight after all this — she'd begun to think they wouldn't find anything about Aya Marga after all.

But there's her name in Annika Lebedevya's

message inbox, going back for weeks. The most recent one is from right before she disappeared.

I'M SO PLEASED YOU BELIEVE IN OUR MISSION, AND I HAVE BEEN HONORED TO CONSULT WITH YOU. I BELIEVE GOD WILL BLESS YOUR GENEROSITY TENFOLD AND DELIVER LOT 131 INTO OUR HANDS. I LOOK FORWARD TO MEETING YOU IN PERSON.

But there's nothing on Lebedevya's meticulous calendar, and a quick search through her messages finds a note to Lebedevya's secretary to remove the meeting with Aya Marga that had been scheduled for last week.

"They were supposed to meet the day Marga disappeared, but Lebedevya canceled it," Las says. "Jay, you haven't found anyone who looks like the aya in the security footage?"

"Negative. I'm still scanning, but — hold on. Las, you need to get out of there. Someone just requested access to the penthouse suite in the lift."

"Is there another way out?"

"Bedroom. Now."

Lasadi yanks the descrambler out of the tablet, shuts it back down, and melts into the bedroom as the lift door opens. A woman enters, having what sounds like one side of a conversation over her comm.

"Sweetheart, I'm so sorry," she says. Her voice sounds familiar, and after a moment Lasadi recognizes it as the speaker who opened the conference. Evelyn. "Her schedule's busy, of course, but I may be able to find some time. You understand moving things around isn't easy, though."

Lasadi presses against the wall beside the bedroom door, scanning the room for an exit — or at least a hiding place. The bed is on a raised dais, with no room to squeeze behind or beneath. A vanity at the foot of the bed is covered in cosmetics and vials — one looks like medicine, labeled Argentias BZ-9114. Lasadi doesn't recognize the name. She snaps a quick still, then risks a glance out the door back into the sitting room.

The woman, Evelyn, seems to be listening to a response in her earpiece; she bends down to straighten cushions, her long dark hair sweeping over her shoulder and nearly brushing the ground.

"Of course, sweetheart," she says, straightening. "I understand it feels like money is tight. But when you joined the Children of Alixhi you made a promise — not to Annika, but to yourself. Annika wants to help you keep that promise. She wants to watch you to grow into your full potential. But how can she do that if you don't believe enough to make even the smallest investment in yourself?"

Evelyn straightens with a smile.

"You will?" she asks. "Oh good, good. Let's meet for dinner and discuss it."

She terminates the connection, then heads towards the bedroom; Lasadi melts into the closet, heart pounding. It's a big walk-in affair, hung with variations of robes in exquisite fabrics. Lasadi hides herself in a cloud of gauzy silk perfumed with heady florals, the bouquet flashing her back to her grandmother's altar, *Lasadi sitting on a cushion in front of the mixla, willing the little house god to do something — anything — to bring the baby back from the hospital, praying the syllables of the baby's name over and over until they lose all meaning on her lips, e-vor-a-faye-e-vor-a-faye, swearing she'll do anything at all if her baby sister lives.* Lasadi tries to shake away the sudden, cloying memory — she'd almost forgotten that moment of childhood terror — and blinks stinging tears out of her eyes.

Lebedevya has awful taste in cologne.

So strong it lingers bitter on Lasadi's tongue, curls through her sinuses like a feather, and Lasadi clamps her hands over her nose and mouth to keep herself from sneezing and giving herself away. Cutting off the scent finally washes away the memory, too, sending her cartwheeling back into the moment just in time to keep from making a sound.

Lasadi holds her breath as long as she dares, heart careening in her chest, taking the faintest sips of air until Evelyn finally calls the lift and leaves once more.

She shakes her head to clear it as she stumbles out of the closet, cologne clinging to her like a malignant, viscous thing.

"You okay, Las?" Jay asks.

"Fine. Just need a shower." When Lasadi glances around the bedroom, though, something tugs at her attention. She turns slowly, trying to figure out what Evelyn was doing in the bedroom while Lasadi was traipsing down memory lane, and finally her gaze rests on the vanity.

The little vial of medicine is gone.

CHAPTER 6
RAJ

RAJ HADN'T BEEN SURE HOW LONG HE COULD STAND TO listen to Annika Lebedevya gush breezily about the vast stores of potential and success Spirit was telling her was in this room, but lucky for him, she moved on to clairvoyance about twenty minutes ago. A lot of ghosts seem to have traveled all the way to Artemis in order to speak with their loved ones, and a surprising number of them have positive things to say about Annika Lebedevya and her organization.

Raj is amazed. Simply astounded.

Right now, Lebedevya's embracing a young man who's sobbing at how proud his dead brother would be of him for taking this step and attending this conference.

Ruby claps along with the rest, eyes wide with feigned wonder, then leans in to Raj. "She's good," she murmurs.

Raj would agree. He's seen cold readings before, and Lebedevya is an excellent grifter. If she's just out to make a living scamming rich people who suffer from ennui, Raj wishes her the best of luck. Only problem is, Aya Marga doesn't fit into that category, and she's not sitting here in this room with the rest of Lebedevya's marks.

So what is Lebedevya really up to?

Raj keeps his expression pleasantly interested in Lebedevya while puzzling over what they know now. They may not be any closer to finding Aya Marga, but phase one — find information — has been successful. They know Marga was supposed to meet with Lebedevya. They know Lebedevya, like Marga, is fascinated by Saint Alixhi. And Raj has an idea.

He claps again as Lebedevya sends the sobbing young man back to his seat and begins a breathy entreaty to Spirit to bring everyone else in this room the wisdom they're seeking. Around the room, voices raise in murmured calls of "Yes, Spirit!"

"What do we know about holy objects associated with Saint Alixhi?" Raj asks.

"She was a prolific painter," Ruby says quietly. "If Lebedevya picked one of her paintings up at auction, she probably didn't have to spend much for it. They're everywhere."

"That's almost true," Jay says over the comms. "Her landscapes are everywhere, since she did so many of those to raise money for her convent. But she didn't do many portraits. Those are prized. What are you planning?"

"Portraits," Raj says. "Got it. Alex, you can paint, can't you?"

"Suuuure," Alex says slowly. "I have definitely painted."

"Then why don't you three go pick up some art supplies, and see if you can get Aya Marga's notes for her book from the Aya Teresa. We'll get ourselves a meeting with Lebedevya and meet you at the bar."

Lebedevya has finished her breathy prayer, and is now shopping a final message. "I sense someone here is seeking answers to a mystery from the past," she says. "A feminine energy. I'm getting the letter *R*. And *Q*?"

Ruby straightens in surprise as Lebedevya scans the room with her piercing gaze. "You wonder why they left you," Lebedevya says in a singsong voice, and Ruby's frowning at her now, lips parted. Raj nudges her ankle under the table. Ruby shakes her head as though surprised to find him there.

Across the room, an older woman with her hair wrapped in a violently purple turban raises both hands. "Me!" she calls in obvious delight. "I'm Raquel."

"Party tricks," Raj murmurs to Ruby, and she nods firmly. Across the room, the older woman is describing her children moving away. Lebedevya gives her a positive message and embraces her, sending her back to her seat to a warm applause.

"There's so much more Spirit wants to tell you all," Lebedevya says as the applause dies down. "I invite you to make yourself open to messages these next few days. Allow yourself to experience vulnerability. I know that's hard for many of you — as successful people, your guard and your skepticism has brought you to where you are. But to fully release your potential, you need to let go and allow room for faith. Remember, you're in a safe place."

"Let go of your rational mind and let us fleece you," Raj translates wryly.

Lebedevya bows to more applause, then drifts off the stage. Someone announces a brief intermission, and the other guests stand to stretch and mingle, but it seems Raj and Ruby aren't the only ones hoping for a chance to speak with Lebedevya. A dense outer ring has formed in her orbit as her handlers work the crowd, intercepting guests and leading a select few in to actually talk with the Voice of Power.

Raj smiles at the handler who greets them: a bubbly young man with a fresh, sharp haircut and acne showing through the powder on his fair skin. He smiles, his teeth gleaming white.

"She's something, isn't she?" The young man is practically glowing with excitement. "Is this your first time seeing the Voice of Power in person?"

"She's amazing," Ruby says; she's pitched her enthusiasm a step below the handler's, a hint of longing in her tone. She glances past the bubbly young man as though seeking a glimpse of Lebedevya through the crowd. "It must be incredible to work with her."

"It's an honor." He smiles. "Are you enjoying the conference so far?"

"It's been very enlightening," Raj says.

Beside him, Ruby sighs. "I'm so disappointed the private appointments are all booked up."

"I know." Raj squeezes her hand. "But you're going to learn so much in the rest of the sessions, Olivia. And we already have a buyer lined up for the collection."

The young man tilts his head at the bait. "A new business opportunity?"

Ruby gives him a nervous smile. "In a way. A family friend recently passed and left a large collection of religious artwork to his children. They don't want to keep them, but I have some connections in the art world. They asked if I could help them sell them, and I confess I'm a bit over my head."

"You're doing fine!" Raj says, squeezing her in a side hug. He beams at the young man. "She's got a buyer lined up and everything. It's amazing stuff. Some of it's even been painted by some saint."

The young man straightens. "A saint?"

"Al—" Raj winces. "Alisha?"

"Alixhi," Ruby corrects; she's got that tone of exasperation with Raj down pat. "And anyway the buyer says he'll *look* at it, he hasn't promised to buy." She sighs, wistful. "I was hoping for some guidance from the Voice of Power."

"Let me see what I can do," the handler says.

Raj winks at Ruby, then turns to scan the room. "That was perfect," he murmurs. "Absolutely brilliant."

"Save your charm for the con, will you," Ruby says. "I know I'm flash."

"Now let's see how good an artist Alex is — oh. *Shit.*" Raj whirls back to Ruby, keeping her squarely between him and the too-familiar face he's spotted in the crowd.

"What is it?" she asks.

"An old childhood friend."

"Will they recognize you?"

"I don't know. Straight behind you — blue suit, gold tie, dark skin. Tall."

Ruby steals a glance as she flags a server for more chai; when she turns back, her smile is still in place, but there's a flash of panic in her eyes. "That's my ex."

"You dated Absolon Chevalier?" Raj asks.

"Ew." Ruby makes a face. "Obviously not. The woman beside him — that's Kitty."

Raj risks another look, and finds there indeed is a woman standing at Absolon's side. She's startlingly familiar in context, but Raj wouldn't have recognized Absolon's gangly little sister as a grown woman if he saw her alone. She's almost five years younger than him, if he remembers right, and was always off in a gaggle of the younger children whenever his family encountered the Chevaliers at social occasions. Which was admittedly rare; Raj's father may have been important, but the Chevaliers are the closest thing the Durga System has to royalty. One of their fathers was a famous singer, the other a diplomat, both roguishly handsome and the darlings of the tabloids.

"You dated Katriana Chevalier," Raj says, two worlds colliding in confusion.

"I've told you about her."

"Kitty? The woman who stole your heart, tore it to pieces, stole it again? The woman who kicked you out of her apartment by tossing your belongings off the balcony and scattering them across the entire neighborhood of Selena's Ante? The woman — and I quote — 'of your most glorious dreams and devastating nightmares'?"

Ruby smiles. "Kitty-Kat — because she — "

"Ruby. Focus."

"It's fine," she says, and lifts her chin to the bubbly young man who's returning with a wide grin on his face. "We get this meeting, we go see Lebedevya in private, and we won't have to come back to the main seminar. They'll never know we were here."

Raj turns his back on the Chevaliers, the skin between his shoulder blades pricking. There's a good chance Absolon wouldn't recognize Raj after all these years, but Katriana — *Kitty??* — is definitely going to recognize Ruby.

The handler is grinning. "You're in luck," he says. "The Voice does have a few free slots for open sessions, and she even said she'll waive the investment fee!"

Ruby's eyes go wide in faux delight. "Really? That's amazing!"

"She is a true believer in Saint Alixhi," the young man says, leaning in with a strange emphasis on the words, like he's imparting a secret.

Ruby nods like she knows what he means, bowing her head and placing a hand over her heart. "Then thank her. I knew there was a reason I was called to come here."

She must have said the right thing, because the young man's smile widens. "Tomorrow morning, in her hotel room. I'll send you the details."

Raj looks as casually as he can over his shoulder as the young man confirms Ruby's — or, Olivia's — information. The Chevaliers are headed out of the conference room; Raj's shoulders relax slightly. They may be able to slip out of the Hôtel l'Eza without their cover being blown after all. Until Absolon pauses in the doorway to say something to his sister, his cold, analytical gaze sweeping over the crowd.

His eyes lock on Raj's, and his eyebrows jolt up in surprise.

Raj squeezes Ruby's arm firmly: *It's time to get out of here.* "Thank you," he says to the young man, then, "I'm starving. Let's find a snack before the next session."

Please don't come over here, Raj thinks, hoping against hope Lebedevya's left a bit of clairvoyance in the room for the rest of them. But Absolon Chevalier ignores the attempted psychic message. He cuts a swath through the other guests, his sister in his wake, and even though the young handler had been about to leave, his attention is caught by Absolon's stony expression.

Raj's heart sinks.

"Well," Absolon says, one brow arched as he looks Raj up and down. Katriana is hanging back a step, watching the scene with pure amused delight, like outing the Alliance traitor Raj Demetriou in the middle of this posh crowd is the most interesting thing that's happened to her all week. "Who would have thought."

CHAPTER 7
RUBY

"DARLING!"

Ruby acts without thinking, stepping past the daggers Absolon Chevalier is glaring at Raj to pull Kitty in for a pair of air kisses. She smells amazing, and of course she looks amazing, slender frame clad in a rich plum jumpsuit, gold bangles gleaming against the dark skin of her upper arms, her normally black hair dyed amber and swept up in a cascade of tight, elegant curls.

"It's so good to see you!" Ruby turns to Absolon. "I'm Olivia," she says firmly, catching Kitty's eye. Her ex-girlfriend teases a smile, and Ruby sends up a silent prayer that she'll be intrigued enough to play along. "And this is my boyfriend, Richard. He's an actor. You might have seen him in *Jewel in the Palace*?"

"It was a small role," Raj says with a self-deprecating smile. He holds out his hand to Absolon, whose mouth pulls into an even more severe line.

Ruby can see the moment Absolon makes his decision — the flash in his dark eyes that says he is absolutely not interested in whatever shenanigans they're pulling. He takes a sharp, angry breath. "I don't know what — "

"Must be why your face looks so familiar," Kitty says, jostling her brother's shoulder with her own, and Ruby melts in relief. "I'm Katriana Chevalier. My brother, Absolon. Nice to meet you, *Richard*."

Absolon blinks at his sister in naked surprise, then grudgingly turns back to Raj and takes his outstretched hand. "Nice to meet you both," he says. His smile is forced.

Lebedevya's handler is watching the exchange curiously, though he doesn't seem suspicious — yet. Ruby and Raj are standing on a powder keg, though, and they need to get to safety.

The last time Ruby saw Kitty, the other woman was sobbing that Ruby could go to hell. But if Ruby knows one thing about Kitty, it's that her sense of curiosity and drive for adventure can overrule her short fuse. Plus, she always did love the feeling that she was pulling one over on the upper class society she constantly rails about — even while she profits from it.

From what Ruby's heard about big brother Absolon, though, he's a buzzkill. And he knows who Raj is, so he could do way more than blow their cover for this job.

"Thank you so much for your help," Ruby says to the handler, and he seems to get the hint. He excuses himself and moves on to intercept the next person trying to get an audience with Lebedevya.

"Kitty!" Ruby exclaims; no one's in earshot, but they can't drop the ruse yet. "It's been so long. And I've heard so much about your brother. Why don't we all go somewhere we can chat?"

"No, Katriana." Absolon's command is sharp. "I don't know what kind of game this is, but — "

"We would love to, *Olivia*," Kitty says, and Ruby sends Absolon silent thanks for his outburst. There's nothing in the world Kitty hates more than being told what she should or should not do.

"You're meant to meet with Evelyn."

"She can wait."

"This is important, Katriana. You are here to get better, not consort with criminals."

Kitty gives him an arch look. "What, I'm supposed to leave that all to you, big brother?" She smiles sweetly at her brother's shock, then turns back to Ruby. There's more than curiosity in her gaze, though, and heat flushes through Ruby at the way her ex takes in the full effect of Ruby's new dress.

"Besides," Kitty says. "I have a few hours before Evelyn and I are supposed to meet up. And I'm dying to know what our two old friends are doing here together."

Raj clears his throat. "Have you been to Segafredo's?" he asks. "Might not be your usual joint, but it's a good spot to talk."

"Kitty loves a good dive bar," Ruby says.

Kitty's gaze holds so much banked fire Ruby's mouth goes dry. She swallows hard, and ignores Raj's amusement.

"I do," Kitty says. "Lead the way."

✳

Segafredo's is *exactly* the sort of bar Kitty loves. A dive, but the type of dive tourists can frequent without being in actual danger — and chock-full of cheesy decor that looks like it was repurposed from a decommissioned mining vessel, meeting tourist expectations for seedy local ambiance.

Kitty's eyes widen in delight, and Ruby knows her instincts were right. The little rich girl still loves slumming it.

"This place is amazing!" she says. She elbows her brother. "This is real Artemis City."

It's not — what Kitty means by "real" Artemis City is the dingy bars where Ruby carries an electric barb and a knife to meetings with shady clients. The sorts of places buried levels and levels below where most offworld tourists would ever dare set foot.

"You still drink silver roses?" Ruby asks Kitty, stepping up to the bar. "I'm buying. Absolon?"

He frowns prissily at the bar, then names a beer from the list scrawled above the taps. When the Chevaliers go to stake out a table, Raj leans in.

"How the hell did you meet Katriana?"

Ruby shrugs. "At a bar. She was giving me looks, I bought her a drink. She told me she was a painter and I didn't ask anything else — I mean, it was clear she was a rich kid playing with the rest of us, but it wasn't until we'd been together a few months that I learned who her daddies are."

"I thought gossip shows were your guilty pleasure."

"Just because I'd recognize her daddies doesn't mean I'd recognize *her* in a dive bar in Artemis City."

Ruby tips a look at him. "You all had playdates growing up, did you?"

Raj shakes his head. "There's rich, and there's Chevalier rich. We didn't run in the same circles, but I did meet them a few times."

"Sounds like a tragic life," she says without thinking, and winces at the darkness that flutters over his face.

"Yeah, it was amazing." He sighs and grabs the drinks. "So what do we tell them?"

"The truth."

"Ruby."

"Mostly the truth. Trust me, Kitty loves a good story, and she's got Absolon wrapped around her finger. C'mon."

His expression says this is a bad idea, but he follows her without another word. Ruby sets one of the silver roses in front of Kitty, Absolon takes the beer from Raj.

"Thank you, 'Richard.'"

"We can drop the game here," Ruby says, holding out a hand. "I'm Ruby."

That flick of his gaze to Kitty, Absolon's heard her name. She hopes whatever Kitty told him, it's not too terrible.

Absolon drums dark fingers against his beer. "I have so many questions," he says. "Starting with why I haven't called the Alliance yet to report a wanted man."

Kitty slaps his arm. "You wouldn't. It's Raj."

"Wouldn't I?"

"No," she says firmly. She twirls a finger to indicate Raj and Ruby. "Because whatever's going on here is bound to be an amazing story. Are you two . . . ?"

"No," Ruby says, as Raj cuts in with an emphatic, "Absolutely not."

"Oh," says Kitty simply, but that curl of her lips makes Ruby's stomach do a fluttery series of flips. Kitty nudges her brother. "Anyway, admit you're curious, Sol." She doesn't wait for an answer before she turns her full, gorgeous attention back on Ruby. "Spill. What's going on?"

Raj leans back in his chair as though trusting her to handle this, and it strikes her that this is . . . new. She's always been a freelancer, hired to do a quick job, follow directions, and keep her opinions to herself. But with Raj — with this whole crew — she's more than that. Lasadi trusts her — hell, Lasadi even trusts Alex. And Jay absolutely defers to her when she speaks up. They consider her their equal, not their hired hacker. On the one hand, that's refreshing. On the other?

This is her third job in a row with Raj and Lasadi and Jay and Alex. She can't remember a single other time she's worked with someone other than Raj more than once. She likes it. And that's a problem, because it's going to be so much harder to give this up when it inevitably ends.

Ruby takes a long sip of her silver rose, coconut and champagne lingering on her tongue.

"You remember Aya Marga?" she asks Kitty.

Kitty smiles. "Of course. She was so sweet, and her partner — Teresa, right?"

Kitty had been with Ruby once to visit the convent, and the memory is bittersweet. They'd been fighting that week, Ruby had almost called off the visit, but as usual they'd patched it up and Kitty had charmed the hell out of the ayas. "Don't lose this one," Aya Julio had told her. And of course, she had. Only a few short months later.

The past is past, though. Time to focus on the present.

"Aya Marga is missing," she says.

"How does an aya go missing?" Absolon asks.

"A convent's not a prison, you can come and go," Ruby points out. "Aya Marga disappeared, along with most of the Aymaya Apostles' funds. Ayalasi Kateri asked me to help find her. As far as we can tell, she was supposed to meet Lebedevya."

"She was going to meet the Voice of Power?" Kitty looks surprised.

"It has something to do with Saint Alixhi."

Understanding flashes across Kitty's face, and she hides her expression with a sip of her cocktail, then frowns at the gold cuff on her wrist when it chimes. "Evelyn," she says. "Asking about dinner. We're just friends." That last to Ruby, pointed. Shameless. Ruby shifts; Absolon clears his throat.

"Evelyn has been more than a friend," he says. "She's been a valuable mentor to Katriana."

"Absolon introduced us," Kitty says. "He heard Evelyn was in Arquelle giving a seminar about tapping into your creativity and finding balance, and I figured why the hell not. I've tried everything else." She shrugs. "The way she and the Voice talk about finding your child self and awakening your dreams, it clicked for me."

"That's good," Ruby says.

She can tell Raj isn't quite following, but she understands what Kitty is hinting at, and why she doesn't want to talk about it openly. Kitty wasn't just slumming in Artemis City as an artist's lark, some rich girl trying to make her parents worry. She was on the hunt for a way to chase away demons only she could see. Ruby knows from experience that when Kitty's feeling good, she shines like gold. But even on her brightest days, darkness always seems to lurk at the edges — Ruby had learned, eventually, that even when Kitty was shining it on for her, an eclipse was hiding around the corner.

Then, Kitty would disappear. Either physically, lost in some manic party scene until Ruby tracked her down, or mentally, lost in her work, forgetting to eat, pushing the darkness away with a medicine cabinet full of mind-altering substances. It was part of why they'd moved to Ironfall, even though it had been harder for Ruby to find work there. Kitty had needed to get away from the too-tempting clubs with their constant flow of party drugs.

The dark times had always passed, but it wore Ruby down. Made her cautious and tentative and ill with worry, until their last epic fight when Ruby decided she couldn't spend the rest of her life picking up Kitty's broken pieces. Kitty had flounced back home to Arquelle, and Ruby had hoped her rich family could help her in ways slumming with Belt trash never would.

Apparently she was right.

Ruby's been searching Kitty's face for the fleeting shadows that used to ghost the edges of her smile, haunt the glitter of her eye, rust the edges of her laughter. She can't find them. Kitty seems . . . truly happy.

"You went to Evelyn's seminar, and then you followed her out here?" Raj asks.

"Evelyn opened me up to a new way of thinking," Kitty says. "It was like, I'd been searching for something this whole time, but I just needed to turn around and look in a mirror, you know? It sounds clichéd — but she was helping me find myself. And I wanted to meet the Voice in person." She gives Absolon a sly smile. "Big Brother was already coming out here on business, so it was perfect timing."

"Business?" Raj asks.

A muscle jumps in Absolon's jaw. "Yes." The coldness in his eyes warns them off.

"The clairvoyance stuff, only?" Ruby gives Kitty a skeptical look. "That's not real."

Kitty shrugs. "I don't know about any of that," she says dismissively. "Some of it's a little strange, but they do good work. For the first time in my life, maybe, I've found someone who can help."

"I'm glad to hear it," Ruby says. She wants to add, *Be careful*, but she knows from experience how poorly Kitty reacts to being cautioned. "But we still have to figure out what they have to do with Aya Marga's disappearance and Saint Alixhi. We think Lebedevya might have scammed Marga into giving her the convent's money."

"And you have a plan to get it back?" Absolon asks, eyebrow raised.

"We do." Raj smiles broadly at him, then lifts his chin to the door, where Lasadi, Jay, and Alex are walking in with their arms full of the supplies Raj asked them to get.

Lasadi and Jay paused in the doorway at the sight of Ruby and Raj's companions, but Alex breaks into a grin.

"Kitty!" he says, dropping his shopping bag on the table and giving her a hug. "What are you doing here?"

Ruby waves Lasadi and Jay over to the table. "Meet Absolon and Katriana Chevalier — *those* Chevaliers. It's a bit of a long story."

Absolon stands, giving a posh Arquellian bow to the rest of the crew. "Not that long a story," he says. "Raj and I have known each other since childhood, apparently my sister used to date your friend Ruby, and we're now — against my better judgement — swept up in some con you're intending to pull on the Voice of Power."

"We're going to help find Aya Marga," Kitty says to him, gently chiding. "We'll do anything we can." She tilts her head down at the shopping bag dropped on the table, then starts pulling out objects: chalks, inks, paints, brushes, and a data stick.

"What's this?" she says, lifting the data stick between her slender, perfectly manicured fingers.

"A copy of Aya Marga's notes on Saint Alixhi's paintings," Alex says.

Kitty breaks out laughing.

"Well," she says, and when she looks back up at Ruby, the mischief in her eyes shivers all the way down Ruby's spine. "This plan seems like fun."

"I'll go get us another round," Ruby hears herself say, and when Kitty smiles back — truly smiles — nothing else matters.

CHAPTER 8
RUBY

CHAMPAGNE DANGER; RUBY FORGOT HOW THOSE SILVER roses go straight to the brain in a heady rush of coconut cream and bubbles and sultry, silken haze. A splash over the rim meant sticky fingers; she'd licked a fingertip clean and looked up to find Kitty watching, and one thing led to the next in a glittering tumble of covert goodbyes and shuttlecab fumbling and then the Hôtel l'Eza's splashy neon lobby and gorgeous satin sheets.

She's made an incredible, monstrous mistake — especially in the middle of a job — but even as the champagne haze ebbs, she can't stop herself from reaching for the curve of Kitty's lean hip.

Kitty's side of the bed is empty.

Ruby stretches lazily, blinking the fuzz out of her head and detangling her limbs from the sea of satin. Warm light blooms in the sitting room, pooling through the cracked-open door, and Ruby waves on the bedside lamp, takes a long, greedy drink of the water Kitty must have left for her. Pulls on a robe and ties it, rakes her fingers through her tousled curls as she pads barefoot into the light.

Kitty is sitting at the hotel table, bare-shouldered in a nightgown. She's twisted and wrapped her hair in a turquoise silk scarf to protect it, so she must be planning on coming back to bed. But for now she's painting. Absorbed in the forgery, graceful neck bent over her work.

Ruby approaches with caution.

Midnight painting means one of two things. Kitty could merely have been unable to sleep, excited by the gleam of a new project. Or she could be painting the demons away, every brushstroke building a wall to isolate her further and further from the people who love her and want to help her.

"Heya," Ruby says softly, approaching her like one would a cat who's likely to startle.

Kitty doesn't turn away from the fine work she's doing, but the curve of her cheek in the lamplight pulls into a smile. "Hey. Look at this."

She finishes the brushstroke, feathering pale blue, and straightens.

"I couldn't sleep, I kept thinking about how even if the Voice believes your story tomorrow, it would be too easy for her to verify whether or not the painting was really Saint Alixhi's. There are a lot of techniques to age a work, but they take more time than we have. And they're not foolproof. But this?"

Kitty leans back to give Ruby a better view of what she's been working on.

The table's covered with sketches. Some are shoved

carelessly to one side, apparently Kitty's earlier practice runs. But a few are set neatly out to dry. Long, bold lines that trace the shapes of mountains and trees, suggesting the sinewy lines of rivers. They look like they were done in a few seamless strokes, without the charcoal lifting from the paper; the lines are smudged in places from the edge of Kitty's palm. Splashes of water-color were added later, the color shockingly delicate against the backdrop of the thick charcoal lines. In several sketches, Kitty added blotches of color haphaz-ardly, as though trying to find the right shade to paint the sky. In the one she's working on now, the technique is more deliberate, watercolors washing into each other in a kaleidoscope of hues.

They're incredible.

"What is this?" Ruby asks, carefully picking up one of the sketches to study the lines.

"I was skimming through Aya Marga's notes about Saint Alixhi and read that she did dozens of sketches for each painting. Mostly she was trying to capture a vision or dream she'd had, but for a few years she experimented with sketching as the medium for vision. She blindfolded herself and let God flow through her to see what happened. She threw out most of her sketches, so they're a lot more rare."

"And easier to forge on short notice."

"Exactly. Show her a holo of the painting I did last night and say it's with the dealer for verification, then take her these."

"Where did you get this paper? It looks antique."

Kitty laughs. "It's from my own sketchbooks. The company has been making art supplies for centuries, and I can't imagine their technique has changed since Saint Alixhi was sketching out her dreams. I used tea to make it seem a bit older."

Ruby tilts her head, studying Kitty. "You've done this before, love?"

Kitty winks. "Not exactly. But I help Absolon sometimes."

"With what?"

"Work."

She's obviously not going to answer, and Ruby doesn't press. Kitty's hinted in the past that Absolon has some rather shady business dealings, but she's never elaborated. Ruby picks up another of the sketches, her attention caught by the symbol in the corner.

A crescent moon turned on its back, balanced on a teardrop. The exact same symbol she'd seen on the conference's site, which had linked them to the protected information about the Children of Alixhi.

"What is this?"

"Saint Alixhi called it the Dreaming Moon," Kitty says. "She wrote that it was difficult to tell the difference between true visions and flights of imagination, and that God of course could influence both. But when she felt certain that a vision was true, she marked it with this symbol. The paintings and drawings marked by the Dreaming Moon are her most valuable — but you won't find many in private collections. The church keeps them tight."

"You read that in Aya Marga's notes, did you?" Ruby asks, and the corners of Kitty's mouth tighten. When Ruby had first brought up Saint Alixhi in

Segafredo's, she'd sensed that Kitty knew more than she was letting on about the saint's significance to Lebedevya. Now she's certain of it.

Ruby settles into the chair beside Kitty and props her cheek on her fist, gambling that Kitty is in one of her chatty, expansive moods.

"Tell me about the Children of Saint Alixhi, love," she says.

Kitty studies Ruby a long time, then tucks her feet up beneath her on the chair. "Now, where did you hear that name?"

"When I hacked into Lebedevya's site," Ruby says. "I found the name, this symbol, and a separate programming track. I couldn't find anything else about it."

"And you won't," Kitty says. "None of it's written down anywhere, and they swear you to secrecy."

"A secret society?" A chill touches Ruby. "You're a member?"

"I haven't decided if I want to take the next step. Evelyn says I can decide once I meet the Voice tomorrow."

"Oh, saints in hell," Ruby groans. "You were supposed to meet Evelyn for dinner last night."

Kitty's smile turns sly, her gaze raking down Ruby's body in a way that turns her spine to liquid gold. "More interesting plans came up."

"Focus," Ruby says, half to Kitty, half to herself. "If we're going to find Aya Marga, I need to know everything."

"I don't know much." Kitty leans back in her chair, stretching lazily. "But you can stop looking so concerned, darling. It's an accountability group for people who want to transform their lives. It's like, we all have bad habits that have been holding us back. Fears, right? What Evelyn has been teaching me is how to face those fears and retrain my destructive habits."

"How?"

"Through dreams. Instead of running from my fears, I face them through dreaming in order to clear their hold on me. Ruby, it's working."

"You seem happy," Ruby says, cautious.

"It's been better than any drug I've ever tried. I feel more alive. More . . . *me*." Kitty's smile glows. "All this time I've been suffering, it's been because of my own choices. It hasn't been real, it was only my fears. And I can choose whether or not to be afraid."

Ruby frowns. "You've learned all this through dreaming?"

"It's a powerful technique. It's worked on toxic relationships, my addictions. Evelyn told me it can even work on illness. It can work on memory loss."

"Course it can."

"Have an open mind, Ruby. Skepticism isn't protection, it's fear."

Now isn't that a perfect line to draw someone into your cult; but Ruby bites her tongue. She still needs information on the Children of Saint Alixhi, and she'd rather not be thrown out of Kitty's hotel room in the middle of the night wearing only her robe.

Though she has a hard time imagining this calm, peaceful version of Kitty sobbing at her to leave. Maybe the dream therapy bullshit is on to something. Least Ruby can do is try to be open to a new idea.

"I'm glad you're happy," Ruby says. "Truly. This dream stuff, though — it's part of the Children of Saint Alixhi?"

"The Children are people who want to go deeper," Kitty says. "More intensive sessions with the Voice of Power herself, stuff like that. I know it sounds silly and secretive, but I've already seen how incredible these techniques are. Evelyn says that what they teach to the Children of Saint Alixhi is even more powerful. You have to be properly trained to explore it."

"Do you think you'll join?"

A flicker of uncertainty flashes over Kitty's face. "I'll do anything it takes to find peace," she finally says. "Evelyn asked me to consider what I'd lose if I stopped my destructive behaviors, and I realized the answer was fear. I want to learn to stop being afraid of the darkness, and learn to be myself again." She tilts her head. "What would you lose if you gave up *your* fear of the past, Ruby?"

"I'm not afraid of the past."

"Sweetheart. You're terrified what you'll find, but you can't stop searching. There's nothing wrong with you because of that, but there is another way."

Ruby breaks eye contact first, soothing her tumble of thoughts by studying the sketches Kitty has scattered over the table. Even though she knows they're fakes, she can't help but picture Saint Alixhi in her cell with a cloth tied over her eyes and a piece of charcoal in her hand. Each bold, sure line sketched fearlessly into the unknown, confident of her direction even as she let her hand move of its own accord.

What would it be like to move that boldly, without overthinking every move?

When she meets Kitty's gaze again, she's surprised to find compassion in her expression. "When you meet with the Voice tomorrow," Kitty murmurs, "try to stay open. I think she could help you."

Ruby clears her throat and waves a hand over the sketches. "If you really think that, then why are you helping me scam her?"

Kitty laughs. "Because Aya Marga is lovely, and I want to help you find her. Besides, saints know the ayas need the money way more than the Voice of Power does. She's filthy rich, she won't miss a few credits." Kitty unfolds herself from her chair and leans forward, long, charcoal-smudged fingers soft on Ruby's cheek. "And maybe because I'm not ready to give up all my bad habits yet."

Ruby shivers as Kitty's fingers trace down her neck, over the gold-ink tattoos on her clavicle; she lifts her chin as Kitty's lips search out hers. "Am I a bad habit?"

"The worst," Kitty murmurs, her fingers on the tie of Ruby's robe. Silk slides over Ruby's skin.

"Sounds like you need to dream about me more, then." Ruby gasps; smudges of charcoal down her breasts, her belly, her thighs. "Face your bad habits, only?"

Kitty laughs and nips her thigh, turning her smile up at Ruby; it's full of mischief and free of shadow. "Might have to do more than dream," she says, and everything else vanishes in glory.

CHAPTER 9
RAJ

RUBY'S NOT IN THE LOBBY OF THE HOSTEL WHEN RAJ COMES down the next morning, but she has sent him a message: MEET ME AT THE COFFEE STAND IN FRONT OF HÔTEL L'EZA.

When he arrives, she's waiting with sunset orange flaring from her hips and swishing around her calves as she laughs with the barista. The top of the dress fastens at the nape of her neck and ties in a bow at her waist, leaving her back bare. She's carrying a large purse of gold-dyed leather, wedge heels to match.

"Good morning." Raj calls, and she lifts a cup of coffee in a salute, polished wood bangles clacking on her wrist. She's perfectly made up, though it doesn't look like she got much sleep last night — clearly in a good way.

Raj lifts an eyebrow and accepts the cup of coffee she puts in his hand. "Did you have a nice night?"

"None of your damn business." Ruby straightens her skirt. "You?"

"Uneventful. But we weren't talking about me," he says. "You spent the night with 'Kitty.'"

"So what if I did?"

"Then I get to mercilessly tease you, those are the rules." Raj holds out an arm to escort her back across the street to the hotel. "Though, seriously — no one saw you? I know I'm a lackluster consolation prize, but you and I are supposed to be a thing at this conference."

"No one saw me," she says. "Though you grew up around famous people. Is it even a realistic relationship if one of us isn't caught having an affair?"

"Fair point."

She pats his arm. "And you're not a consolation prize, love. The captain'll come around."

Raj shoots her a sharp glance. He's not so certain, and either way, he doesn't need thoughts of Lasadi distracting him right now. When he'd told her to take her time in getting back to him, he hadn't meant for her to keep him in limbo the rest of their lives.

He shakes the thought off, attention back on the job at hand. "Tell me you at least got a painting out of it."

Ruby pats the oversized gold purse as they walk into the Hôtel l'Eza lobby. "I've got something even better. Ready for showtime?"

They're slightly earlier than the day before, and most of the guests in the Nebula Room are milling about, networking, catching up with old friends, and discussing the events of the day before. Raj overhears one woman in a flowing pantsuit and caked-on makeup discussing her private session with the Voice of Power, and motions for Ruby to slow. They pretend to peruse the snack table.

"She didn't even have to speak, and I knew exactly what I was meant to do," the woman says. "I sold my shares in the company, and I've never felt so light in my life."

Raj leans in to Ruby as the woman walks on. "Was Katriana always into this stuff?"

Ruby pauses, considering. "We had a fight once," she finally says. "I told her to stop running off, that if she was trying to figure out who she really was, she should look in a mirror." She waves a hand at the crowd around them. "Maybe this is her way of doing that. I mean, Lebedevya is a fraud, isn't she, with the mind reading? But Kitty was happier last night than I've seen her in ages."

"Lebedevya is fleecing these people," Raj says.

"So it's expensive. Kitty can afford it, only, and it's better for her than some of the other highs I've seen her chase."

"Are you having a change of heart?"

"Absolutely not, love. I'm keeping an open mind, aren't I."

Raj has been scanning the crowd, searching for the Chevaliers — and on high alert for any other unpleasant surprises from his past. Absolon finally enters the conference room a few minutes before the first session is supposed to start. Alone. Raj nudges Ruby. "Did you wear Kitty out?"

"She had an early appointment with Evelyn," Ruby says primly. She smiles at Absolon, whose expression of measured annoyance doesn't change.

"Morning," Raj says, holding out a hand; Absolon

doesn't shake it. Raj lets his hand drop back to his side. "Will your sister be joining us today?"

"She's with her mentor," Absolon says. "I don't expect I'll see her until this evening." He glares pointedly at Ruby. "We have firm dinner plans."

"I'm surprised you came to the seminars anyway," Raj says. "Doesn't quite seem your style."

"My sister finds comfort in these teachings, so I would like to know more. Call it curiosity in the thing that finally gave her some inner peace." The lines of his mouth sour. "Unlike you two, I have a certain amount of respect for the work being done here."

"For the color theory and the clairvoyant act, sure."

Absolon leans in close to Raj, malice sparking electric between them. "The sole reason I haven't hauled you in to the nearest Alliance outpost myself as a filthy traitor is because of my sister," he says, voice deadly low. "Give me one reason, Demetriou, and I will destroy you." He straightens, bowing sharply to both of them in turn. "Good day."

Someone strikes a chime as Absolon stalks off, and a staff member appears to usher Raj and Ruby to the same table they sat at the day before. Interesting that there's assigned seating. Probably helps with the fake clairvoyant readings.

They're welcomed with the same enthusiasm as yesterday, and Raj pays only half attention to the speaker. He's watching Absolon, who's sitting in straight-backed attention on the other side of the room.

Absolon may not be going to turn him in to the Alliance, but that doesn't mean he's happy to be mixed up in their plan — and Raj isn't thrilled about his and

Katriana's involvement, either. Absolon's diplomat father was entrenched in Alliance politics, and Raj remembers everyone assuming Absolon would follow his path, since Katriana clearly got their singer father's artistic genes. Raj hasn't followed Absolon's career — he's been too busy trying to keep himself out of trouble to care what any of his old peers are up to. If he'd been asked, he would have assumed Absolon was working some enviable political appointment some-where posh.

And yet.

He's been awfully cagey about the reason he's actu-ally here in Artemis City, and Katriana left some juicy hints that her brother's business may not be entirely aboveboard. Raj would love to know more.

His attention returns to the stage when the speaker introduces the Voice of Power once more.

"Another session of parlor tricks?" Ruby murmurs; Raj shrugs, claps politely as Annika Lebedevya takes the stage with deliberate grace. Today she's dressed in pale lavender, a flowing robe made of layers of shifting gauze. She holds her arms out and it shimmers around her, ethereal and impossibly light. Her glossy blond hair is left loose and soft, her dark slash of eye makeup a moody contrast.

"My dear ones," Lebedevya says with a beatific smile. "Welcome to the second day of this incredible event. I am feeling the excitement and joy even more than yesterday. More of you are committing to your power. I love to feel this energy!"

A smattering of applause, a couple of excited whoops from a table near the front that gets Lebedevya's sweet smile and scattered laughter from the rest of the room.

"Yesterday, I spoke to many of you individually of spiritual healing," Lebedevya says. "I heard a theme. Many of you brought up a troubled soul connection with the spirit of wealth, and that is something I wish to speak with you all about this morning. Maybe you came today because you heard of a friend who was in financial troubles before I asked the spirit of wealth to help them. Maybe you read of someone whose business was failing before I helped them connect with the spirit of wealth so they could transform their business into a beacon of good in the world.

"Maybe you came, wondering if I could help you heal your spiritual connection with wealth in your own endeavors." She smiles at the rapt crowd. "I can."

Raj keeps from rolling his eyes by cataloguing the language she uses as she slips into a series of stories about nameless actors she helped into successful careers, heirs she helped turn their family businesses around, politicians she helped win elections. Their private session with her is right after this, and Raj wants to be able to speak her language when the time comes.

And he's still trying to get a handle on her game.

Yesterday, he'd pegged Lebedevya as a common charlatan, using simple psychology and cold reading techniques to bring a sense of wonder over the crowd. But this crowd is filled with smart, savvy people, who have traveled — like Katriana — from as far away as Indira to seek out her wisdom. Parlor tricks will only work on them for so long.

Raj scans the faces in the crowd around him. Some

people seem to be fully immersed, with a desperate or hopeful look in their eyes. Others seem skeptical, and it's those Lebedevya's speaking to right now.

"If you are wondering if my power is real, to you I would say the same thing I told the executive of a Teguçan company who came to see me last week. You've sacrificed so much to be here today. Trust yourself, and have faith to step the rest of the way."

Raj catches faint nods on some of the people he's clocked as holdouts. Her reasoning is compelling: They've already sunk a ton of money into attending this conference, they might as well go all in and see if her magic formula works for them.

"We all have the ability to see success like I have been speaking of — or even greater," Lebedevya continues. "We all have a divine spark calling for us to live our greatest lives so we can make a positive impact on the world. Our one goal — our calling — is to stop smothering that spark and allow it to grow into the vibrant, divine Power it wishes to be.

"You are all savvy with your money, that is what has gotten you this far. You invest in the markets, in your businesses, and expect a return. Maybe of five, ten percent? Maybe twenty? But what if I told you I had an opportunity that would return your money tenfold? You would call me a liar."

She smiles gently, there's friendly laughter around the room — at this point in her speech, nearly everyone's on board with her.

"What if I told you the investment was yourself?"

The room stills as her words sink in.

"How much do you believe in yourself? It isn't easy.

For myself, leaving my past behind to invest in this spiritual journey saved my life. I invested in myself, and I can tell you for certain the investment you're making in *your*self today will come back to you tenfold. The greater the investment, the greater the return, which is something I know you all understand. And I already know you believe in your own potential or you would not be here this morning."

She presses her hands together, and around them, others do the same — quite a few more than yesterday. Ruby's quick to follow; Raj glances at her and then awkwardly presses his own hands together, still playing the part of the actor boyfriend uncertainly supporting his true believer heiress girlfriend.

"May Spirit bless your investments today," Lebedevya says, holding her hands up as though to bless the crowd before walking off the stage.

Before Raj has time to comment on the theatrics to Ruby, she's turned her face to someone behind him with a bright smile; Raj shifts to see the bubbly young man from yesterday.

"The Voice of Power is ready to see you now," he says.

CHAPTER 10
LASADI

"KITTY TOLD ME SOMETHING WILD LAST NIGHT," ALEX says.

He's flipping through Aya Marga's notes on a tablet as they walk, having gone from mildly interested in the artistic endeavors of saints to completely obsessed overnight. "She said Saint Alixhi never left her cell, so all the landscapes she painted came to her in visions. They were all of real places — though some of them hadn't been discovered yet when she painted them! Some of it was even old Earth stuff, historians found matches when they went back through the archives."

They're on the hunt for a lead on Aya Marga, having found the name Lupita's Hotel in her notes. Turns out Lupita's is in the sector that immediately surrounds the dockyards, the busy, cavernous ring corridor off which hundreds of warehouses, shipping offices, inspections centers, and cheap flophouses and body lockers are located. It's busy as always with pedestrians and mototaxis; driverless cargo trains zip along an invisible track through the center of the chaos.

Jay grabs Alex's elbow, gently steering the kid around a buttress and through a line of hopefuls applying at a recruitment center. The sign above the door promises Short Runs, Home Every Month in neon green letters.

Alex holds up the tablet, which is open to a surreal landscape of translucent blue ice cliffs, the faint silhouettes of bulbous buildings trapped beneath the ice. "Did you know Saint Alixhi painted alien planets, too? Look at this."

Lasadi squints at the tablet, trying to makes sense of it. "Is that on Indira?"

"It's alien," Alex says. "If the other stuff she painted turned out to be real, then the alien planets must be, too." Alex flips to another painting, this one featuring blackened spears of what might be lava spiking into a sulphur-yellow sky, purple vines choking the spears from the jungle below. "She wrote about even more alien planets than she painted. Get this — "

"Step up," Jay says, and Alex steps over a tangle of cables, keeps reading without missing a beat.

"'On the moon of a gas giant far from this system, the trees reach to the heavens, ancient and yet aware, the tendrils of their roots holding vast secrets.'"

"I thought you were trying to find information on why her relics were cursed," Lasadi says.

"That was before I knew about the aliens," says Alex, like his intellectual derailment is the most natural thing ever. He slips the tablet back into his satchel. "But I did learn about the curse. She made a vow never to leave the convent in New Manila, and in her later life she became an anchorite. She — "

"I'm sorry, what?"

"An anchorite. Literally walled into a single room. Like, without a door."

Lasadi suppresses a shudder. "Why?"

"So she could get high and talk to God."

"I don't know much about your God," Jay says. "But I'd be worried about getting hit by a meteor for that kind of joke."

"I mean, it's true. She took mushroom teas and did these extreme breathing exercises to put her in a meditative state. I'm not saying her visions were faked, though — maybe that's how God works? I don't know. Anyway, someone stole her bones a century ago, and they haven't been found since. Legend says she'll bring misfortune until they're returned home."

"So the patron saint of travelers doesn't like traveling herself."

Alex taps a finger against his temple. "She traveled in her mind."

"Is the curse real?" Jay asks. Lasadi shoots him a look; he shrugs.

"Of course not."

"Okay," Jay says. "Curse is fake. Aliens are real."

"You got it. Can we stop for some dumplings? Those smell amazing."

"No," says Lasadi. "It's just a few more blocks."

"You don't want to eat anything in this part of town anyway," Jay says.

They've passed by the more legitimate establishments in the sector, entering a no-man's-land full of cheap accommodations and transient food carts peddling deep-fried meals to the dockworkers, belt drifters, and few non-union sex workers too desperate to ply their trade in the sanctioned establishments.

The place Marga listed in her notes, Lupita's, is a no-frills body locker, private bunk shelves rented by the hour with shared toilets and the main garbage chute for the block located beside the locker's front door. Charming. The sort of place you stay if you're completely broke, on the run, or a mercenary who's used to sleeping in worse.

Lasadi would have to be desperate to stay some place like this, and she's stayed some pretty rough places. She can't imagine how Marga must have fared.

Lasadi stops down the corridor, assessing.

The pale-skinned woman behind the bulletproof screen at the front desk has her cheek propped on her fist, like she's playing a game on her tablet rather than working. Las glances between her and Jay, sizing up the situation. This morning he's wearing a dark blue shirt advertising a classic kafusa group. It's snug enough to show some definition on his abs and pecs, the short sleeves rolled tight against his biceps. His shaggy black hair falls fetchingly into his dark, narrow eyes.

"This one's you, pretty boy," she says, propping her shoulder against the wall to wait.

Jay crosses to the woman, brushing his hair back as he does. "Excuse me, ma'am," he says in his most charming Coruscan lilt.

"I need an accent," Alex says, watching the woman's body language change from bored to extremely interested.

"I think it's the muscles."

"So muscles, and an accent."

"A certain New Manilan girl seemed to think your Artemis City accent was cute, even without the muscles."

The tips of Alex's ears flare red and he ducks his head. Across the street, the woman laughs at something Jay says; he leans against the desk casually, smile dimpling in his cheek. A minute later he thanks the woman and heads back to Lasadi and Alex.

"Did you get a date?" Las asks.

"I got something better: information. Marga *was* staying here, under an assumed name. She checked out two days ago. Becca said she rented one of the few actual rooms they had, and didn't leave much. She said she seemed nervous."

"Becca, huh?" Lasadi lifts an eyebrow at him; Jay ignores her teasing.

"Becca was worried about her — said she stuck out like a sore thumb around here."

"We'll find her," Alex says firm, as though to reassure himself. "If she was using an assumed name, Ruby should be able to track her down."

"We can do some digging, too," Lasadi says. "Every minute counts, and if Aya Marga was using a fake identity, she got it from someone in Artemis City." Lasadi checks her comm; Raj and Ruby should be meeting with Lebedevya right now, and they haven't sent out any urgent calls for rescue. "Let's go chat with Rizzo."

Rizalino Yu's studio is inside the dockyards. Officially, he's a customs lawyer. Unofficially, he helps customers who have gray market cargo and excellent financing navigate Artemis City's bureaucratic red tape around imports and exports by making sure bribes get to the right people without offending the delicate sensibilities of the local customs officials.

After all, this isn't Ironfall or Bulari, where a brutish exchange of money for favors is business as usual. Bribes are still expected, but Artemis City has standards.

Of course, Rizzo consults with clients on much more than how to pay the proper bribes. Step past his very classy main office and into his shielded back room and you've entered one of the most sophisticated identity forging operations in the Pearls.

Rizzo greets Las and Jay with a grin and a bear hug. He's lanky and dark-skinned, with a tidy beard, a shaved head, and the exact level of suit you'd expect to find a shipping and logistics consultant wearing. A flash of puzzlement creases his forehead when Lasadi introduces Alex, but it passes quickly and Rizzo ushers them into his main office.

"I hear you're working on your own now," he says to Lasadi. "Tora didn't give you a good enough deal?"

"It was time," Las says, though she doesn't particularly like Rizzo knowing her business with Tora Garnet already. "Her offer was good, but I'd rather be on my own. What have you heard about it?"

"I heard Tora's coup was mostly bloodless — I think everybody but her father thought it was time for him to hand down the reins. Tora's been spreading around that you parted ways amicably and are still doing odd jobs for her."

Lasadi lets herself relax slightly. The odd jobs detail is good; it'll keep Tora's enemies from assuming Lasadi and Jay are a threat, while implying that anyone who messes with them outright will earn Tora's wrath if they do. Tora's watching out for them. That's probably a good thing.

"Glad to hear it went well," Lasadi says. "I always liked Nico."

"Did you, then." Rizzo grins. "You're an odd bird. What can I help you with?"

"We're looking for a friend. Last we heard she was checked into a body locker called Lupita's, under an assumed name."

Jay swipes the name and Aya Marga's image onto Rizzo's desk, and the other man leans in. Rizzo never asks why they need to find someone, and no matter who they're looking for, it's always "a friend." His fingers blur over the keyboard as he cross-references the image, the name, running various permutations and swiping potential matches to the side. Once, his fingers still over an entry and his gaze flicks to Alex, then he swipes the entry onto the side of his desk and keeps searching.

It's a few minutes before Rizzo sits back, cracking his neck.

"The aya's left Artemis City," he says; that he figured out Marga was an aya isn't much of a surprise. But the steely look he shoots at Alex is. "And I've got a question for the kid. Who the hell are you?"

Alex's eyebrows shoot up. "Alex Quiñones?"

Rizzo's eyes narrow. "And?"

Alex glances at Lasadi, who gestures for him to answer. She has no idea what Rizzo's getting at, but she isn't getting a sense of threat off him. Presumably Rizzo has plenty of security measures to protect him in his own office, but she's never heard of him attacking first. Still, she shifts in her seat so she's got easy reach on her gun.

"And nothing," Alex says. "I'm just Alex. We're looking for Aya Marga because she helped raise me and my sister."

Rizzo swears. "Older sister," he says; it's not a question. "About ten years older?"

"Twelve."

"Rizzo?" Las asks. "What's going on?"

"You look exactly like your dad," Rizzo tells Alex, and the kid's jaw drops. Lasadi's heart pounds in her ears in the silence.

"What do you mean?"

Rizzo doesn't take his eyes off Alex. "You're what. Eighteen? Twenty? About that long ago, a couple came into this office. Gave me birthdates and pictures of their kids and said, 'They're called Alexander Abdul and Ruby Nicole. Help us hide them.' So I did. I gave you all new identities — different last names, made sure nothing linked you with them. I didn't ask what they were going to do with you, but my secretary told me later she'd suggested the Aymara Apostles. I told her off for getting involved." Rizzo tilts his head; Alex has gone ashen beneath his dark skin, sitting straight and still. "I always wondered what happened."

"Where did they go?" Lasadi asks when Alex doesn't speak.

"No idea. I offered to sell them passage off Artemis, they said they had their own ship. Seemed like they were running from someone — your dad especially was in bad shape, someone'd done a number on him a few days earlier. I almost turned them away — I don't need that kind of trouble — but then they showed me those photos of you and your sister."

"And did you catch trouble?"

Rizzo nods. "Yeah. Big fucker. Wore a full face helmet and never told me who he was working for, but he broke my arm when I wouldn't talk."

Alex winces. "Sorry," he says.

Rizzo shrugs. "Don't worry about it, kid. I've got one rule. I'll help you find someone, and I'll help you hide your identity — but I'll never pollute those two revenue streams, everybody knows that. No one's going to hire an identity fixer who rats out his clients. Getting an arm broken over it gives you cred."

"What were their names?" Alex asks. "I know you said you don't tell. But I have to know."

Rizzo frowns at him, silence stretching over a dozen heartbeats before he breathes sharp through his nose, types something quick, and slips a chip out of his desk. He slides it across to Alex, but doesn't lift his fingers when Alex reaches for it. "Kid — "

"Are you going to ask if I really want to know what's on this chip?" Alex's jaw is set, grim. "Because of course I want to find out what happened to my parents. What kind of asshole would say no to that question?"

Rizzo lifts an eyebrow, then smiles. "Of course you do. I was going to ask if you have anything that can access HPSI format."

"Oh." Alex blushes. "Yeah, my sister has basically every gadget."

"Thanks, Rizzo," Lasadi says. "We owe you."

Rizzo holds up a hand to wave away payment. "This one's on me." He gives Alex a sad smile. "Wish I could help you more, but do me a favor and don't ever come back here."

"You think whoever was hunting for my parents might still be out there?"

"I don't know anything except I've seen a lot of people come through this office searching for someone, and most of the time it ends badly."

"You said Aya Marga left Artemis City," Lasadi says. "Where'd she go?"

"Boarded a transport yesterday afternoon, didn't she. To Sapis."

"Sapis?" Lasadi groans. Olds, they'd been so close, only to find Marga shipping out deeper into the black. "What's on Sapis?"

"Ice? Bixian weirdos?" Rizzo spreads his hands. "No idea. But I like you, Las, so my advice to you is the same as it is for the kid. Whyever the aya left, she's probably trailing more trouble than it's worth. I'd think long and hard about whether it's best just to rest easy knowing where she went."

CHAPTER 11
RUBY

RUBY'S ALWAYS BEEN FASCINATED BY THE CASUAL WAY people like Kitty and Raj go through life. Sure, Raj may not have much money these days, but he still has the carefree attitude of someone who's always had a safety net. Even now, when he says he can't go back to Arquelle, she doesn't quite believe it. If he were in serious trouble, someone back home would bail him out — even if he didn't want to owe them for it.

And Kitty, she's never once checked the price of an item before ordering off the menu. Her room at the Hôtel l'Eza must cost per night what Ruby's flat costs in a month, and Kitty probably doesn't even know how much she's paying. Raj at least knows what it's like to be strapped.

Not that Kitty cares about luxury. She'd been equally at ease in the ritziest restaurant as she ever was curled up in the corner of Ruby's broken-down couch eating noodles from the corner stand and watching vids on Ruby's staticky holoprojector. But that's the point. Kitty doesn't have to care.

It's hard for Ruby to stay jealous of Kitty's *things* when she's also enjoyed the parties and the fancy meals and the Hôtel l'Eza's incredibly luxurious bedding and room service. But she'll always be jealous of her casual inexperience with normal worries like hunger or losing your place to live.

Annika Lebedevya, Ruby would guess, is the sort of woman who knows what it's like to covet wealth from the outside. She doesn't carry herself like someone born wealthy, but she's certainly flaunting it now. No more corner-stand noodles for Lebedevya, no more broken-down couches and cheap, noisy hostels. And as the lift opens in Lebedevya's penthouse hotel suite, Ruby wonders what the Voice of Power will do to keep this access to luxury now that she's gotten it.

Ruby holds her head high, her shoulders back, and channels every ounce of the indifference she's learned from Kitty as she walks into the room.

Lebedevya is sitting in the main room of the penthouse suite, which has been cleared of furnishings; only simple cushions and a serenely patterned rug remain. It reminds Ruby of Ayalasi Kateri's quarters, though it's hardly so rustic. The cushions are slubbed silk woven with gold threads, the rug thick, expensive wool.

Lebedevya is barefoot, so Ruby slips the wedges she borrowed from Kitty off in the entryway, then turns to bow over Lebedevya's hand like she's seen others do. "It's so good of you to see us."

"Welcome," Lebedevya says, generously letting Raj bow over her hand as well before waving them to the cushions. Ruby sits awkwardly cross-legged, smoothing her skirt over her thighs; Lebedevya sinks into a graceful prayer pose. "Richard, Olivia. Tell me about your goals for our session today."

"I'm looking for clarity," Ruby says timidly. "Maybe this sounds silly, but a family friend died recently, and it made me start thinking about whether I'm spending my life the right way. I inherited means from my parents, and I want to make sure I'm using them well."

"Death is a powerful catalyst for reflection," Lebedevya says in her strange, breathy accent. She smiles at Raj. "And you, Richard? You're an actor, correct?"

Raj dials his grin a touch too bright. "Living the dream."

"It can be hard to find success without losing your way," says Lebedevya. "Society encourages it, in fact, but I have worked with many seekers who came to realize the greatest successes in their careers arrive when they stay true to themselves and to Spirit."

Raj lets his smile falter with the perfect hint of confusion. "Olivia's the seeker here," he says, patting Ruby on the knee. Lebedevya follows the intimate gesture with faint distaste; Ruby tucks that away to wonder about later. "I'm here for moral support."

"Yes?" Lebedevya turns her attention back to Ruby. "I understand you've come upon a new business opportunity?"

"The family friend I mentioned," Ruby says. "He was a fantastic collector of religious artifacts in his life, and his children aren't interested. I have some art connections, so they came to me for help. I felt like Spirit was saying to me, these could have gone to a museum where they'd be gawked at and misunderstood by the masses. Instead, I chose you, to help them find the right home where they'll be cared for by someone who understands their true value."

Lebedevya nods serenely for her to continue.

"Finding a buyer hasn't been a problem," Ruby says. She smiles fondly at Raj. "Between my family and Richard's, we know practically everyone. My challenge is that I want to make sure I'm on the right path. There's a lot of spiritual energy in this collection."

Did she overdo it with the mumbo-jumbo? For a split second she worries she has, but Lebedevya only smiles and holds out her hands to Ruby and Raj. Ruby places her hand carefully in Lebedevya's; if the other woman is as sophisticated a con artist as she seems, she's probably looking for sweating palms, elevated heart rate. She doesn't seem to be wearing a lens or scanning their biosign any other way, but Ruby wouldn't rule it out.

"You want to live up to your true potential, Olivia," she tells Ruby, who nods attentively. "You described a crossroads — many of us find ourselves standing there at some point in our lives, after blindly following what society has prescribed for us for so long. We wonder which way to go, and we ask ourselves, 'What would my true self do?' But we don't understand our true selves enough to answer."

Lebedevya takes a peaceful breath, and Ruby follows suit, glancing at Raj. He looks every bit the part of the supportive partner: not bought in, but curious and willing to play along if it makes "Olivia" happy.

"The best time to access our true selves is during

childhood," Lebedevya continues. "Of course, none of us are children anymore. But I can teach you ways to unlock the energy of your child self and release the lessons held there." Lebedevya opens her eyes and locks her gaze on Ruby. "The idea bothers you?"

Saints in hell, she's good. Ruby's been trying to keep her reactions under control, but she tensed involuntarily, and Lebedevya obviously picked up on it. Ruby firmly pushes away panic. There are tons of reasons a person might not want to talk about her childhood, she tells herself. Lebedevya probably gets this reaction all the time.

"How does it work?" Raj asks with genuine curiosity, like he hasn't noticed the strange new tension between the two women. "Like, hypnosis?"

"Close your eyes and let Spirit flow," Lebedevya says. She releases their hands and gracefully rises, crossing to the wet bar where she's prepared a small tray with a stick of incense. She lights the incense and sets the tray in the middle of their small circle; a thick, floral smoke coils into the air, tickling Ruby's nostrils. She wrinkles her nose to avoid sneezing. Lebedevya wafts her slender hands through the smoke, humming.

Finally, Lebedevya stops humming and says breathily, "Tell me the earliest thing you remember, Olivia."

The first thing Ruby remembers is the door to the Aymaya Apostles convent, that welcoming, peaceful blue, the sensation of fear and worry and hope about who would be on the other side. She's not going to say that, though. Ruby opens her mouth to offer something innocuous about her mother's hug, and hears herself say:

"Gardenia and beeswax," and she's yanked into tangle of sensations: the rich, warm scent of her mother's hair products, the feel of the stiff new jumpsuit with the too-tight neck and scratchy zipper, the ache in her neck and scalp, and the taste — "and strawberries? Ice cream, I think. My mother tugging on my scalp braiding my hair. If I sat still without complaining she'd buy me ice cream."

There's another person in the scene, Ruby has a brief impression of her mother's voice and a man — her father? — laughing. Ruby can feel the rich vibration as he says her name, touches the tip of her nose with a strong finger that smells faintly of sulphur and iron. She reaches, hungry, but the more she tries to grasp at the scene, the deeper it vanishes into the foggy veil of her memory.

Ruby opens her eyes; Raj is watching her curiously. Lebedevya has a faint smile on her lips.

"You learned from your mother that if you were disciplined you would get a reward," Lebedevya says. "What you need to learn now is that discipline is its own reward. Good. And how about you, Richard?"

"Water," Raj says slowly, closing his eyes once more. "Standing in the tide with my nanny's hands under my arms, the way the outgoing tide sucked the sand from under my feet. I remember being afraid it was going to suck everything away and me with it." He opens his eyes. "I remember screaming, or at least that's what they tell me. My parents teased me about it for years."

A real memory? Or something nice Raj thought

Lebedevya would like? Ruby's not sure how anyone can think with the reek of incense so thick around them.

"Even as a child you sought stability," Lebedevya says with a knowing nod. She holds her hands over her heart and bows. "Thank you for sharing. We learn so much about our path when we embrace the lessons of our child selves." She reaches for the incense, grinding it out on the tray; Ruby blinks as the air clears, takes a grateful breath. "I have methods to help you connect deeper, of course. Through your dreams. It works best individually, however."

"Sounds interesting." Raj's tone says he will definitely not be signing up, but Lebedevya isn't speaking to him now; all her attention is on Ruby. Lebedevya's a professional. She's not going to waste time on a skeptic.

"We should talk more," Lebedevya says to Ruby. "Alone. Did you bring the painting?"

"The painting?" Ruby's as surprised by the quick change of subject as she is Lebedevya's blatant attempt to separate her and Raj. She shakes her head. "Oh, I don't have the painting, we're having it verified with an expert right now. But I brought a taste of the collection."

She gets to her feet much less gracefully than Lebedevya and retrieves the black artist folio from Katriana's oversized gold leather purse. "A few old sketches," Ruby says. "I wasn't sure if they would be worth anything."

She hands it to Lebedevya, who opens it curiously. And for the briefest of moments, Lebedevya's serene mask drops in pure amazement.

Thank the saints for Kitty.

"These are Saint Alixhi's sketches," Lebedevya says.

"The charcoal, the brush strokes in the watercolors — these are from her automatastic phase, I believe."

"You really know her work."

"I was taught by one of the best experts alive." Lebedevya smiles, and a shiver runs down Ruby's spine. Does she mean Marga? The message Lasadi had found yesterday suggested that the aya had been consulting with Lebedevya. "There are others?"

"Just the painting," Ruby says. She slips a mini holoprojector onto her palm and sets it to display the painting Kitty finished late last night.

Lebedevya barely glances at the holo before turning back to the sketches. She carefully turns the page to reveal the one with the moon-and-teardrop symbol, and her lips part in surprise before she schools her expression back to pleasantly interested. Ruby pretends not to notice the Dreaming Moon. Let Lebedevya think she's pulling one over on an ignorant socialite.

"You said your goal was to make sure the spiritual energy of these relics flow the right way in the world?" Lebedevya smiles gently. "This is important to me, too, which is why Spirit has moved me to make a sacrifice of funds to protect these pieces from negative energy."

"Really?" Ruby lets her eyes go wide. "That would be such an honor! I can forward you the appraisal paperwork as soon as I receive it, and we can make an appointment to see the painting. Maybe next week?"

"Olivia," Raj cautions. "You promised the other buyer he could view them."

"Yes, but we could put him off for a little bit," Ruby says. "Don't you think?"

Lebedevya's hands tighten slightly on the artist's

folio. "I'm afraid I'm scheduled to leave as soon as the conference is over this evening."

"Oh?" Ruby puts disappointment in her tone, and Lebedevya waves a hand.

"But any item from Saint Alixhi is too precious to let languish, even a simple sketch." *Especially* a simple sketch, if Kitty's right. Particularly if it's marked with the Dreaming Moon. Ruby can see the glimmer of greed in Lebedevya's eyes as the con artist scents she's close to closing a deal. "Allow me to pay you a deposit, and hold the painting for me to consider."

Ruby presses her lips together in feigned worry. "I don't know," she says.

"I understand your hesitation," Lebedevya says. "Your mother taught you the lesson of staying with a course in order to reach a reward, and I'm showing you an alternate path from the one you already began walking down. But I sense great potential in you, Olivia, if you give yourself permission to look deeper and see it."

She glances at Raj, then returns her attention to Ruby. "The reason I'm leaving so soon is that I'm holding an intensive retreat with certain members of my community. People who want to delve deeper into their own child selves, and unlock the power held deep within them."

Ruby doesn't think she reacts, but something in Lebedevya's smile says the other woman saw straight through to her soul. Alarm bells clang through Ruby's skull.

"Where is the intensive?" she asks.

"Paradise," Lebedevya says with a smile. "My organization rents a ring on Sapis Station." Sapis — one of Bixia Yuanjin's moons — isn't Ruby's idea of paradise. It's absurdly far out into the black. "I can have my assistant transfer the deposit immediately. And I will waive the fee for the retreat if you wish to join us. You are welcome to take the time you need to consult with Spirit about whether or not to invest in yourself by attending."

"I'll sell you the painting and sketches," Ruby says. "But we'll need to talk about whether we'll come to the retreat."

"It should be an individual decision," Lebedevya says. "But of course you both are welcome to come."

She stands abruptly, and Ruby and Raj follow her to the lift. They both bow over her hand once more, but when Ruby begins to pull away, Lebedevya leans in closer. "I have watched the light of too many true believers dim because they let skeptics hold them back," she murmurs. Lebedevya touches Ruby's cheek with a gentle hand, and Ruby catches another whiff of the strong incense, still lingering in the sleeves of Lebedevya's robe. "Tend to your own child self, dear one."

They don't speak until they're both out of the hotel, until Raj hails a shuttlecab and squeezes Ruby's elbow. "You all right?" he asks. "You looked like you'd seen a ghost when you started sharing that memory."

"An act, only."

Raj obviously doesn't believe her, but she doesn't want to talk about it. The memory wasn't her parents, it couldn't be, she doesn't remember anything before she was twelve. It must be of the ayas — there were plenty of times she let Aya Teresa braid her hair. But Aya

Teresa never bribed her with ice cream for sitting still — Ruby remembers always being too proud to complain no matter how badly Aya Teresa pulled.

And none of the ayas had fingers that smelled like fresh gunpowder.

Ruby pulls out her comm, checking the account she set up for this job. She shows it to Raj, triumphant, and thrilled at a chance to change the subject. "There's the ayas' money back," she says with a grin. "I hope the others have a lead on Marga and we can be done with this lot."

"Same." Raj hands back the comm. "What did Lebedevya say to you right before we left?"

"Some prattle about how she'd like us to go to the retreat, only. I don't know about you, love, but I'm ready to call this one quits. I'm dying to take these heels off."

She flashes him a wink, then turns her face to watch the glitter of Dāl Sector fade, Lebedevya's words echoing in her mind. *Tend to your own child self, dear one.*

Something's skittering in her mind beyond the words, some hint of a memory: Raj hadn't wanted to come here in the first place; hadn't they had an argument about returning to Artemis City? Or was it about coming to this conference?

Of course it wasn't; they hadn't known about the conference before talking to Aya Kateri and Aya Teresa, yet she clearly remembers fighting with Raj about it. Not the words they said, but emotions painted in broad strokes: frustration that he didn't understand her, fear he never would.

Ruby shakes her head. She and Raj may not have

fought about this job, but they've fought about plenty of others, and she's exhausted. "I need a nap. Or a coffee."

"Didn't get enough sleep last night?" Raj teases.

Ruby laughs, and the feeling of unease slips its grip in her mind. "Mind your own damn business, love."

Tend to your own child self, dear one.

CHAPTER 12
RAJ

"ALL RIGHT," LASADI SAYS. AROUND THE TABLE, HEADS turn her direction. "What have we got so far?"

They're back at Segafredo's, circled up with a new face in the group: Aya Teresa. The aya is out of place here in her sky-blue robe and veil, but the sort of people who frequent Segafredo's have some seriously ironclad respect for others' privacy. No one's given them a second look.

Raj's feeling more relaxed now that he and Ruby are both back in their usual clothes: a comfortable button-up with the sleeves rolled for him, a low-cut tank top and red leather jacket for her. She's got her black boots kicked out in front of her, and she's slouching back in her seat and chewing on a thumbnail. The rest of them are sharing a pot of slightly oily, slightly grassy tea.

"We recovered the convent's funds," Raj says; Ruby doesn't seem like she's about to respond. "Along with a nice cut which will keep us all fed and the *Nanshe* fueled for another few months." He tries to catch Ruby's eye to see if she has anything to add, but she's frowning at the table.

Something about the visit to Lebedevya has her spooked, and he'd bet it was the memory session. She tried to play it afterwards as nothing, but something was off about that memory exercise Lebedevya led them through. He'd chosen the memory of the nanny holding him in the surf because it was one his parents always dragged out for a smile at parties even though he barely remembered it. But as soon as he'd started sharing it, he could feel the nanny's hands under his arms, feel the sand washing away, feel the pure terror rabbiting through his tiny chest.

Raj shakes the memory away.

"Lebedevya also said she's leaving tonight for some kind of intensive retreat," Raj continues. "She invited us out, but personally, I'll be glad to have some distance between us."

"Same," says Lasadi. "She didn't say anything about Aya Marga? Or Lot 131 from the auction house — they were supposed to meet to discuss that specifically. It sounds like Marga might have been consulting with her about Saint Alixhi's artifacts."

Raj shakes his head. "Not while we were there."

"And if she met with the aya in the last day or so, she didn't do it in her room," Jay says. "I've been through all the hotel's security footage, and all the audio from the mic Las put in her room. She hasn't said anything about ayas in general or Lot 131 in specific."

"We figured out where Marga was staying, though,"

Lasadi says to Aya Teresa. "At a body locker near the docks, under an assumed name."

Aya Teresa goes pale, and Alex gives her an encouraging look. "It sounds worse than it is," he says reassuringly, though Raj has spent a night or two in shitty dockside body lockers, and he doubts that. Alex has a good heart, though he seems as distracted as his sister today. He's tearing a napkin to meticulous shreds. A habit he learned from Ruby? Or a genetic fidgetiness inherent in the Quiñones family?

"The person at the body locker told us Aya Marga was staying there alone," Lasadi says. "No one came to visit her."

"So she wasn't kidnapped?"

"Not from the convent, at least. She did buy a ticket off Artemis — or at least, one was bought for her assumed name. We have no way of knowing if she left willingly. Do you have any idea why she'd go to Sapis?"

Raj straightens, but Ruby jolts out of her distraction to say it first.

"She went to Sapis? Saints in hell — sorry, Aya."

But Teresa seems more worried about Marga's destination than Ruby's cursing. "What's on Sapis?"

"That intensive retreat Lebedevya's holding, on Sapis Station," Ruby says. "That's where she invited Raj and I to meet her."

"We have to go," Aya Teresa says.

Lasadi leans forward. "Aya," she says carefully. "Bixia Yuanjin and its moons are a long ways away. It's not so easy to fly out and have a quick look — especially if Marga doesn't want to be found."

"She would never leave without telling me why," Teresa says. "Not unless something bad was going on."

"We *said* we'd bring her back, Cap," Alex says.

Lasadi glances at him; Alex's jaw clamps shut against further protests. "We said we'd find out what happened to her," Lasadi says. "And as far as I'm concerned we haven't yet. It doesn't change the fact that this has gotten more complicated."

She takes a deep breath, and spines straighten expectantly around the table. "Ruby. We have the money from Lebedevya? Get it transferred to the ayas."

"On it, Cap."

"Raj, we need to know what was in Lot 131 that had Aya Marga talking with Lebedevya in the first place. Jay's been digging into it, but we need better intel. Those antiquities dealers you know, could they help us?"

"I'll get in touch. If we're going deeper into this job, we'll probably need their help shoring up our fake collection of artifacts, too."

"You trust them?"

"Absolutely."

"Thank you. Alex, keep digging around in those notes and work with Raj. We need to know everything we can about Saint Alixhi's art." She turns to Aya Teresa. "We'll find her. We'll make contact. And if she wants to come back, we'll head out to Sapis and get her ourselves. Now if you'll excuse us, we should probably get to . . ." Her gaze shifts past Teresa to the door. "Work," she finishes, then lifts her chin to Raj. "Your friend's here."

Raj turns to see Absolon Chevalier in the door of

Segafredo's. He's scanning the bar, clearly looking for someone, and when his gaze lands on their little group he takes a sharp, almost disappointed breath. He stalks to them, dark gaze pinned on Ruby. "Where is she?"

"I haven't seen Kitty since this morning," Ruby says.

"You shouldn't have even seen her then," Absolon says, voice low and even. Deadly. "She's here to study, not so you can take her out partying."

"So *I* can take her out?" Ruby asks. "Kitty does whatever she wants, maybe you've noticed."

"*Katriana* is susceptible." His nostrils flare. "And you know that."

Absolon's standing a touch too close to Ruby, using his height and the fact that she's still seated to intimidate her. Lord knows Ruby can fight her own battles, but Raj has had enough of Absolon's mood. He pushes back his own chair to stand, forcing Absolon to step back.

"None of us have seen your sister," Raj says. "And you're way the fuck out of line here." He glances over his shoulder. "Sorry, Aya."

"That's rich, Demetriou. A deserter telling me I'm out of line."

Two weeks ago, that knife would have cut to the quick. Now, surrounded by people who know the truth and welcome him anyway, the opinions of people like Absolon Chevalier no longer matter to him.

"What's your problem with me?" Raj asks.

"I have no patience for a man who betrays his country."

"That's not what happened."

"Then explain it to me, because all I see is a coward

who ran away from battle. Do you know what you've put your mother through? She's locked herself away in shame. And it destroyed your father. He's taking longer and longer deployments. People are saying that when he's home, they don't even sleep in the same wing of the house."

"I didn't think you were the type to share gossip."

"I'm saying that you've brought shame on your home. Your parents would have done anything for you and you threw it all away."

"My father tried to have me killed because I wasn't going to stand by and let him commit a war crime," Raj says calmly. "Is that part of the sob story he tells?"

Absolon blinks at him, lips parted.

"Boys," Lasadi says before either of them can continue the argument. She's leaning back in her chair, arms crossed like she's watching a dull chess match. "Why don't you both grab a seat?"

Raj would rather send Absolon out of Segafredo's with his haughty nose bloodied, but that wasn't a suggestion, it was an order. Raj pulls over another chair to their little group; a muscle jumps in Absolon's jaw, but he sits stiffly. Raj settles cautiously beside him, aware of the waves of animosity rolling his way. Though it's not just anger. If Raj had to hazard a guess, he'd say Absolon isn't upset with him at all. Raj is simply the closest target on which to work out the fear that clearly has Absolon in his grips.

"Your sister's missing," Lasadi says; Absolon nods woodenly. "Tell us what happened."

"Katriana has always been a bit wild," he finally says. "Moody and stormy, sometimes quite depressed, other times playful and fun. I've worried about her my whole life, and tried my best to guide her. But of course she didn't listen to her older brother."

"She doesn't listen to anyone," Ruby says, her tone gentle. "But she respects you."

The corner of Absolon's mouth twitches; he doesn't look her way. "When I saw the seminar Evelyn was offering back home, I suggested it but assumed she wouldn't go. I'd never seen her sit through a single lesson with one of our tutors, but she attended the entire weekend and worked through the lessons at home. I was amazed. And I wanted to be supportive — parts of it were scammy, but if it genuinely helped her, I didn't care. Evelyn has been different here, though. More demanding of Katriana's time; when she couldn't get in touch with her yesterday" — now he shoots a glare at Ruby — "she hounded me instead."

Lasadi nods. "Have you asked Evelyn where Katriana is?"

"She's not answering me, either." He takes a deep breath. "Katriana left me a message and said she was doing some deeper work with Evelyn, and that I should finish up here and head home myself. She said she and Evelyn would travel back together after."

"After what?"

"Some sort of retreat on Sapis. I thought it was a joke and she was with Ruby — who the fuck goes to Sapis?" He seems to notice Teresa for the first time, and straightens. "My apologies, Aya."

"Sapis?" Ruby's eyes are wide. "Lebedevya *is* holding some sort of private retreat. She invited us to go with her."

"Oh, right," Absolon says, voice dripping with disdain. "I forgot to ask how your day of fleecing went. I trust it was lucrative?"

"It went wonderfully, thank you," Ruby says.

"And thank *you* for making my sister a criminal." Absolon pushes back from the table. "This was a mistake."

"Hold on," Lasadi says, and Absolon stills, hope and frustration warring in his expression. "We've been digging into Lebedevya, and we still aren't sure what her game is, but you're smart to be worried about your sister. Aya Marga also went to Sapis without telling anyone beforehand, and from where I stand, that's not much of a coincidence."

"What is Lebedevya doing out there?" Absolon asks.

"We don't know. You feel like finding out?"

"Yes." Absolon takes a deep breath. "Will you help?"

"Will you play nice with my crew?"

Absolon's gaze cuts to Raj, then back to Lasadi. "Of course."

"Costs a fair amount to run a ship out to Sapis."

"Money's no issue."

Lasadi looks around her crew, getting nods from everyone. Raj gives his assent wholeheartedly. He'd much rather be avoiding Absolon on the *Nanshe* for a few weeks than worried he was out changing his mind about calling in a traitor to the Alliance. And somewhere, back in the annals of their youth, he and Absolon had enjoyed each other's company.

"Then we're in," Lasadi says. She turns to Aya Teresa. "It looks like we'll be going to find Aya Marga in person after all. The repairs on the *Nanshe* will be wrapped up tomorrow afternoon. That won't put us too far behind Lebedevya, and we can spend the time getting any gear we might need. Everyone get Jay a list tonight — be creative and think of *anything* that might be useful. Sapis is a long way from anywhere if we suddenly decide we need a field disruptor or a paint-brush or a set of mystix cards or whatever it is you need to finish out this con."

"Well, the coffee maker's moxed," says Jay, then winces. "Sorry, Aya."

"I don't even know what that one means," says Aya Teresa.

"Like, corroded beyond repair. You'll have to throw the whole thing out."

Aya Teresa smiles sweetly. "So, 'fucked'?" Ruby snorts into her tea; Raj grins at a stunned Alex. "You all can stop watching your language around me, I've spent plenty of time with Aya Julio and his stable of choice curses."

"You got it," Lasadi says with a smile. "Equipment lists to Jay, people."

"A privacy sphere would be useful," Ruby says. "We don't know what they'll have bugged."

"Good idea."

"Can I have a frog's tongue?" Alex asks.

Lasadi frowns at him. "Do I want to know what that is?"

"For if you're in zero G and drifting. It's sticky, like."

"Then sure."

"And we'll definitely need weapons a scanner won't

pick up," Raj says; beside him, Absolon clears his throat.

"If I may," he says, prim and coy as a cat. The others look to him expectantly. "I might be able to help with any equipment you need."

CHAPTER 13
RUBY

"So. Big brother Absolon's an arms dealer."

Ruby's perched on the lid of one of the crates Absolon has loaded into the *Nanshe*'s cargo hold, scrolling through the manifest. Absolon had been right that he could help with the equipment list — nearly everything Ruby could have asked for was in the hold of his ship, meticulously catalogued. Guns, hacking rigs, stealth tech, armor, along with some highly sensitive technology that Ruby's not sure any private citizen should have access to.

"I'm a specialty equipment distributor," Absolon says.

"Sure." Ruby lifts an eyebrow at one item on the list. "You have silverfish? Give us a look."

"What do you need those for?"

"Spying on Alex."

Ruby catches the packet of remote-controlled microtransmitters he tosses her way, slipping one of the silverfish onto her fingertip. "Flash. I haven't been able to find these for years, I thought they stopped making them."

"They did." Absolon clears his throat. "I have excellent relationships with my suppliers."

"And some interesting clients, if this is what you're peddling." Ruby tosses back the packet and closes the manifest, satisfied that whatever she'll end up needing on Sapis to finish this job, she'll find it in the *Nanshe*'s cargo hold now. It's stuffed full; Absolon's crates of "specialty equipment" aren't the only thing they're taking to Sapis. Jay called on some of his contacts to swing a few private courier jobs and earn some extra cash, too. Always thinking ahead, that one.

Ruby's spent the morning restless as a caged animal, trying to lose herself in planning and prep work, but mostly distracted by her worries. She'd tried to get in touch with Kitty all night, in the hope that she was just teasing her brother with the nonsense about going to Sapis with Lebedevya. She may have given her brother the slip, but she wouldn't vanish without a word to Ruby. Right?

But every one of her messages has gone unanswered. Like Aya Teresa's messages to Marga.

Ruby's kicking herself for not asking Kitty more questions about the Children of Saint Alixhi, about Lebedevya, about her mentor, Evelyn. Ruby had never had a good idea of what was going on in Kitty's head, but she could have pushed her to open up more. She should have spent more time reading up on Lebedevya's organization, she should have had a better plan going in.

Well, she'll have plenty of time for reading and planning in the next week.

Sapis, one of the larger moons orbiting the vast ice giant Bixia Yuanjin, is nearly seven days' journey from the Pearls — farther out into the black than Durga's Belt is from Indira. The Bixian moons have been inhabited as long as the Pearls have, though much more sparsely. It takes a certain sort to want to make their home so far from the cradle of human life in the Durga System, and the handful of Bixians Ruby's met over the years confirm they're an odd bunch.

The moon of Sapis is the breadbasket of the black, blessed with a saline sea below the icy surface that intrepid settlers tapped centuries ago. Few people live on the surface to tend the agricultural operation; the majority live in Sapis Station, the enormous city-in-the-sky that orbits the moon itself. The station is owned and run by the agricultural collective, Sapis Cooperative, though they rent parts of it to many different groups. Including, apparently, Annika Lebedevya.

What the stars is that woman doing out there?

Ruby pushes away the feeling of unease, pouring herself back into her work. The maintenance crew left the *Nanshe* an hour back, and the sooner they can get everything secured, the sooner they can get started on the horribly long business of flying and *waiting*.

"Here, you'll like this." Absolon tosses her a small circular device. It nestles in her palm, a glossy black egg banded by blue light. "Twist the segments until the bands line up."

Ruby does, and the light pulses twice, then gives off a steady glow. Her ears pop, and she yawns her jaw to release the sudden pressure. "A privacy sphere," she says. "I've never seen one so small."

"The range isn't much, but it's powerful. You can speak freely as long as you're within one meter of the device. My sister and I both carried one from an early age."

"Why?"

"Everywhere was potentially hostile territory. Our fathers' enemies could have been listening in, or some tabloid reporter. We were trained it wasn't safe to speak freely unless we were in our own home."

"What a terrible way to grow up."

Absolon shrugs one shoulder. "We both turned out fine."

"Did you?"

He turns a level look on her.

"I'm not throwing shade at your parents," Ruby says. "And you're probably lovely company when you don't have a stick up your ass, but Kitty is — not always well."

She expects a biting comment, but Absolon swallows hard, shoulders dropping slightly in a minute gesture of defeat. A chink in his armor; it takes ten years out of his face, and Ruby catches a glimpse of the boy he must have been. The boy who was taught he was entering battle every time he left his home, with one hand holding a privacy sphere and the other clutching his sister's, trying as hard as his young heart could to protect her from a world that wanted to tear them apart for entertainment.

If he still goes too far trying to protect Kitty, rather than letting her be her own person, well. Ruby certainly can't throw stones. She's got a little brother of her own.

"I owe you an apology," Absolon finally says. He straightens once more, no defensiveness in his posture. "You were good for her, and I've treated you poorly."

"We're both scared for her. I'm not being a dick about it, only."

Absolon's cheek tugs into a smile, and when he lets the rigid muscles of his expression relax, he looks exactly like his sister. Ruby's heart breaks for them both.

"We'll find her, Sol. And we'll bring her back."

Footsteps ring on the cargo bay ramp, and the moment's over; Absolon stiffens his shoulders again as Raj and Alex return from the grocery run. Ruby holds out the device on her palm to show them. "Privacy sphere," she says.

"What did you say?"

Ruby grins and twists the device back off, popping her ears once more. "Privacy sphere." She tosses it to Alex. "Turn it on in your room at night and spare us your snoring."

"That's great," Raj says. "But how will we get it in? We have to assume Lebedevya might search our bags."

The corner of Absolon's mouth curls into a smile. He sets his own suitcase on a crate, snapping it open to reveal the false bottom beneath his precisely stacked clothes. He pulls out a handgun, along with a number of other strange devices Ruby doesn't recognize but now desperately needs to own.

"Unscannable, undetectable," Absolon says. "Responds to a precise series of inputs coded to a specific set of fingerprints. The compartment's also blastproof, which makes it good for transporting delicate or sensitive items in potentially dangerous locations."

"That's extremely impressive, and I would like one," says Raj.

"I have a few more," Absolon says, then hands Ruby one of the small cases he pulled from the secret compartment. "Extendable shock baton designed to be concealed in a cuff, holds up to twenty charges."

"These are very illegal," Ruby says, admiring the sleek case. She flicks it out experimentally, admiring the satisfyingly sharp *phwap* it makes, then slips it beneath her own cuff.

Raj takes the translucent blade Absolon hands him, turning it in his palm appreciatively. "Nerve blade," he says. "Only other time I've seen one of these was when an Alliance special ops soldier was showing off to a bunch of us at the officer's academy. It's impossible to get your hands on one if you haven't gone through a lifetime of special ops training."

"Sol has excellent suppliers," Ruby says playfully, and is pleased to win a smile from the dour-faced man. Maybe with a week together, she can get him to loosen the hell up.

"And here I thought you were an Alliance patriot."

"We can fight later, boys," Ruby says. "But I'm ready to fly."

She helps Raj and Alex stow the groceries while Absolon finishes securing his crates of goodies in the smuggler's cache, then calls up to the captain that they're ready. She heads to the galley, settling herself into one of the crash chairs with a deep breath.

"Strap in," Lasadi says over the comms, and the hard bud of nervous anticipation that's been lurking under Ruby's sternum all morning blooms as always into full-on anxiety.

It's just flying, she tells herself. Just a rush of thrusters and the choking pressure of too much gravity, and then they'll be floating blissfully, pretending not to notice the fact that there's only a few millimeters of the *Nanshe*'s hull between their tiny fragile bodies and the cold dead vacuum of space.

Alex drops into the chair next to her with a grin. "You good, sis?"

"Course I am, aren't I." Ruby's heart throws itself against her chest, like it does every time, like it hasn't been through dozens of launches and come through fine on the other end, like it didn't survive the *absolute nonsense* that was Lasadi flying the Liluri Star Run. Ruby curses her hyperactive lizard brain and breathes like the ayas taught her, four-count in, four-count hold, four-count exhale.

"You want a distraction?" Alex asks, and there's a serious catch around the edges of his tone that makes Ruby open her eyes to meet his, liftoff anxiety ebbing lower as curiosity takes its place. "Because I learned something about our parents yesterday I've been meaning to tell you."

CHAPTER 14
LASADI

LASADI HAS SPENT A LOT OF THE LAST THREE YEARS WITH this view in her screen; whether coming or going, the Pearls are a lovely sight. The dwarf planets are all lit up and sparkling. Artemis covered in a diamond layer of glittering blues and gold. Dima dark beyond it with glimmers of orange in red in its crevasses, the spike of Ironfall glowing like a forge. Meilikki glinting in the distance, twins Nerrivik and Nujalik distant specks against the blanket of stars beyond.

Only this time, Lasadi's destination isn't somewhere in Durga's Belt, or even sunward towards the inner planets. She's aiming the *Nanshe* deeper into the black, where Durga's burning flame will seem just another star in the distance.

Lasadi is equal parts excited and unsettled by the thought of the vast, untroubled darkness beyond Durga's Belt. She sensed a similar unease in the rest of the crew during dinner in the galley earlier this evening — aside from Absolon, whose family apparently vacationed at Bixia Yuanjin when he and his sister were children, none of them have been out that far. Dinner was a crowded affair with six people, though slightly less awkward than Lasadi had been expecting. Absolon has toned down his posturing, and even laughed once or twice. Maybe bringing him with wasn't a terrible idea after all.

Now, as far as she can tell, the others are on their way to bed, settling back into their cabins with ease. Las doesn't need to be up here, but she's not quite ready for sleep. Her mind is racing, and not with anticipation for the trip.

She could ignore Raj when they were both distracted, focused on finding Marga and winning Lebedevya's confidence. But now that he's back on the *Nanshe*, she can't keep putting off the conversation they need to have. She should have dealt with this days ago, but she didn't have the guts. She's been telling herself she was still thinking things over, but that wasn't true. She's made her decision, and has been too terrified to follow through.

She opens a new message.

YOU STILL UP?

YES.

She takes a deep breath.

COME CHECK OUT THIS VIEW, I NEED TO TALK TO YOU.

She hears the door to his cabin open almost immediately, a creak of the ladder behind her as he floats himself into the bridge. She wants to watch his face when he sees the view, but that feels too dangerous; she turns back to the screen.

"Wow," he says. His hand touches light on the back

of her chair, and the closeness to her shoulder is electric. She takes a breath when he moves away to take the co-pilot's chair.

"You think of the Pearls as home?" she asks, and he shakes his head, silken strands of black hair drifting around his face. His skin is kissed to golden brown by the few days they were on the surface of Indira.

"No," he says. "I mean, it's been a good place to take off my boots for a bit. But Ironfall never felt very homey. Doesn't even matter about the accent, if you haven't lived in a hub for at least three decades, everyone thinks you're an outsider. People are nice, though."

Lasadi allows herself a glance over at him, and immediately regrets seeing the gentle, curious way he's watching her.

"So how'd you get to know Ruby?" That's not what she meant to say — not what she'd steeled herself to say — but her traitorous heart is stalling for time.

"Met her through a job we were both hired for," Raj says. "Next time I needed a hacker, I asked her. Time after, too, but she told me she was too busy. I kept asking, and I started to figure out she just doesn't like to get trapped working for one person." He looks thoughtful. "She *didn't*, at least."

"She's good at keeping people out. Not you, though."

Raj laughs. "It took a while, but I got under her skin."

Which is the exact same thing he's been doing with her. Since leaving Indira, Lasadi's been dissecting her attraction to him, studying it, hoping that if she ran the numbers enough times she'd come up with the correct solution to this problem. Her attraction to Anton had been closer to girlish obsession, and it had taken her years to realize she was in love with the image in her mind more than the man he was revealing himself to be. The problem she has with Raj is the opposite: the better she gets to know him, the more attracted she is. Anton had been so insistent on her attention she'd never had time to think through how she really felt. But Raj?

Lasadi's made a tactical error by waiting so long. She thought she was giving herself more time to make a clearheaded decision, but in the end she's given Raj's quiet charm more time to work.

She takes a deep breath, readying herself.

"I wanted to revisit our conversation from the other day," she says. She almost clarifies which conversation, but there's only one with the capital *C*, and anyway he nods, expression neutral. It must be obvious why she asked him up here. *Just say it, Las.*

"I don't think it's a good idea for us to . . ." She rolls a wrist, not sure how to finish the sentence.

"To date," Raj clarifies. The easy, open expression he'd had when talking about Ruby has turned serious, but he doesn't seem upset. She might as well have been talking through their flight path.

"Yes." She owes him an explanation — or maybe she owes herself one, so she keeps talking. "So much is changing right now. A new crew, this job, owning the *Nanshe*. And I'm still trying to sort out some personal things."

He's still relaxed in the co-pilot's chair, but tendons

flicker on the back of his hand, belying his outward calm. She tears her gaze away; thinking about those fingers isn't helping.

What she desperately needs right now is for him to brush this off. To tell her it's no big deal, he was just giving it a shot. That he didn't really have any feelings for her but the usual hormones you'd expect when two people are thrown together in a few life-or-death situations. She needs him to say something to make them both laugh at how absurd the idea was from the beginning. So she can finally get him out of her mind.

He's studying her face. Surely he can see through her fracturing resolve. And if he asks even one simple question — "You sure?" — she's going to lose it and say, *No, I'm not. I'm full of shit. I want you desperately and I'm terrified.*

He doesn't ask, and he doesn't toss out a joke to help her brush it off.

"I understand," he says.

"Okay." Her mouth is dry. "Good. I wanted to clear the air. Are we . . . ?"

"We're all good." He opens his mouth as if to speak, shuts it again. Clears his throat. "To clarify, is this a 'not now'? Or a 'no.'"

"It's a no." She says it to them both, firm. She's proud of how steady her voice sounds. "I'm sorry. I'm looking for something different."

A muscle jumps in his jaw, and a vise squeezes around Lasadi's heart. She's *not* looking for something different — it was a bullshit line to fill the silence, and she's about to take it all back when Raj gives her a broad, easy smile.

"I get it," he says. "And like I said before, most important thing is this crew. You don't have to worry about me — I'm happy being friends."

How can he be so relaxed? It can only be that he truly means what he's saying, and he really was taking a casual shot. That's good. That helps. She doesn't need a relationship with someone who's only casually interested.

Or he's a good actor, trying to make this easier on you.

Lasadi wills that small voice to stay quiet. "Thank you."

"Of course." He smiles again at her, the same smile he'd give any of the rest of them, and spins in the chair. "I'll catch you in the morning," he says. "Night, Lasadi."

She almost loses it at the sound of her name in his mouth, but he mercifully turns away and slips down the ladder to the crew level, and she doesn't have to hold on to her mask any longer. She hits the button to close the hatch behind him, then buries her face in her hands, the heels of her palms pressing into her eye sockets to keep renegade tears from seeping out.

The bridge suddenly feels too loud, the pings of equipment and whirring of electronics driving home the fact that she's alone. She could always talk to Jay — but he's in the engine room, and getting there means passing the crew quarters. She won't be able to keep it together if she sees Raj again. Plus, she already knows what Jay will say. He'll tell her she's an idiot, and she already knows that.

She made the right decision. There's no point in crying about it.

So she leans back in her chair and stares out at the black, ignoring the ache in her throat and the stinging in her eyes. It fades as she breathes, calming her mind until only she, the *Nanshe*, and the stars remain.

It's Coruscan tradition to sleep on the bridge the first night of a trip, she tells herself, and although she's certainly done it before, it's normally because she's exhausted rather than out of superstition. But tonight she doesn't want to pass Raj — or anyone — in the hall. And she did change out the captain's chair for a more comfortable one, like she'd promised herself ever since she first started dreaming about owning the *Nanshe*. Might as well enjoy it.

She can't talk to Jay about this, and definitely not Ruby. But there *is* one truly safe person she can tell her feelings to.

Lasadi calls up a screen on a whim and hits Reply, begins to type out a message she promises herself she'll never send.

Hey Evvi Faye,

You're right, I totally hate your ex, and agree with Grandma that he's completely awful for you. But you already know that — that's why you wrote to me. You're smart, compassionate, and you know your own mind. Plus, you have a generous heart with so much love to give — if he's not willing to see that, walk right out that door and find someone who will. I swear I'll come back as a ghost and haunt you if you stay with him. He's not worth it, sister.

And now I have something I want to tell you.

WHICH IS GOING TO SHOCK YOU, BECAUSE I NEVER REALLY CONFIDED IN YOU ABOUT STUFF LIKE THIS, BUT I NEED TO TELL SOMEONE. AND I'M DEAD, SO IT'S NOT LIKE THIS MESSAGE WILL EVER GET SENT.

I MADE A HUGE MISTAKE OF MY OWN WITH A GUY. UNLIKE YOU, THOUGH, MY MISTAKE WAS RUNNING HIM OFF. JAY SAYS — I HOPE YOU CAN MEET JAY SOMEDAY, HE'S OUR MECHANIC AND I LOVE HIM LIKE A BROTHER — THAT I SHOULD FOLLOW MY HEART AND "BE HAPPY." WHATEVER THAT'S SUPPOSED TO MEAN. BUT THIS DOESN'T FEEL CUT AND DRIED TO ME. IT'S NOT JUST ABOUT ME. I HAVE A CREW, NOW. I NEED TO BE SURE I'M NOT JEOPARDIZING US ALL BY MAKING A BAD RELATIONSHIP DECISION. I'VE BEEN ALONE FOR THREE YEARS — AND LET'S FACE IT, BEING WITH ANTON WAS SOMETIMES WORSE THAN BEING ALONE. I CAN HOLD OUT A LITTLE LONGER.

UGH, I HAVEN'T EVEN TOLD YOU ABOUT ANTON.

YOU KNOW WHAT, I SHOULD PROBABLY START AT THE BEGINNING. OR, AT LEAST, THE BEGINNING OF THE CURRENT MESS I'M DEALING WITH, ANTON'S A WHOLE OTHER MESS. SEE, I MET THIS GUY "R" WHEN I WAS WORKING A JOB FOR A GANGSTER NAMED NICO GARNET —

YEAH, I CAN SEE YOUR FACE AT THAT. I SHOULD PROBABLY GO BACK FARTHER.

POUR YOURSELF A DRINK, EV.

CHAPTER 15
RAJ

RAJ'S PLAN IS TO GRAB A BOTTLE OF WHISKEY FROM THE galley and head to his quarters to throw back shots until the world seems fine again, but his smooth exit is ruined by Ruby and Absolon. They're sitting at the galley table, talking in low tones, a bottle already floating between them. Ruby looks up when she hears Raj in the hallway, gaze flicking to the closed bridge hatch above him.

Her expression turns compassionate at whatever she sees on Raj's face, and without a word she pushes over to the cabinet and grabs a third bulb, pulling him a healthy shot of liquid gold and floating it to him with the perfect flick of a finger.

"Sorry, friend," she says as she raises her bulb to him. Absolon's frowning at them both.

The burn of the whiskey somehow makes the ache in his throat worse, not better. "That obvious, huh?"

"I'm honestly surprised. I thought for sure she — "

"That's not helping." He takes a longer draft of the whiskey, coughs on the fumes. "And I'm good."

Ruby tops his bulb off with a skeptical look, which Raj ignores. "Do you want to talk about it?"

Not in front of Absolon, whose expression of confusion has shifted to understanding; he's wisely keeping his mouth shut. And if Absolon wasn't here? No, Raj doesn't want to talk about Lasadi. He'd been completely convinced there was something between them — that she'd felt it as well. But obviously he'd been wrong. A hopeful little voice reminds him she'd had to take over a week to think through her decision, but his cynical side suggests she was probably just trying to gin up some enthusiasm to match his own.

Either way, she's told him what she wants, and he'll respect her decision. Rehashing it with Ruby won't change Lasadi's mind. It won't change what she said: She's looking for something else. Some*one* else. He could say that out loud and forestall any more of Ruby's questions, but the whiskey's closing his throat up around the words. Instead, he takes a page from her playbook and deflects with a subject change.

"What are you two still doing up?"

"Drinking and talking," Ruby says. "Have a seat, you, unless you'd rather go sulk."

Raj flips her a rude gesture, but he settles at the table. She laughs.

"Alex told me something as we were launching," she says. "That identity fixer who helped them find Marga? He recognized Alex. Apparently our parents went to him when they needed new identities."

"You're kidding."

Ruby shakes her head. "They had him make false identities for us, too."

"So you're not . . ."

"I'm still Ruby Nicole, but at least now I know why I got nothing but dead ends anytime I tracked down someone named Quiñones with a connection to Artemis City." She sighs. "The fixer told Alex the false names he'd given our parents, but it's not any better of a lead. They picked about the most common names in the Durga System — Abdul and Maria Devi. Even cross-referencing to the right timeline and with the passenger manifests of ships leaving the Pearls the year I was twelve doesn't do anything. Records are already shaky, and there are too many people out here who'll falsify a registry for a couple of credits."

"Did the fixer say anything else?"

Her lips press into a firm line, and she takes a long pull of the whiskey. "It seemed like they were running from something. Apparently our father was injured."

"Have you tried searching the bounty boards from back then?"

"That might work. I wish — "

Raj tops off her bulb, waiting.

"I wish I could remember," she finally says. "I keep thinking I could shake something loose in my head." Her dark eyes are glazed and glittering. "That memory I told Lebedevya?"

Raj glances at Absolon, whose expression says he's heard this story already. "Your mother braiding your hair."

"I remembered my father, too, didn't I. I couldn't see his face, but I heard his voice. He tapped a finger on my nose and his hands smelled like sulphur and iron. What else might be locked inside this brain?"

For a brief flash, Raj feels that vivid pulse of childish terror, the retreating surf sucking at his feet. He shakes his head. "Lebedevya is a fake," he says. "Hypnosis, memory recovery — you know how that works as well as I do. Even if you worked with someone you trusted, how would you know what memories were suggestions and what were real? Even the memory I told Lebedevya, of being afraid of the waves — do I really remember that? Or have I heard my parents tell the story enough times that I can picture it myself."

"I know. But this is the first clue I've had in years and I can't *do* anything about it now. What have I even learned?"

Absolon clears his throat. "You learned they didn't leave you willingly," he says, voice gentle. "They were trying to save your lives."

A sharp snap as Ruby flicks her pinkie nail against her thumb. "Well, they still left."

"And we'll help you find out why."

Ruby finishes her whiskey, but waves off Raj when he reaches for the bottle again. "In more practical news, Sol's been helping me polish up our own false IDs with juicy insider gossip. Check this out."

She swipes through her tablet, then presses Play on a vid clip she's queued up. It's a cheesy romantic drama, Raj recognizes the brooding opening music of *Jewel in the Palace*. He sits back in surprise when his own figure walks out on the screen.

"Is that supposed to be me?"

"Ruby's certainly got talent," Absolon says; she waves him off.

"I doctored a few clips and scattered your name around the audition circuits and in a few minor profiles. It'll do on a medium dive into your identity." She swipes to a new screen. "I was easier — just write up a couple of puff profile pieces on a rich heiress with faked quotes from people they might actually recognize — Sol was lovely help there. I wrote a piece to link us, too."

Raj skims through a quick hit of celebrity gossip to find his alias's name.

"'Tam's boyfriend, Richard Cason Smith, was most recently considered for the leading role of *In Their Shadow*, which goes into production later this month. The movie will star heartthrob Paulo Sabine,'" he reads. "Thanks, Ruby, I needed a good ego boost."

"No offense, love, but it's Paulo Sabine. He's gorgeous, isn't he." She takes the tablet back. "I left spiders to notice if someone goes searching, and I've already gotten some hits. They're digging into my financials, mostly."

"And what are you finding out about Lebedevya?"

It's Absolon who answers. "She's actually been the subject of several lawsuits, all dismissed. A fraud suit from years ago, which took some digging to uncover. But in the past month, several prominent families have claimed she brainwashed their loved ones into leaving Indira with her."

"Another lawsuit?"

Absolon nods. "The judge sided with Lebedevya; the families face fines if they bring it up in public anymore — but several families have taken the fight to

Sapis. Also unsuccessfully, it sounds like. Sapis Cooperative is the local authority, and they aren't willing to cross Lebedevya either. They say they interviewed the 'missing people,' and none of them want to speak to their families."

Raj shares a look with Ruby. "Why not?"

"Several of them have some upsetting stories about abuse; they claim Lebedevya is protecting them."

"I can see why Sapis Co-op wouldn't want to get involved," Raj says. "Have you gotten in touch with the families there?"

"I'm trying to; they're rightfully suspicious."

"That could help us." The whiskey and this puzzle are doing their best to distract Raj; he wonders how much of this next week he can lose himself in planning.

He's not the only one who will need the distraction, it looks like. Absolon's proud shoulders are slumped, a sharp line sketched between his brows as he frowns at his hands.

"Your sister's going to be okay," Raj says quietly.

Absolon's dark eyes flash anger. "I should have known. The signs were all here — the families, the lawsuits — and I missed them. If I'd known, I never would have brought Katriana with me to Artemis. I never would have encouraged her to attend that first seminar with Evelyn."

"You said the lawsuit was last month," Raj points out.

Ruby squeezes Absolon's arm. "Kitty'd been attending the seminars long before then. You can't blame yourself, you were trying to do what was best for her."

"By introducing her to a cult."

"You didn't know, Sol. You were acting out of love." Ruby takes a deep breath, then turns to Raj. "I'm for bed. You need something to keep you busy for a while?"

"Gods, yes."

"When we get to Sapis, we need to give Lebedevya a list of artifacts that are legit flash if we want to keep up the ruse. Have you talked to Vash and Gracie yet about our mysterious lot from the auction house?"

Raj shakes his head. "I'll message Vash right now, and ask her if they can help us come up with some more artifacts."

"Good. Sol? Keep trying to make contact with the families, they could be a valuable resource." She pushes herself up from the table. "And if either of you need to talk, you know where to find me."

"I am absolutely fine," Raj says. He gives her his most charming grin, nods to a storm-faced Absolon, grabs his bulb and the bottle, and heads back to his quarters. "Night, everyone," he calls cheerfully, maybe a touch louder than he needs. Just to be sure anyone else listening knows he's absolutely fine, too.

Raj manages to keep himself busy as the days stretch long and changeless into the black. He spends time learning about their targets and internalizing every-thing he can about Lebedevya and Saint Alixhi. He straps himself in the resistance bands and works out until his muscles scream, then fires up the treadmill until his brain stops positing what-if scenarios about the captain that really aren't helping. He jokes with Jay and Alex and finds himself unexpectedly connecting with Absolon — who's taken it down quite a few notches since their fight in Segafredo's.

And, after the first few days of subtly avoiding Lasadi, the awkward tension finally begins to dissipate. Raj greets her with an easy smile. Forces himself to relax, to treat her the same way he'd treat Jay or Ruby or Alex, to let her know they're all good. After all, this is what he wanted, right? A crew he can trust and count on, no matter what Lasadi ends up feeling about him.

After his conversation with Ruby that first night, he'd recorded a chatty vid to Vash and Gracie explaining why it's taken him so long to get back to see them, and what he needs from them now. He'd meant to keep it on topic, but whiskey'd loosened his tongue and a lot had happened since he last talked with them. He caught them up on the *Nanshe*, on his new crew, on his general outlook in life — which, despite the splinters of shattered hope still lodged in his heart, is better than it has been in years. He's pretty sure he kept it professional when it came to telling Vash and Gracie about the *Nanshe*'s captain.

They're less than a day out from Sapis when he gets a response from Vash; he settles in at the galley table to watch. In the vid, Vash's silver hair is wound in a bun at the base of her neck, her face softly lined around her hooded eyes, the corners of her smiling mouth. Her camera has been knocked off-center, her gaze drifting offscreen.

"Raj, it's good to hear from you," she says. "And

don't worry about the delay, come by when you can. We'd love to meet the new crew, and we may have something you can help us with. Gracie is in the shop at the moment, but we did check into the question of Saint Alixhi. Thank you for that rabbit hole, by the way. Very fun."

Vash blinks and feels for something offscreen: a glass. She takes a sip of water. "Two things to tell you. Thing number one, I'm attaching a list of the most probable Saint Alixhi relics your fictional friend might be selling. Thing number two is why it took me so long to get back to you.

"My friend at Thierry et Zhang's auction house was cagey about Lot 131 — kept telling me it was a custom private sale and he didn't know anything more about it. He did tell me he was glad to have it gone, though.

"I finally traced Lot 131 to an antiquities broker Gracie used to work with years ago. He's crooked as they come, but he keeps good provenance records and owes me a favor. He told me it's a reliquary, he got his hands on it from some rich widow after her husband was killed in an accident right after he brought it home. She thought it was cursed."

The fine hairs stand up on the back of Raj's neck.

"I'm not going to tell you Lot 131 is Saint Alixhi's actual relics," Vash continues. "But everyone who's handled them thinks they're the real deal and believes in the curse. I sent you everything I could find. And Raj. I know you're good at getting out of trouble, but Gracie and I are both a little worried about this one. Be smart, okay? And come visit soon."

Vash's forehead creases as she fumbles to stop the

recording, and a pang of nostalgia pierces his heart. It's been far too long.

"Is that your antiquities-dealer friend?"

Raj jumps, not realizing Lasadi had entered the galley.

"Yeah. Vash — she and her wife, Gracie, got us some intel."

"She's blind?" Lasadi asks; Raj nods. "Do they live in Ironfall?"

"No — you know if you're heading from Dima past Nerrivik, you'll pass those asteroids that have been bound together, like rocks stacked on each other? There's a sign: Stop at the Traveler's Emporium, and kind of the weird, ah . . ." Raj pauses, searching for the word.

"Sculptures?" Lasadi asks. "There's a neon pink spaceship sliced into pieces, and an enormous welded . . . I don't know. Is it a parrot?"

Raj snaps his fingers. "That place. Have you ever stopped?"

"No, because it looks like a serial killer lives there."

"It's Vash and Gracie's place. Gracie is the sculptor and collector, Vash is the inventor. You'll like them." *And they'll love you,* he wants to say — but that sounds presumptuous. Like he still has expectations. *Absolutely no expectations here.* Raj clears his throat. "Apparently the word is that Lot 131 is actually Saint Alixhi's relics."

"Seriously?"

"Vash didn't believe it, but everyone she talked to was treating it that way."

Las shivers. "I hope it's not true — I don't want

those remains on my ship." She shoots him a look. "Don't you dare tell Alex I said that."

He smiles. "Your secret's safe with me."

She laughs, and it's almost perfectly nice. Raj takes a sharp breath. It *is* perfectly nice. They have rapport. They have camaraderie. And the one thing getting in the way of him appreciating her company is his expectations.

"I actually came to get you because we're coming up on Bixia Yuanjin," Lasadi says. "Can you grab Ruby and meet me on the bridge? I figured you'd appreciate the view, and we can go over our plan one last time."

"Of course, Captain."

She gives him an easy smile and disappears back up the ladder to the bridge. And it's good. Everything is absolutely, perfectly fine.

Raj takes a deep breath and goes to find Ruby.

CHAPTER 16
RUBY

RUBY DOESN'T THINK SHE SWEARS OUT LOUD WHEN SHE arrives on the bridge, but the way the captain looks over her shoulder and laughs, her astonishment must be clear on her face.

Sapis Station, framed through the screen of the *Nanshe*'s bridge, is absolutely incredible.

Growing up, Ruby'd believed what everyone in Artemis City did: Artemis was a gem, but the rest of the Pearls, everything else in Durga's Belt, all the settlements deeper into the black, were nothing but primitive backwaters, hastily constructed and janky as hell.

Ruby's traveled a bit since. Ironfall is fantastic and sophisticated, even if it lacks the flash and dazzle of Artemis City. Visiting Meilikki is actually a pretty great time. There's plenty to love about the many modern free-floating stations and asteroid colonies scattered throughout the belt, like Maribi Station and Tos.

But if you'd asked her to describe the settlements around Bixia Yuanjin, she would have guessed they were cobbled together out of space debris and ruled by roving drifter gangs, where rolling life-support brownouts and freeze-dried rations for every meal were a way of life.

She hadn't expected the approach to Bixia Yuanjin to be so gorgeous. The ice giant swirls with vast clouds of turquoise and deep, rich blue, drizzled through with threads of white. From a distance the rings appear flat, but now that they're on the same plane, Ruby can make out towering ice sculptures that glimmer in the reflected light of the planet, casting shadows on the diamond fields below.

And Sapis isn't too shabby, either. The moon is much bigger than Artemis, though it seems a mere speck compared to the enormous planet it orbits. Its surface gleams, blistered with glass agricultural domes and desalination plants pumping the saline oceans from beneath the icy crust.

Their destination is Sapis Station, the enormous city-in-the-sky that orbits the moon. It's the largest station Ruby's ever seen, built like a sphere sliced into rings, which are slightly offset around a central spindle. Shuttles trail down to the moon's surface from the station's cargo and shipping hub. It looks every bit as sophisticated as what she'd find closer to home, and the luxury cruisers twinkling in the moon's orbit are just as glamorous as anything Ruby would see orbiting Artemis.

"Wow," Ruby says. She settles into the co-pilot's chair, Raj standing behind her. "Where are we docking?"

"Public dock in the upper level," Lasadi says. "Lebedevya's levels have a private docking station, but this will give Jay and Alex and me a bit more freedom to come and go without Lebedevya and her team tracking us."

They're approaching the top of the spherical station; a hundred ships the *Nanshe*'s size could dock at the airlifts around the upper level, and the docking ring is busy with other small cargo haulers, private passenger ships, and bulky public shuttles like the one Aya Marga flew here on. An enormous Ganesh-class cargo hauler is lurking beyond the station, locked in synchronous orbit around the moon.

"The size of that hauler," Ruby says, shaking her head. "I've never seen one up close."

"Sapis Station is the central hub for distributing goods to the rest of the Bixian settlements," Lasadi says. "And for collecting goods to be shipped back. I read somewhere a Ganesh comes out here every other month."

"I had no idea." Ruby watches the Ganesh's slow dance of robotic arms and cargo pods with fascination. So much for the rustic backwater of her imagination.

"Are you two ready to meet Lebedevya?" Lasadi asks.

Ruby nods. "I checked back through her welcome packet — the rules she has would make your head burst. No tech unless it's approved assistive or prosthetic devices, simple clothes, no outside food or medicine. Thank the saints for Sol, we should be able to sneak everything we need in his fancy suitcases with their secret compartments."

"And we'll do our best to make contact from outside," Lasadi says. "The station's run by Sapis Cooperative, same outfit that runs the agricultural operation on the moon. All their ag offices are on the lower levels, and they run station security and logistics out of the offices in the upper levels. A few other levels are reserved for co-op housing, but the rest of the station is rented out."

"Who are some of the other tenants?" Raj asks.

"Handful of tech companies and mining ops. Things like that." Lasadi points to a level near the top, with a busy private dock and the snake-and-staff logo outlined in gold. "Sulila hospital and research facility," she says. "The co-op has a small clinic for members, but Sulila's got a monopoly on healthcare for the rest of the Bixian settlements. The handful of levels below the hospital are all resort condos."

"I remember hearing there's a fair amount of medical tourism out here," Raj says. "Family friends would come out for experimental treatments."

"And that'll be where Sol's contacts are staying," Ruby says. Absolon had finally connected with the families who had traveled out here to extract their loved ones from Lebedevya's brainwashing. It didn't sound like they'd had much luck petitioning the Sapis Cooperative for help, but they could be valuable allies.

"Then his view won't be bad," says Lasadi. "And neither will yours. Lebedevya has the two levels below the resort condos — forty-seven and forty-eight. Jay and Alex have been going over the station schematics, and it doesn't seem like there's an easy way in besides the front door. We're hoping we can find something more when we get access to the station's system — see if Lebedevya filed any building applications, if there are any special mods, that sort of thing. Today we're gathering information. So be safe, and we'll figure out an extraction plan once we know what we're dealing with."

"Got it," says Raj. "Get the lay of the land and try to make contact with our three ladies."

Lasadi turns back to him. "Three?"

"Aya Marga, Katriana, and Saint Alixhi."

The captain suppresses a shudder, and Ruby tilts her a smile. "You're superstitious, are you?"

"Of course not."

"Relax, Cap. Even if Lot 131 really is Saint Alixhi's relics, we'll be taking her home."

Before Lasadi can answer, a voice crackles through her comms.

"Sapis Station to *Nanshe*," says the controller. "You're clear for Bay G7."

"Copy G7," Lasadi replies, and reaches for the controls. "I'll see you two in cargo."

Ruby's managed to keep her anticipation under control all week; now, nerves churn like caged mice below her ribcage. *I'm coming for you, Kitty,* she promises. And if Lebedevya's done anything to her, no amount of holy mumbo jumbo in the system will protect her from Ruby's wrath.

CHAPTER 17
RAJ

IT'S NICE TO BE BACK IN ARTIFICIAL GRAVITY AFTER THE time on the *Nanshe*, but more than that, it's nice to be *doing* something again. Raj has spent enough time researching and preparing, poring over contingency plans and rehearsing possibilities — and yes, the prep work is necessary, but in a job like this, everything hinges on the interaction and thinking quick on your feet, and that's much more his style. As the lift descends to Level 48 — the upper of Lebedevya's two levels in Sapis Station — Raj feels blissfully alive.

"How do I look?" he asks, and Ruby gives him a critical once-over. Flicks a speck of dust off his lapel and straightens his collar, then brushes a strand of hair out from behind his ear so it falls across his cheekbone.

She stands back, a hand on her hip, then draws a circle in the air around him with a finger. "Lasadi is crazy to pass on this. Tell her even a lesbian knows you're a catch."

"Not helping." Raj keeps his smile wry and light,

but that wound's not anywhere near healed. Doesn't matter how well he cleans up, he's still Raj Demetriou, and Lasadi made it clear she wants something else. If only it were so easy for him to start fixating on something else, too — but that's the other reason he's glad to get back into action.

"Sorry, love." Ruby tucks her hand into his arm. "Ready?"

"More than ready."

The lift doors open into a reception room, and tranquility hits Raj like a physical thing. The knot below his sternum untwists, his shoulders fall a notch, he takes a reflexive breath that's deeper, calmer than any breath he's taken all week. The reception room is peacefully decorated: pale golds and warm sands, abstract blown-glass sculptures suspended on the walls. Serene music plays softly in the background. The air is perfumed with sandalwood and honey.

Beside him, Ruby takes a quick breath of surprise, the faintly sketched worry lines around her eyes vanishing, her fingers relaxing on his arm.

The woman behind the desk looks up with a broad, restful smile, left eye glimmering with the subtle light of a lens. Raj recognizes her with surprise as the same woman who'd introduced Annika Lebedevya at the conference. Katriana's sponsor, Evelyn. Today her glossy black hair is braided into a crown around her head, a few long curls hanging loose to frame her fair cheeks.

"Welcome to Paradise," Evelyn says; the same phrase is subtly embossed in gold across the wall behind her. She stands with arms wide to embrace them both. "Olivia, Richard. It's nice to meet you. I'm Evelyn."

"Oh!" Ruby says. "I can't believe we're finally here — this place is amazing."

"It's a lovely space," Raj says. He's not having to fake being impressed. After the last few long, fraught days, stepping into this room feels like a weight's been lifted from his shoulders. *You're finally home,* whispers a voice in his head. *You're safe here.*

Raj keeps his smile peaceful as he lets his gaze wander over the room. There's something in the color scheme, in the subtly embossed phrases on the walls, in the abstract glass sculptures, in the incense. Lebedevya's engineered this room to give guests exactly this disarming reaction when they enter; it would be fascinating if it wasn't so dangerous.

Evelyn's smile broadens, the lens over her eye flickering again. "I received word your bags have been placed in your rooms. Why don't I show you there so you can get some rest? I'm sure it's been a long trip, and in station time it's rather late."

Evelyn turns to palm open a door to their left, then leads them through. Raj hangs back a step while Ruby engages Evelyn in small talk, taking a last close look at the reception area. He can't see any obvious security, though his brief inspection of the glass artwork makes him suspect they're obscuring origination points of trip fields. Likely impossible to pass without setting off the alarm system.

Even as he studies the room, he can't shake the warm glow of peace, and he can't identify where it's coming from. Is it situational priming? Or is the explanation simpler, and he's simply able to finally relax after a week of pretending everything was fine on the *Nanshe*?

He hears Ruby's gasp of delight and follows her out of the reception room. His own eyes widen. The room off the reception is about ten meters long and half as wide, decorated in the same warm neutrals and dotted with low, cushioned chairs and tables in muted jewel tones. The air smells like jasmine and mint, probably from the tea service at the side of the room.

The dazzling showpiece, however, is the floor-to-ceiling windows to their left, the chromothermatic glass dimmed slightly against the glorious swirling brilliance of Bixia Yuanjin.

Raj lets out a low whistle. "Incredible."

"This is the observation room," Evelyn says. "Our social area, where you're welcome to meet any time. Most of the other areas of Paradise are meant for silent meditation, so if you do feel like talking, please do it here."

A handful of people are taking advantage of the room. A trio on the far side of the room are chatting over tea; they wave in greeting as Evelyn leads Raj and Ruby past. They seem relaxed and happy, unlike the lone woman at the other end of the room. She's curled up on an amethyst-colored chair, pretending to read a book, though her clear green eyes flash suspiciously to Evelyn. She's not as well put-together as the others, either. Her nails are chewed short, her gaunt, pale face is framed by choppy brown hair that looks like she's attempting to grow out a shorter haircut without the guidance of a stylist.

Raj nods a greeting to her and her gaze flashes back to her book, though her attention trails after them.

"That's Marissa," Evelyn says; she's noticed the exchange. "Several of our members have taken vows of silence, so don't be offended if Marissa doesn't speak to you."

Raj smiles at Evelyn, then gives the room one last good look before following on. There are three ways into the observation room: the reception area, a perpendicular corridor to the right, and a gently curving corridor straight ahead. Evelyn leads them into the curved corridor, which is bright and clean, still with no visible security features.

Raj had spent some time studying the layout of Sapis Station's levels — the information was easy to find on the cooperative's commercial real estate site — and found that most of the levels have the same basic floor plan. A circular corridor around the outer edge allows access to two rows of offices or living quarters, the outer ones with external views. Two cross corridors, like the one leaving from the observation room, divide the section into quarters, letting you cross to the far side of the circular level without having to walk all the way around, as well as allowing access to the smaller hub of operational rooms at the center.

They hadn't been able to find a plan of Lebedevya's levels specifically, but so far it seems to conform to the basic plan.

"Is a vow of silence required?" Ruby is asking Evelyn.

"It's not for everyone," Evelyn says. "But it can be restorative. The first time I met the Voice of Power, she took one look at me and said, 'You have no trouble speaking, but you have not learned to give voice to your soul.' I spent a month in silence after that."

"I don't think I could do that."

"When someone wants badly enough to heal, they'll do what's needed." Evelyn's calm surface fractured at that, revealing enough hidden pain for Raj's instincts to sit up and take notice. Since he first saw Evelyn at the conference back in Artemis City, he's been wondering if she's Lebedevya's partner in this con or a true believer. He's beginning to err on the side of believer.

As they walk the corridor, they pass doors on both sides, each closed and all whimsically labeled: Lotus, Saffron, Buttercup, Pear, Coral.

"Are these residences?" Raj asks.

"Some," Evelyn says. "Others are teaching spaces, or private offices."

"How can you tell which is which? The labels don't tell you anything."

Evelyn laughs. "You won't have to worry about that. One of us will bring you anywhere you need to go."

"Perfect," Ruby says politely. She shoots Raj a glance behind Evelyn's back. So they'll always have a chaperone. Good to know.

They pass another cross corridor — which must mean they've walked a quarter of the way clockwise — before Evelyn slows her pace and her chatter of tour-guide niceties. She palms open a room labeled Lavender. "Here is your room, Olivia."

The room is small and simply decorated, but the furnishings are all up to the standards Raj would have expected in a place like this. The walls are a dark faux wood grain, with recessed vertical lights casting a serene glow. A door on the far wall leads to a private toilet, with a vanity and sink that slide out of the wall to save space.

That saved space makes room for the centerpiece: a comfy-looking bed draped in a blue down duvet, with a padded white faux-leather headboard and matching dressing bench at the foot of the bed. Ruby's suitcase is sitting on the end of her bed.

Raj frowns at it. "And my suitcase?"

"Is in your room. We all stay separate here. Even couples. But don't worry, you'll be close — your room is down the hall."

Ruby's brows draw together. "We weren't told that."

Evelyn is unperturbed. "We find that most people who come to stay with us have profound shifts in how they think about themselves and their goals. It's easier to have those shifts — to really reach your potential — when you have a bit of extra space to think."

"Oh," Ruby says; Raj can't tell if her discomfort is real or feigned.

"It's fine, babe," he says, channeling every ounce of his overconfident yet mediocre actor persona into the sly grin he turns on Evelyn. "I'm sure we'll have the same epiphanies."

"Of course," Evelyn says mildly. "Richard, if you'll follow me."

His room — labeled Sunflower — is a few doors down from Ruby's. It has the exact same layout and color scheme, along with his suitcase. When Evelyn leaves him with a bow, hands pressed together over her heart, he closes the door and presses a thumb to his suitcase's biolock.

And frowns at the contents. There's no sign of the lock being tampered with, but someone has gone through his things. Raj's suitcase may look like chaos, but it's *organized* chaos. And things weren't put back in the right order.

They didn't find the false cache, though. Absolon's magic tech worked. Raj enters the code and slips a thumbnail in the catch, easing the compartment open without removing his clothes. He didn't spot any cameras in the room, but he wouldn't put it past Lebedevya to be surveilling her guests even here. His fingers brush past the pistol — too bulky — and close over the translucent nerve blade Absolon had given him.

How the hell Absolon got his hands on one of these is beyond Raj. The Alliance special ops types Raj had met tended to be extremely protective of their fancy gadgets.

As a nonlethal weapon, nerve blades are extremely debilitating. They don't draw blood, but getting slashed by one feels like getting lashed by lightning and fire and ice all at once, and it leaves the muscles spasming for a solid minute. Raj has had the pleasure once, and he'd appreciate never experiencing it again.

But he sure would love to try being the one with the handle in his hand.

Raj slips the blade and an earpiece into his sleeve, pulls out his toiletries bag, and heads to the bathroom to freshen up.

Probably no cameras here, he hopes; he runs the

water to brush his teeth, fastens the blade's slim holster around his calf, pops the earpiece in.

"Can you hear me?" he asks under the sound of the running water.

"We've got you," Lasadi says in his ear; relief floods through him at the sound of her voice, and he tells himself he's just happy the comms are working. There's no shielding in Lebedevya's levels to shut them down. That's all.

"They put us in separate rooms," Raj says. "Has Ruby checked in?"

"Not yet."

"I'll go see what she's up to. They didn't say we couldn't talk."

Raj finishes brushing his teeth, checks his appearance in the mirror — Ruby was right, he's looking like quite the catch today, not that it matters, and not that Lasadi can see him. He double-checks that the secret cache in the suitcase is secured, then heads into the hallway.

Ruby's door is open. "Olivia?" he calls brightly as he knocks on the wall beside it. But she doesn't answer. She's not in the room, and she's not in the bathroom; the door is open and there's nowhere else she might be hiding. Her suitcase appears untouched.

She's gone.

Someone clears her throat behind him, and Raj whirls. It's a young man wearing the same flowing robes as Evelyn. "Can I help you?"

"I had something I wanted to tell Olivia."

"Olivia said she wanted to talk with her friend,

Katriana," the young man says. "Evelyn showed her to Katriana's room."

Without her earpiece? Without telling Raj? A thread of unease coils beneath Raj's ribcage.

"I'd love to see Katriana, too. We'd meant to go together."

"I'm sorry." The young man doesn't look sorry; he's serene and impassible as a mountain. "Olivia wanted to go alone. I'll let her know you'd like to speak to her."

Lasadi's voice sounds in his ear. "We've got her," she says quietly. "She doesn't have her earpiece, but she did activate a beacon."

The young man is still smiling at Raj. "Why don't you get some sleep," he says. "We'll call you for breakfast in the morning."

"Great, thank you."

When Raj closes the door behind him this time, he hears the young man's footsteps pause outside his door. Guarding him? Or making sure he doesn't try to go wandering again on short notice. Raj would put money on an alert popping up anytime he opens his door.

He could make a scene, demand to be taken to Ruby. Or he could trust that she can handle herself and continue with the original plan of taking it slow and gathering intel.

He stretches out on the bed, hands behind his head, staring up at the ceiling.

Back to waiting. Lovely.

CHAPTER 18
RUBY

THEY TOOK NO TIME SEPARATING RICH HEIRESS "OLIVIA" from her actor boyfriend; Ruby'd barely slipped off her heels before Evelyn returned and said Kitty wanted to see her right away. Could Ruby have a second to freshen up? Of course, Evelyn said, and stood politely in the doorway to wait. So much for any chance to access the secret cache in Absolon's suitcase.

According to Evelyn, "Richard" had decided to go straight to bed and said he'd see Ruby at breakfast. She doesn't believe that for a second, but the risks of calling Evelyn out on her lie seem greater than the risk of following her to see Kitty. And Ruby can probably get more information out of Kitty alone than if Raj were with her.

At least she was already wearing the wooden bangle with the tracking beacon in it. The captain and Jay will be able to follow where she's going, and she could probably even signal for help if she needed it. Flicker it on and off, that sort of thing, like Alex used to do with a torch to signal his friends in the convent — oh!

That might just work.

Ruby takes a deep breath, bare feet padding along the corridor as Evelyn slips her tidbits of the history of Lebedevya's Paradise, unease flickering down her spine. She didn't see which room Raj was given, but all the doors in this hallway are shut anyway, and the labels tell you nothing at all. Almost like they want to keep you on your toes, sure.

When Evelyn opens a door labeled Sage, it's not another bedroom, it's a staircase that leads down to the lower of the two levels Lebedevya rents on Sapis Station.

"We're entering an area of silent meditation," Evelyn says over her shoulder, and Ruby nods her understanding, then flickers her beacon and follows Evelyn down.

If the upper level was designed to be inoffensively relaxing, the lower level ticks the vibe a few more notches into moody introspection. The staircase opens into a large room of navy blues and deep turquoises and faux walnut. The lighting is dim, glinting dully off brass accents and — there it is. The lens of a camera, tucked into the corner. Ruby flicks her beacon and follows Evelyn through a set of doors that slide seamlessly from the wall, closing behind them as invisibly. Now they're in a corridor, as dimly lit as the room before; Evelyn palms open another invisible door a few meters down.

They seem to be working inward, concentric rings of corridors and interconnected rooms all decorated with the same moody hues. Several seem like meeting rooms, with thick rugs and scattered cushions similar to the ones Lebedevya had in her penthouse at the Hôtel l'Eza. Others are completely unfurnished, and Evelyn doesn't give her a clue what any of them are for. Occasionally they pass people: some seem to be staff, in robes like Evelyn's, though others must be guests. A few greet Ruby and Evelyn in silence with a bow; most ignore them.

The rooms down here have more visible security than the ones above, and Ruby surreptitiously clocks it as she follows Evelyn. She's not certain Evelyn isn't leading her in circles — hasn't she seen that mandala tapestry before? This place is a maze. When Evelyn smiles back at her, Ruby tries to keep her expression bright and delighted with the new wonders of Paradise, rather than unnerved by the fact that she's quickly losing her bearings. Another turn or two into identical rooms and she'll never be able to find her way out of here on her own.

Finally Evelyn pulls back a curtain to reveal a circular room with thick, plush carpeting and a domed ceiling. Unlike the sparsely decorated rooms Ruby has just passed through, this one is filled with artwork, carefully hung and lit to give it the feel of an exquisite museum.

A museum dedicated to a single artist, Ruby realizes with a shiver. She recognizes the style, after studying Aya Marga's notes, and she even spots a few familiar paintings. There's Saint Alixhi's *Dawn Meditation*, which went missing from a museum in Bulari a decade ago. Her *True West With Dancers*, which has been thought lost for nearly a century. And, on the far wall, a series of lovingly framed sketches Ruby recognizes as Kitty's work.

A simple wooden crate sits on a raised dais in the center of the round room, on top of a gold-edged cloth. The crate is perhaps a meter long and half as wide, three handspans tall, and Annika Lebedevya is kneeling in front of it with her eyes closed in prayer.

Evelyn gestures for Ruby to step forward and closes the curtain behind her; Ruby kneels awkwardly on the second cushion beside Lebedevya's. She spares a glance at Lebedevya — the other woman doesn't acknowledge her — and begins to bow her head, too.

And stops, her attention caught by the crate.

On a closer look, it's not just a rough container. It's been decorated, with thin whorls of wire now tarnished with age and lack of care. The wood is ancient, darkened with time but polished bright at the corners and the top as though touched by a hundred thousand venerating hands. Ruby's heart begins to pound in her throat.

She can't help herself, she reaches for the inlaid design at the head of the crate, which a hundred thousand people before her have touched. A crescent moon, lying on its back, balanced on a teardrop: Saint Alixhi's Dreaming Moon.

If this is a forgery, it's phenomenal.

"What do you feel?"

Ruby snatches her hand back as though burned; Lebedevya is watching her with a curious expression.

"I'm sorry," Ruby says.

"Don't apologize when the Dreaming Saint moves you. What do you feel?"

"You'll say this is foolish."

"Of course I won't."

Ruby takes a deep breath. "I feel . . . her. I've been to her shrine in New Manila, but it felt so jarring to be there with hundreds of others gawking at her cell, at the gardens where she used to walk." Ruby's seen pictures, at least, even if she hasn't personally had the honor of visiting the shrine. She lays a hand back on the wooden crate; electricity shivers up her spine. "Is this a replica of her reliquary?"

Even as the words leave Ruby's mouth, she knows it's not a replica. She's seen replicas. They don't hum with holy purpose. They don't sing to your heart. They don't make your soul tremble beneath your skin.

"I, too, have been to Saint Alixhi's shrine," Lebedevya says. "I imagine her heart must break to see so many tourists in her beloved gardens, shattering the peace she enjoyed in her life. The first time I traveled to Bixia Yuanjin, I knew in my soul that it was holier out here in the black. Easier to dream. And so I created a shrine truly worthy of a dreaming saint."

She lays a hand on the lid of the crate.

"Traditionally, the reliquary was displayed without the lid, to allow the saint to see all who came to visit her. But that seems irreverent, doesn't it?"

"She's here?" Ruby's voice is barely a whisper.

Lebedevya smiles at her. "She's here." She bows her head to the reliquary once more, then rises to her feet. "Did your expert finish verifying the rest of the collection?"

Ruby looks up in surprise, mildly horrified to discuss business in front of the saint. "He did. It was difficult to verify provenance for some, but overall he was thrilled with the authenticity. I knew as soon as our family friend asked me to help them sell the collection that I needed to make sure it went to the right person. I always felt I had a special connection with Saint Alixhi, ever since I was a girl." Ruby shakes her head. "I'm sorry, that must sound silly."

"Why do you say that?"

"Richard always says so. He wants me to be more business-minded about it."

"I believe by giving you access to this collection, Spirit is saying you do have a connection to Saint Alixhi, and that following Spirit's guidance is the best business decision you could make."

Ruby lets her expression soften in hope. "You think so?"

"And by staying true to your morals and finding the right buyer for this collection, you've strengthened that bond."

"Richard doesn't believe any of this."

Lebedevya takes Ruby's hands; hers are cool, paper-dry. "It's upsetting when the ones who are supposed to support our spiritual journey turn out to be the ones who are holding us back. But unfortunately, it's common." Lebedevya takes a sharp breath as though something's just occurring to her. "You mustn't tell him about Saint Alixhi's relics. She has enemies who would throw her carelessly back to the masses."

"Of course I won't," Ruby says. Lebedevya smiles gratefully, and Ruby studies her, trying to figure out her next move.

Lebedevya had wasted no time separating "Olivia

and Richard" physically, and now, as she had in the penthouse, she's testing the strength of their emotional bond. It's textbook. Isolate the mark from anyone who loves her, convince her that only Lebedevya understands what she's going through, and give her a deep secret to keep on Lebedevya's behalf.

Little Miss Heiress Olivia Tam should be feeling quite the bond with Lebedevya now, and if Ruby wants to get to the bottom of this, she needs to sell it.

Good thing she's got plenty of reserved frustration and regret around Kitty; she conjures a flood of it to spark tears in her eyes, delicately flicks them away. "I'm sorry," she says. "But this trip has been hard on Richard and me. When we first met, I told him how important my spirituality was to me, and he seemed excited to come to the conference on Artemis. But he's done nothing but make jokes. I'm beginning to think he's after my family's money and I've been an idiot." She screws her eyes shut, takes a sharp breath. "I'm sorry, this isn't a therapy session."

"It's important to leave behind the things holding us back," Lebedevya says. "And sometimes the people, too."

Ruby shakes her head. "I couldn't. He came all the way out here with me, and breaking up now would certainly make the return trip awkward."

"We can help you make arrangements," Lebedevya says. "If he wishes to leave, he's free to go. You should make the decision that's right for you, not him. Tend to your own child self, Olivia."

Ruby puts on a show of pulling herself together. "What do you mean?"

"Do you remember the dreams of your childhood? They were vivid, wild, full of fears and mysteries and hopes. Most of us forget what we once dreamt as we get older, but I never forgot." Lebedevya lays her hand on the reliquary, fingers resting gently on the Dreaming Moon. "When I was a child, I dreamt the truth: that I am the reincarnation of Saint Alixhi, come back to do her work in the world."

A chill traces its way down Ruby's spine.

"You don't believe me," Lebedevya says.

"Oh, it's not that." Ruby's trying for polite — she doesn't think Olivia would buy this nonsense, not yet — but Lebedevya waves her concerns away with a smile.

"You do not have to accept it in order to accept my help. My role is to help Saint Alixhi's children find wholeness and healing through dreaming." Lebedevya tilts her head, eyes bright as she studies Ruby. "I can tell you feel you're missing something. An emptiness where memory used to be? I sense in you an inability to connect with your inner child, with your childhood. I can help."

Ruby swallows hard.

"Don't think about Richard right now," says Lebedevya. "Think about your own connection to Spirit. You invested in coming all the way out here, so trust yourself to continue the rest of the way. Your entire life, you've been living a dream of who someone else thought you were. Isn't it time to wake up and discover who you really are?"

Goosebumps down Ruby's arms, even though she read through Lebedevya's course materials on the way here. This is language Lebedevya always uses. *She doesn't know anything about your past.* But that doesn't matter. Lebedevya may not know what Ruby has in her past, but she can clearly sense how desperate Ruby is to remember it. And she's circling her like a wolf.

"I want to wake up," Ruby says, and Lebedevya's smile glimmers bright.

"I shall show you how."

CHAPTER 19
LASADI

"So hear me out," Alex is saying, his voice echoing in the airlock chamber as the doors to the *Nanshe*'s cargo hold cycle back open. "I think she actually traveled to some of the places she painted."

Lasadi looks up from the portable desk she's unrolled on a table in the now-empty cargo hold, nods a greeting to Jay and Alex. The two men have been gone the past hour, unloading the legitimate — and illegitimate — shipments they'd brought out to Sapis Station and trawling for intel.

"Like, physically?" Jay cycles the airlock doors shut once more. "You said she was walled into her cell."

"I've been reading about astral projection — Saint Alixhi could project her soul anywhere in the universe."

Alex keeps going, but Lasadi tunes him out, frowning down at the moving dot on the desk. Ruby may have managed to activate her beacon, but something's wrong. It's shorting out, and every time it blinks, Lasadi's heart lodges in her throat with the worry it'll be the last.

Raj's beacon is staying still and steady in his room, and Absolon's is ensconced in his posh suite on the resort levels. He's already reported back that he made contact with the families who have been here petitioning Sapis Cooperative to help them get in touch with their loved ones in Lebedevya's "Paradise," but that the co-op had interviewed the individuals in question and refused to intervene unless they asked for help directly.

"Can souls travel faster than the speed of light?" Jay asks.

"Of course." Alex perches on a crate next to Lasadi. "They have no mass."

"I thought you said a soul was just energy."

"It depends on who you ask. According to one paper I read — "

"Successful trip?" Lasadi asks, loud enough to cut though the riveting metaphysical argument Alex is clearly gearing up for.

"Sapis Station people are weirdos," Jay says. "But we got the rest of the cargo unloaded."

"Who're weirdos, the staff?"

"Staff, the long-haul pilots, everyone."

"Sure." Lasadi shrugs. "You've got to have a few bolts loose if you want to come all the way out to Bixia for a delivery run."

"And apparently we do," says Jay.

Alex leans in to study the blinking dots on Lasadi's desk. "Where's that?"

"They separated Raj and Ruby," Lasadi says. "Raj

has his earpiece, but Ruby didn't activate hers before she started wandering. Her beacon's still working, she's on the lower level, but it keeps shorting out. It's been steady for a few minutes now, though."

"Show me?" Alex asks.

Lasadi keeps the live feed running in one corner in case Ruby starts moving again, then plays back the recording from the moment Ruby left her room. Alex tilts his head. "Holy shit. She remembers."

"Remembers what?"

He pauses the recording. "When I was little, right after she left? A friend and I at the convent had made up a code where we'd blink lights at each other after dark. The ayas hated it. But I taught it to Ruby so we could write secret messages to each other while she was gone." He points at the desk. "Here. When she left her room, she signaled: 'I am safe.'"

Alex grabs a tablet and begins to scrawl out the key, a series of pulses in intricate patterns. He licks his lips, erases and rewrites a few, then hands Lasadi the tablet.

"I'm pretty sure that's it."

Lasadi starts the playback again, jotting down the series of blinks and pulses from Ruby's beacon while Alex translates.

"'Two cameras,'" Alex says. "'Scanner.' She's helping us map security on the lower level. Yeah. This is flash. I can work with this."

"We need to find a floor plan of that level."

"I left a flea in the dockmaster's terminal while Jay was distracting him, so we should have access to all Sapis Station's files now." Alex's tongue darts over his lower lip as he studies the series of pulses Ruby made right before her beacon stopped moving. "'Heavy sec floor sensor trip field shrine.'"

"Shrine?" Lasadi pushes herself back from the desk, sorting through the next steps. The good news is Ruby can communicate with them, the bad news is they can't get any information back to her. "Start going through those floor plans and maintenance records to find us a way in. Ruby's not signaling for help yet, but I don't like how quickly they separated them. We need to be ready to go if they need us. Jay, what else have you got?"

"I made a new friend," Jay says. He swipes a file from his comm onto the portable desk, then settles with the chair turned backwards, bare arms crossed on the back of the seat.

"A lady friend," Alex says, jerking his chin at Jay's crossed arms. "It's definitely the muscles."

"It's the dimples," Lasadi says.

"I'm naturally charming," Jay says. "Shar works in the station's distribution center — right now she and her team are up to their ears sorting through shipments from the Ganesh and delivering them to the station's renters. I gave her a hand loading up one of her pallets, which just happened to be going to Lebedevya's levels."

Lasadi glances down at the file Jay threw onto the desk.

"And got your hands on the manifest."

"That I did."

"He got Shar's number, too," Alex points out.

"It could come in handy. Maybe we need more info."

"Did your new lady friend say anything about Lebedevya?" Lasadi asks.

"She was happy to gossip. The word in Distro is Lebedevya and the rest are weird but harmless. And constantly high — nobody likes doing that delivery run. The maintenance guys think the level is cursed. Soon as you fix one thing, another goes wrong."

Alex looks up from the desk, eyebrows high.

"Don't get any ideas," Las says to Alex. "There's no such thing as curses."

"I've met plenty of cursed engines," Jay says.

"You're not helping."

"Why do you think Coruscan mechanics always have a shop mixla? Doesn't matter if you believe in the old ways or not, it doesn't hurt to burn a bit of incense and keep the old ones happy so they don't start doing mischief."

"Superstitious nonsense," Lasadi says.

"Says the woman with a mixla on her bridge."

"It's pretty and reminds me of home."

"Yeah?" Jay grins — there's that dimple — and reaches to tug on her bare earlobe. "Then where's the little opal earring you always wear?"

Lasadi bats his hand away. "Focus." The earring, of course, is in the stasis field at the base of the mixla, along with a dash of whiskey in a thimble as a request to return them all back to the *Nanshe* safe and sound. It feels wrong not to, since she rescued the little house god. And it doesn't hurt anything to follow the old ways — but she definitely does not want to talk about it.

"So none of the station staff want to go to Lebede-vya's levels," Lasadi says. "We can use that."

"I'll round us up some maintenance jumpsuits."

Lasadi leans into the table, studying the manifest Jay swiped from his new lady friend. The shipment headed to Lebedevya's level contains all the usual supplies you'd expect, as well as a medication whose name catches Lasadi's attention. Argentias BZ-9114. Lasadi gnaws on the inside of her cheek, trying to remember, then pulls up another screen and scans through the stills she took in Lebedevya's penthouse at the Hôtel l'Eza.

There, among the makeup cases and tubes on Lebe-devya's vanity, is a vial of medicine with the same label.

"What does it do?" Jay asks.

Lasadi pulls up a search; it's not hard to find. "Some sort of neural blocker that stops you from being affected by hallucinogens. Why would she need that?"

"Probably because of this." Jay points to another line on the manifest, listed as a chemical formula. "Kids these days call it white flame. It's a neurotoxin, power-fully hallucinogenic — really more of a designer drug since it's expensive as hell and it doesn't have as many side effects as the stuff your average brain-melter would be able to afford."

"That can't be legal."

"Not in the Pearls or any Alliance country," Jay agrees. "But out here? There's no central government for the Bixian settlements. Sapis Co-op's bread and butter comes from their tenants who do experimental medical treatments — I bet if you checked the manifests on shipments heading to the Sulila hospital you'd find all sorts of drugs you couldn't get legally, not even on New Sarjun."

"Can you find old manifests? She must have ordered this before."

Jay scrubs a hand over his jaw, light from the desk flickering in his dark eyes. "Yeah," he finally says. "Not in this quantity, though. She must be expanding her operations."

Lasadi takes a deep breath. "Well," she says. "I really don't like any of that." She opens up the connection. "Raj? Come in."

Her heart beats into the long silence; Jay cracks a knuckle.

"Raj?"

When Raj finally answers, his voice is bleary. "Yeah, sorry. Dozed off."

"That's fine," Lasadi says. His beacon is still active in his room, and it's well past midnight, *Nanshe* time. Maybe this could have waited until morning. "Wanted to let you know Ruby's communicating with us via her beacon, and we're formulating a plan to get in after you."

"Mmm-hmm. Whadya need fr'm me?"

"Nothing for now. Get some shut-eye and ping us when you wake up in the morning."

"Kay. G'night, Las."

The glimmer of warmth she feels at the casual, comfortable way Raj says her name is almost immediately drowned out by warning bells. He's been careful to call her nothing but captain since she shut down his advances a week ago. And that slurring. She's seen him after a few friendly drinks. She's seen him worn to the bone with exhaustion. She's never heard him lose control of his speech.

She meets Jay's gaze. "He sound okay to you?"

Jay presses his lips together. "Tired," he says, careful.

He called me Las, she wants to point out, but saying that aloud betrays far too much. And Alex is listening, too.

"I don't like this," she says. "Alex, find us a clear floor plan and start working on breaking through the security. Jay, get us some maintenance uniforms and a reason to be nosy."

"On it," Jay says. Alex nods sharply. He seems about to say something else when Ruby's beacon — the one in the live feed — begins flashing once more. All three of them stare at the desk, attention darting between the flashing beacon and the tablet where Alex had written the key.

Lasadi scrawls down each letter as it comes, hairs rising on the back of her neck.

S-T-A-L-I-X-H-I-I-S-H-E-R-E

"Saint Alixhi is here," Alex says.

Lasadi takes a deep breath. "There's one of our ladies found," she says. "Two more to go." She opens the channel again. "Raj?"

There's no answer.

"He just fell asleep, Las," Jay says; but the way Raj said her name, the way he and Ruby have been separated? Something's gone wrong, and her people are vulnerable in the enemy's lair.

Lasadi pushes back from the table. "Get me in there. Now."

CHAPTER 20
RAJ

THE CAPTAIN'S CALLING HIS NAME, HER VOICE THIN AND liquid, threading through dreams bloated with strange imagery: salt waves crashing into candyfloss froth Raj is trying to collect and sell, rooms that spiral inward like a shell, a family party where everyone in attendance has been turned into enormous walking sea spires and keeps trying to hug him with the fleshy, spiny tentacles growing where their hair should be.

Raj presses his face deeper into his pillow, mind swimming in that liminal state where fragments of real memory spark against dream imagery — the beach, the rooms, the pier, the balcony, all real places from the resort town his parents used to take him on summer holidays when he was a child, remixed by his subconscious into a bizarre wonderland.

Raj! Come in!

He blinks heavy lids open at Lasadi's voice, rational mind trying and failing to make sense of the images that still feel more real than the bed he's lying in. He can only dimly make out the room around him when he tries to focus.

The meaning of the dreams escapes him. Why sea spires, those leathery, elongated creatures tethered to the sea floor, which serve as perches for much more beautiful anemones? Is it a deep, soulful metaphor for the stagnation he'd felt in his former life in Arquelle? Or simply a fancy sparked by the fact that even as a child he thought sea spires resembled people with their anemone hair.

Wait. Hadn't his mother actually been a sea star? She'd been cartwheeling through the room, crashing drinks out of guests' hands — she and Raj's father would definitely fight about it later.

Raj!

Raj wrenches his eyes open with a sharp gasp, fills his lunges with cool, clean air.

Clean air.

The last thing he'd noticed before falling asleep last night was a strange scent in the air, cloyingly floral. Perfume — or incense.

"Raj!"

He touches his ear; the earpiece is still there, but the voice calling his name isn't coming through it. It's Ruby, sitting beside him on the bed, shaking his shoulder.

"Raj," she says; her voice sounds exactly like Lasadi's — has it always? "If you can hear me, let me know. We're coming in."

"Ruby?"

Ruby smiles at him.

"Course I am, love." He shakes his head to clear the confusion; she doesn't sound like Lasadi in the slightest. He struggles to sit, clawing away the tangle of blankets and assessing his state. Is he decent? Shirtless. Ruby won't care.

"Did you find Katriana?"

"I came here to tell you something," Ruby says. "Are you listening? It's important."

"I'm listening." Raj runs a hand through his hair, smoothing unruly strands out of his face. He cracks his neck; it's always stiff the first night spent sleeping in gravity again.

"I needed to tell you about the water. You need to remember that you can breathe underwater."

Raj frowns at Ruby, trying to get the joke. "I just woke up. You're going to have to be a lot clearer."

"Remember, love. You used to be able to breathe underwater, when you were a child. You still can if you don't let fear get in the way."

"What are you talking about?"

"We're underwater now," Ruby says, and suddenly he notices her hair is floating — not in the weightless, buoyant way of zero G, but twisting and dancing in invisible currents like kelp leaves. The light from the bedside lamp dapples her dark cheeks. She takes a breath and lets it out slow, then laughs. A thin trickle of bubbles escape her lips and whirl upward towards the surface. "See?"

"Ruby, what the fuck?"

"It's fine." She takes his hand; hers is cold as ice. "Just breathe."

Panic thrashes in Raj's chest, but that's the animal part of his mind, right? The rational part of his mind notes he must have been breathing underwater this whole time — look how the bedsheets are tangled in the currents, see the colorful reef fish glinting in the recessed lighting. *You're drowning,* shouts the animal part of his mind. *You're drowning.*

He tries to take a breath, but cool bitter salt floods his mouth and nose; he chokes on it, lungs burning, and tries to claw himself free from the bedsheets that twine around his legs and arms like fishing nets.

"Oh, Raj," Ruby says sadly, her eyes sinking deeper into her sockets with every breath, collapsing like a corpse's. "Have you forgotten how to breathe underwater?"

She keeps speaking to him, tiny bubbles dancing between her lips, and somehow Raj knows she's singing him a lullaby even though he can't hear a word over the sound of blood rushing in his ears.

CHAPTER 21
RUBY

ANNIKA LEBEDEVYA LOCKS THE DOOR TO THE SHRINE behind them with the most amount of security Ruby's seen since she arrived; Ruby pulses her beacon to let the others know: "Biolock phys key retina scan." She has no idea if her messages are getting through — or if Alex will even remember the ridiculous code. Even if Alex and the others are reading her, they don't have any way of responding.

Ruby keeps an easy, curious smile on her face when Lebedevya leads her back into the maze of moody rooms that make up the lower level. She's about to report on the camera she spots above a door when Lebedevya falls back a pace, linking her arm with Ruby's to walk shoulder to shoulder like conspiring sisters.

Ruby's pulse rabbits; she forces herself to stay calm and return Lebedevya's smile. That warm pressure of Lebedevya's arm linked through hers, Ruby's suddenly thrown back to the convent.

She'd made her decision to leave when she turned eighteen, but before then, she'd been just another student. A child to be taught and trained up and pruned so she could bloom strong on her own like any of the other flowers in the convent's garden — Aya Julio's metaphor.

Ruby had left a child, but every time she returned, the ayas welcomed her as an adult. Marga would ask her opinion on politics. Julio would ask her to "sneak" him in chocolates he could easily have purchased himself. And Ayalasi Kateri would take her arm to walk in the garden, ask how Ruby was settling in outside, solicit her advice on how to deal with Alex. At first, Ruby hadn't had anything to hide — making ends meet was a struggle, but she'd found a pod in a not-too-horrible neighborhood, she'd found work, she was eking by doing odd freelance jobs — not hard to do in a tech startup mecca like Artemis City.

But eventually she'd began to find a more lucrative niche, and she hadn't been proud of it. It started with forging visas and customs inspections for some of her neighbors. Moved on to identity fixing, corporate espionage, information sabotage. She'd stopped telling Ayalasi Kateri about her work, but for the first time, she'd been able to contribute money to the convent for Alex's stay — money the ayas had never asked for — while still eating well herself.

Ruby hadn't had to rely on the charity of others anymore. She'd paid her own way without having to ask for help, and had started paying back what she couldn't help but think of as her insurmountable debt to the ayas.

Aya Marga had once hinted she knew where the money was coming from, but she hadn't pressed too hard; knowing the convent's financial troubles now, Ruby wonders if the ayas had always needed her tithes, badly enough not to ask.

She channels the calm of walking the garden with Ayalasi Kateri. Maybe it's something about Lebedevya's floral perfume, but she can feel the sensations almost as though she were there now: the crunch of the composite pathway under her boots, the gentle humidity of the misters on her skin, the warmth of the false sun streaming from the ceiling, the gentle trickle of the fountain, the hyacinth and rose and jasmine perfuming the air. The soft warmth of Kateri's arm through hers, the words she'd spoken when Ruby had come to collect Alex for the last time: "It's been a blessing to watch you learn yourself, Ruby Nicole. I trust you'll find your path. I'm proud of you."

Ruby takes a deep breath to clear away the memories, but Aya Kateri's calm lingers. She smiles serenely at Lebedevya, and for the first time Ruby sees her without any of the mystique. The perfect blond hair, the ridiculously dramatic eye makeup, the breathy accent — this woman isn't a priestess. She's a grifter who can't hold a candle to the gentle grace and wisdom Ayalasi Kateri embodies so naturally. Kateri walked arm in arm with Ruby out of love and friendship. Lebedevya's doing it to hack Ruby's sense of intimacy — and to get close and personal with Ruby's physiological reactions. She's a con artist, and she's scented blood.

Come and try me.

"I commend you coming here, Olivia," Lebedevya

says airily. "This experience will be transformative for you, if you're willing to release the things that hold you back. Tell me more about Richard. How involved in your business ventures is he?"

"Oh, hardly at all," Ruby says. "We haven't been dating for very long, but he comes from an entrepreneurial background, so he's been helpful." She frowns. "Although he's done nothing but be skeptical since we arrived."

"It's common to realize uncomfortable truths about your partner when you begin learning about yourself. It's good he's not more involved in your business venture. Is anyone else in your family involved?"

Lebedevya's probing for who else might be keeping an eye on "Olivia's" whereabouts. "No, I'm working alone," Ruby says; let Lebedevya think she's an easy target whose absence won't much be noticed. "I love not having to run decisions by anyone else, but it's been a bit exhausting. I've been meaning to hire a secretary."

That satisfies Lebedevya. "And, of course, your parents are passed." She pats Ruby's arm before Ruby has realized she stiffened. "You told me you inherited the family fortune, so I assumed your parents had gone. I'm sorry for your loss."

"Right." Ruby laughs. "Of course. I have a few cousins left, but no one I'm close to. I suppose that's why I find the idea of your community so appealing."

"Many of Saint Alixhi's children are independent people like you. Self-directed and self-sufficient, but looking for a community."

Wealthy people with weak family ties, Ruby translates. People with no one to fuss about how they spend their fortunes.

Lebedevya slows, and Ruby takes the moment to study her surroundings once more. They've arrived in front of yet another door, this one labeled Orange Blossom.

"Here we are." Lebedevya releases Ruby's arm and smiles ruefully as she pulls out a vial of pills. She palms one and swallows dry. "A genetic condition, I'm afraid. I'm prone to migraines, which the dreaming room sometimes triggers."

"I'm sorry."

"It's such a small sacrifice for this work."

The door slides open, and a rush of fresh paint hits Ruby, mingling with the thick floral perfume of incense. She sneezes, then frowns at the room, confused. This level is a maze, but she still thought she had a better grasp on the direction. She thought they'd been going inward, but they seem to have entered the antechamber to an airlock. Except that instead of lockers with environment suits, the room's cold metal walls have been draped with violet curtains, thick white rugs laid out over the floor and dotted with purple cushions for people to sit. Another piece of abstract glass art is backlit against one wall.

It's odd, but it doesn't matter. Because she's found Kitty.

Ruby's ex stands in front of the airlock door, paintbrush in hand, working the delicate lines of a mandala in intricate concentric circles around the doorframe. She's alone.

Ruby's relief sours as she approaches; Kitty turns

glassy eyes on her, blinking slowly as though trying to remember where she's seen Ruby before. Her lips hold a dreamy smile, her movements are slow and precise.

Cold, aching fury unspools in Ruby's gut.

Kitty's high, which was the very thing she'd hoped Lebedevya's program would help her stay away from. Ruby hadn't much faulted Lebedevya for taking advantage of rich folks with too much time on their hands, but Kitty had come here looking for a way to find herself without the help of pills. And Lebedevya drugged her.

Ruby wants to deck Lebedevya's perfectly painted lips and break that dainty nose, to grab Kitty and run for the *Nanshe*, spring her from this trap and find someone who will *truly* help her. But Kitty's not the only one trapped here — they still haven't found Marga. Ruby needs to keep her anger in check a little bit longer.

And despite the glassy eyes, Kitty looks happy — she's always been the happiest when she's painting, riding high on whatever substance helps her tap into her creativity, even if it leaves her shivering and twitchy and screaming at Ruby for some imagined slight hours later.

Ruby's heart tightens, but she keeps her smile on for Kitty. And for Lebedevya.

"Kitty!" she exclaims. "I bet you weren't expecting to see your old friend Olivia here." She puts subtle emphasis on her fake name — please let Kitty still be coherent enough to remember their ruse.

"Livvy!" Kitty draws Ruby in for a hug, careless of the paintbrush in her hand; Ruby catches it before it glops green paint on her dress, but not before Kitty swipes it across Ruby's forearm. "I was so thrilled when Annika told me you were coming to Sapis. I think you're going to love it here."

"It's been amazing so far." Ruby stands back to admire the mandala. "This is gorgeous." And her heart lurches as her attention shifts past the painting to the view through the window. There's no double door beyond this one — just the vast expanse of space stretching dark and sparkling with stars. They're not standing in the antechamber to an airlock; this room must itself be the airlock. Although the door they walked through wasn't rated for pressure. Is this door decommissioned? Even if it is, there's no way this would be considered up to code anywhere in the Pearls.

Something floats out the window, barely out of view, perhaps a twist of wrapping plastic from a shipment, or some other bit of debris cluttering the space around the station. Ruby can't make it out in the darkness; she turns away, shaking her head at the bout of sudden dizziness. Bad enough being near an airlock — even worse to be here with no safeguards.

Kitty's hand in hers grounds her, and it occurs to Ruby that the gesture is too intimate for the role she's supposed to be playing. Too late to hide it now, though. With any luck, Lebedevya will take it as more evidence the relationship between "Olivia" and "Richard" is on shaky ground.

"Are you all right, Liv?"

Thank the saints Kitty is sticking with the con despite whatever chemicals are floating through her veins.

"I'm fine. How are you?"

"I'm amazing, love. I feel incredible."

"Are you taking something?" Ruby asks it delicately — she doesn't want to provoke Kitty's temper, or Lebedevya's suspicion. But she needs to know.

Kitty shakes her head. "Nothing," she says. "It's the dreams. When Annika tells you she can help you recover your past, she means it. There were vast swaths of myself I didn't remember — that I dulled over the years. Sometimes I treated you so poorly . . ."

"It's all forgiven," Ruby says quickly; Lebedevya's watching them curiously.

"But the memories — I know you don't buy it yet, but if you let Lebedevya work with you, you'll remember your past." Kitty lifts her hands to cup Ruby's face. There's a smudge of paint on the inside of her left wrist, a little splash of yellow glowing like a sun against her dark skin. "Whatever happened to you, it's in here." Her voice is husky, thrilling through Ruby and turning her knees to water. "Those memories aren't lost, they're blocked. Lebedevya can help."

She smiles, that mischievous smile Ruby knows so well, and Ruby feels herself melt. Her lips part for Kitty's, savoring the familiar taste, the softness, the playful way Kitty's teeth catch her lower lip before she pulls back, leaving Ruby dizzy for more.

Just plain dizzy, actually. And mortified at the impulsive slip in front of Lebedevya.

Saints in hell, what's gotten into her? It's been ages since she ate, she tells herself, and she must be hungrier than she feels. It's late, Sapis time, and she can't calculate how long it's been since she slept. Add to that the cloying incense, no wonder she's a bit off her balance.

Kitty's smile sparkles at her and the dizziness resolves into euphoria, a warm, golden joy that they're here together. She could stay here, she thinks, fantasies of things finally working out with Kitty singing in her skull. She could take Lebedevya up on her promise to help her reclaim the lost memories of her childhood. Let Raj and the others head home with Marga, and she and Kitty can finally be happy. The thoughts crowd together in her mind, a jumbled, peaceful blur.

Ruby coughs and steps back, blinking.

"You feel it, don't you?" Lebedevya says. "The joy of Saint Alixhi? I can show you more."

It's the incense, Ruby thinks. She looks back at Kitty, who's smiling like the sun. There's something in the incense.

Ruby steps back; she needs to get out of this room if she's going to keep her head. "I think the incense is making me a bit dizzy," she says. *Get out of here, Ruby. Something's not right.*

"Of course," Lebedevya says. "You've had such a long trip. But there's one thing left I want you to see before it's time to rest. You want to remember, don't you?"

"Yes," Ruby says tentatively. She breathes shallowly, trying not to fill her lungs with whatever Lebedevya's incense is pumping into the air. She's still stronger than Lebedevya, she tells herself. The woman may be taller, but she's willowy and probably hasn't ever had to hold her own in a bar fight. Ruby could use the element of surprise, grab Lebedevya by the hair and drive a knee into her gut, push past Lebedevya right now and make a run for the door, dragging Kitty with her. But if she does, she blows her cover — and Raj's.

When Ruby turns back to Kitty, the piece of space debris outside the airlock catches her attention again. It's not a twist of plastic, as she first thought. It's human hair — a long, blond curl drifting weightless in the vacuum. As Ruby watches in horror, the side of a woman's face comes into view. Pale skin, eyes closed. She could be sleeping — if you could call what happens in the vacuum of space "sleep."

Ruby startles back, eyes wide, to realize Lebedevya has moved to stand beside the airlock, pale hand gripping the switch.

"Do you trust me?" Lebedevya says, and Ruby lunges for her — but Kitty's grip on her wrist is iron.

Lebedevya throws opens the airlock.

CHAPTER 22
RUBY

RUBY USED TO HAVE THIS NIGHTMARE.

Sometimes, when the stress of stretching every credit or managing a dangerous boss's ego or hustling for seedy contracts got too bad, she'd dream she was scrambling through her day, petty frustrations piling up along with her blood pressure until a wall tore open and she was suddenly sucked into the void.

Not many girlfriends had lasted through their first experience of Ruby's night terrors. Kitty hadn't balked. Every single time, she'd shaken Ruby awake until she stopped panting for breath. Held her until she calmed back down and believed again in the air — and the strong arms — around her.

Ruby's been terrified of the void since she was a child: that drifter's death with your blood boiling out and eyes frozen open to stare forever into the nothingness that killed you, your body just one more piece of debris that might be discovered some day, or might be left to break apart over aeons until you're finally dust.

She's died in the dark a thousand times in her dreams, but this bitch Lebedevya isn't killing her this way.

Ruby pushes all the air from her lungs, a lifetime of emergency depressurization drills sending her body into the conditioned response, but the air inside the room doesn't rush past into the vacuum of space beyond. It doesn't pull her and Kitty — who's still gripping her wrist — out into the void.

Kitty is laughing. Ruby stares at her, blood slowly pulsing back to her cheeks to blaze raw heat, then turns bewildered to stare out the door of the "airlock." The room beyond is painted black, stars glimmering softly against the far walls and ceiling. Even the floor is painted black and pricked with tiny pinpoint lights. When she focuses she can see the artifice; the glimpse she'd gotten through the window had been terrifyingly realistic.

Bodies are floating in the room — about a half-dozen. There's the blond woman Ruby had seen through the window, hair floating out from her shoulders, a peaceful smile on her face. Her eyelashes flutter gently in her sleep, eyes moving beneath her lids. She's wearing headphones over her ears.

"I'm sorry, Livvy, but the look on your face." Kitty jostles her with her shoulder, playful, teasing out forgiveness for what apparently was just a shitty, shitty joke. "I thought Annika told you."

Lebedevya steps past Ruby and slips her feet under the mesh of nearly invisible straps that crisscross the floor, then reaches to caress the blond woman's cheek.

She gives the woman a small push so she drifts farther from the door.

"This is our dreaming chamber," Lebedevya says. "The station's artificial gravity ceases beyond these doors, allowing the body to completely relax so the subconscious can do its work."

Kitty slips an arm around Ruby's waist, drawing her close. "You'll love this," she murmurs in Ruby's ear. Her eyes are glossy black pools. "Sometimes you need to stop using a magnifying glass and start using a mirror."

"Kitty. Love. What are you talking about?"

"This is what I've been learning," Kitty says; Ruby's seen this intensity plenty of times, the euphoria and revelation brought about by whatever designer drug is ricocheting through her neurons right now. "*This*. I've been searching outside myself to find out who I am, but the secrets are in my dreams. They've been in me the whole time."

Every response Ruby wants to have dies on her tongue; Lebedevya is watching them. She clearly now knows their relationship goes deeper than friendship, but that won't blow Ruby's cover. What'll blow Ruby's cover — saints give her strength — is launching herself across the room to slap that beatific smile off Annika Lebedevya's perfectly made-up face.

Ruby will get Kitty the help she *really* needs, but she won't throw this job, not yet. The others are still depending on her.

She lets Kitty lead her into the room; Kitty pushes off as gracefully as though she was born off-planet, making micro-adjustments with her long, lithe limbs. She stretches out and shivers, black skin inky in the cool blue light so she seems to be dissolving into stars herself, points of light shining through her skin like diamonds. Goddess of the night sky, Ruby thinks, reaching to stroke Kitty's bare arm.

At the touch, the vision vanishes and Kitty is a normal human once more. Ruby shakes her head. "There's something in the incense," she says, and Kitty smiles at her. Her image doubles, and when she speaks again her voice sounds impossibly far away.

"Of course there is, silly."

Lebedevya's still watching them. The incense keeps making her forget she's supposed to be Olivia.

"This place is amazing," Ruby says. She catches her bare toe in a loop to anchor herself, coming around to face Lebedevya. "I really did think you were opening an airlock."

Lebedevya studies her, blond hair floating behind her like a cape. "Why are you so afraid of the void?"

"I grew up in the Pearls," Ruby says. "Everyone is."

"Not like you are. Did something traumatic happen in childhood?"

Easy guess, something traumatic happened to everyone in childhood. But Ruby pretends to ponder the question, spins to take in the room. The illusion is still enough to drive flickers of panic through her, but she ignores the stars and studies the floating bodies. How did Lebedevya lure them all here? What promises did she give them, and what did she earn from them in return?

Ruby doesn't recognize any of the faces, all so relaxed in gentle repose. At least none of the ones who are near enough, though maybe one of the figures floating near the outskirts is Aya Marga. Saints in hell, how big is this room?

"I watched a thriller vid when I was too young," Ruby says; Lebedevya is still waiting for an answer for her question, so Ruby gins one up. It's not a real trauma, but it'll work, and the plot of the vid is still clear as day in her mind. "About a little girl on a ship with her parents. Someone was firing at them, the father was trying to steer them through the missiles while the mother was trying to repair something in the engine. Some shrapnel punched through the wall of the ship and the little girl was trying to cover it with a temporary patch — saints know where she found it, but she was holding it on with her bare hands. She was afraid to move in case the patch didn't hold, and she was terrified another piece of shrapnel was going to tear through the hull. And her." Ruby smiles at Lebedevya, going for lighthearted. "I remember thinking when I watched that vid, human skin is so much more fragile than metal, and even metal didn't do much to stop shrapnel."

"I can see the scene made an impression," Lebedevya says. "What was the name of the vid?"

"It was called — " The name's there and gone off her tongue, though Ruby can still see the scene as clear as day. Only now her own hands are on the patch, her mouth dry and bitter with fear, snot running from her nose and tears from her eyes and she couldn't do a thing about it because her mother — belly bulging with child — had stuffed her in an environment suit and sealed the helmet and told her to hide, *hide*. But the hull in the supply closet had been breached and air was hissing out, and by the time her mother had come to tell her it was safe Ruby's arms were shaking with exhaustion. Ruby had been elated and proud she was able to help. She hadn't understood why her mom had started sobbing.

Oh, fuck.

Fuck.

"I don't remember the name," Ruby says lightly. She fans at herself. "I think this incense is making me dizzy."

"And I think you're remembering."

"I'm remembering?" Ruby laughs. "I told you I *forgot* the name of the vid."

"It's natural to be afraid of remembering," Lebedevya says. "Most of the people who come to me find they're remembering darkness as well as light. Our memories have a way of repressing the things that happened when we were too young to comprehend. With your friend Katriana, we've been unearthing the childhood traumas that have made it so hard for her to feel whole in adulthood."

Ruby twists to look over her shoulder; Kitty has drifted away to the far side of the chamber, she's speaking with a figure who seems to be attending the floating dreamers. "Like what?"

"I'm sure she'll tell you when she's ready. But her brother Absolon is not the man you think he is."

Ruby glances back at Lebedevya, puzzled. Sure, Kitty's childhood wasn't as fairy-tale perfect as it seemed from the outside. Maybe her fathers had been a bit too focused on their own careers, maybe their desire to protect their children from the world's eyes had instead created a pair of awkward young people who didn't know how to engage with anyone. Kitty had rebelled by drinking the world in as fast as she could, Absolon had learned to hold everyone who crossed his path — or his sister's — at rapier's length.

But they'd all loved each other. The idea that Absolon had ever, *ever* hurt Kitty is ludicrous.

Kitty's already floating, though. She smiles at Ruby across the room, and an attendant gently slides a needle into her arm. Kitty's eyelashes begin to flutter; Ruby fights down panic.

"Are you ready to learn the truth?" Lebedevya asks.

Ruby could defer. Tell Lebedevya not yet and ask to go back to her room. Or she could scream and yell and insist Lebedevya wake Kitty back up so the two of them can get safely back to Absolon. But she hasn't found Aya Marga. And even if she had, she's beginning to suspect that whatever con Lebedevya is running is far more dangerous than any of them have realized.

She needs to understand what Lebedevya's end game is, and there's only one way to do it.

Ruby takes a deep breath.

"I'm ready," she says.

The attendant, who has finished with Kitty, floats over to Ruby, catching his feet gracefully in the loops on the floor. Ruby's suddenly grateful she wasn't able to get an earpiece; there's nothing to keep Lebedevya and her people from searching her while she's sleeping, but they'll find nothing but an innocent-looking gold bangle that serves as her beacon.

"Let go," Lebedevya murmurs. "Relax."

Ruby releases her foot from the loop on the floor, pivoting gracefully to horizontal and taking deep breaths. The attendant helps Ruby float, steadies her with soothing hands massaging her temples, thumbs stroking between her brows, cradling her — so safe, so safe.

Ruby slides a hand over the bangle on her wrist as though adjusting it, blinks out a series of flashes. "Im ok found k."

"Dream well," Lebedevya says, and Ruby feels the barest pinch in the crook of her arm as the attendant inserts the needle.

And then she's gone.

CHAPTER 23
LASADI

Lasadi doesn't like any of this. Ruby's stopped communicating with them and Raj is either sleeping soundly through this entire job or has been drugged. She'd prefer the former, but she knows by now he's not the type to leave the rest of them hanging. Which means he's in trouble, and Lasadi's done watching from the outside.

Fortunately, it turns out every level on Sapis Station has a separate maintenance access, and by contract with the Sapis Cooperative these are available at all hours and restricted to co-op employees.

Or, at least, to people wearing Sapis Cooperative maintenance jumpsuits and holding the right access cards. Jay used the flea he'd left in an unattended terminal to log an urgent complaint about the recyclers in Lebedevya's section, then intercepted the ensuing maintenance request. It'll get them in and give them a seemingly legitimate reason to be traipsing around the hallways this time of night. The maintenance gear they've loaded up with lends them an air of legitimacy, while also disguising the weapons they're carrying.

Alex shifts uncomfortably under the weight of the welding harness he nicked from olds know where. "This is awkward," he complains. "Next time can I play the part of the ritzy socialite who gets to stay in the flash hotel?"

"Tell me about it," Jay says. He's pushing a janitorial cart with a moxed wheel that bucks the whole cart every few steps. "Up ahead on the left."

"We definitely get dibs on the fun part of the job next time." Lasadi says it to keep the mood light, though nothing about the sustained false identities Ruby and Raj have been wearing sounds appealing to her. She'd much rather be getting filthy in a maintenance jumpsuit than sipping tea and trading niceties with an oiled snake. She had enough of that for a lifetime with Anton.

"Hey!"

Lasadi tenses at the voice behind them. Beside her, Jay slips a hand into the pocket of his borrowed coveralls. "No guns," she warns him and Alex both. They need to get a lot farther in before they risk tipping their hand.

She waits for a second "Hey!" before she turns back to find a lone figure flagging them down with the circular arm wave spacers tend to use. It's a portly man with thinning gray hair, wearing the same Sapis Cooperative maintenance jumpsuit they've procured. He must have come down the lift right after them.

"I got this," Jay murmurs, then raises his voice. "What's up, man? You here for the recyclers, too?" His accent has become passably Belt drifter, which should work. Much more likely someone from Durga's Belt would be out working on Sapis Station than someone from Corusca.

"Yep," the older man calls back. "Just saw the job come through."

Jay shakes his head, annoyed. "Second time this month the main office has double-booked us on a call. I'd like to know who's sleeping on the job up there."

The older man's studying them with a faint frown, and Lasadi counts heartbeats while she decides if she's going to need to act. Sapis Co-op employs a few thousand people, but there's still a chance he calls their bluff if he's the kind of guy who thinks he knows everyone on the maintenance crew.

"Happened to me earlier," the guy finally says, and Lasadi relaxes her grip on her stunner. "Some kind of bug in the system, I think. But, hey. I get paid by the job even if it's a false alarm — time and a half when they drag me out for a night call."

"Ain't that the truth," Jay says.

"Anyway, better you than me." The older man stifles a yawn. "I hate calls on this level. Place is cursed — something's always breaking."

"Cursed like haunted?" Alex asks.

The older man gives a noncommittal shrug. "Keep your eyes to yourself down here, got it? Watch your tools and each other's backs and you'll be fine."

"Thanks for the advice," Jay says, and the older man turns back to the lift with an arm raised in farewell. As soon as the lift closes behind him, Jay starts pushing the cart again. "Security office is down this hall. Third door

on the left, malfunctioning recyclers are across the hall."
He pokes his head around the corner; it's clear. "We're
up," he says to Alex.

He scans a stolen keycard over the door to the security room. When the door slides open with a hiss, Jay
pushes the cart through without looking inside.

"Blue Warps are completely screwed this year," he
says over his shoulder to Alex; Lasadi vaguely recognizes the reference to a New Manilan sweeps team.
"Without Elena Brava? She was the only one keeping
the team together."

"Her and a half-dozen other killer players," Alex
shoots back, crowding after Jay and the cart into the
security room. It's basically a closet, barely big enough
for a half-dozen screens, a desk, and the woman who's
spun in her chair, eyes wide in surprise. Alex ignores
her, attention on his argument with Jay. "And Brava's
dislocated her shoulder, only. She'll be wiping the field
with your Crows again by the time playoffs roll
around."

"You remember how long Ling was out," Jay
points out.

"Excuse me?" The woman's half out of her chair,
face flushed red and expression mildly panicked.

"Ling *separated* his shoulder. That's — "

"Nah, I saw the hit that took Brava out, man, there's
no way it's a simple dislocation. She — "

"Hey!" The woman inside the security room has
found her voice. Jay and Alex both trail off as though
shocked anyone's inside the room. "You can't be in
here!"

"Look, I got a maintenance order." Jay shoves the

janitorial cart out of his way with a grunt and holds out his comm.

The woman leans forward, squinting. She's balanced awkwardly, blocked in her chair by the cart, and Alex edges behind her as though he's trying to give her space. Even though Lasadi is watching for it, she doesn't see him slipping a transmission chip into the panel behind the woman.

The woman hasn't spotted Alex, either. He gives Lasadi a thumbs-up behind the woman's back.

"Your order says recyclers," the woman says, flinging an arm out to point to the door across the hall. "That door. This fucking co-op, when are they going to send us someone who actually knows what they're doing? Get out of here. Now."

Jay maneuvers his cart out of the room, cursing at the bucking moxed wheel and grumbling at Alex; the woman glares after them until the door slides shut. Lasadi swipes the recyclers door open across the hall and the three of them crowd inside. There's a bit more breathing room than in the security cubby, but not much.

Lasadi pulls the cover off the cart and fires up the desk unrolled across the top. "Code?" she asks Alex, who reads a string of numbers off his comm. One by one, the cameras and controls from the security room begin to populate on the desk.

Alex sidles up next to her. "Give us a look."

"Lots of dark spots," Lasadi says. "Not nearly as many cameras as we expected. But at least we now have the exact layout of the place." She maps Raj's location beacon on her comm to the schematic on the security screen. "Here. His room is locked." It's also pulsing a pale green. Lasadi matches the color with another button on the dashboard, labeled Dreaming.

"What does that mean?" Alex asks.

"It means they're drugging him," Lasadi says. She really hadn't wanted to be right about that. "That white flame, or whatever Jay said the kids call it — they must be pumping it into his room." And sure enough, when she calls up stats on his room, the dose is listed along with a timer. He's been under almost two hours.

His isn't the only room pulsing pale green; apparently Lebedevya's people are sending multiple guests on a hallucinogenic trip tonight. Lasadi reaches for the button to stop the cycle short, but Jay holds out a hand.

"A thousand credits says Lebedevya gets alerts from the main system," he says. "We shouldn't mess with anything until we're ready for her to know we're here."

Lasadi takes a sharp breath. He's got a point. As much as she wants to get her crew out of here, they have no evidence anyone's in immediate physical danger. *Think with your head, Lala,* her grandmother would have told her. *Not your heart.*

"Are the rest of those rooms occupied?"

"Looks like it." Jay's scrolling through a hand terminal that's also tapped into the transmitter Alex left in the security room. "I found a guest list — room locations, meal preferences, medical treatments."

"Any schematics of the lower level?" Alex asks.

"One sec." Lasadi sweeps away the upper level and finds the lower one without difficulty. "Let me get that recording of Ruby's movements queued up."

"I'm all good." Alex frowns down at the schematic,

slim finger tracing what could be arcane sigils while he concentrates on retracing his sister's steps from his memory of the recording. "Here's where she entered," he finally says. "Then she walked here — 'Camera,' she signaled — and down this hall." His finger stops on a small circular room. "This is where Saint Alixhi is."

"Can you get to it?"

"Easy, Cap."

"Get in position and wait for my signal."

Alex nods and gives the schematic another once-over — presumably filing every detail away into his library of a brain — then slips back out into the hallway.

Alex may not have needed the recording of Ruby's movements to figure out where she went on the schematic, but Lasadi does. She queues it up, then traces Ruby's steps from the moment she left the small room with Saint Alixhi's relics to a large chamber at the center of the second level. It's not labeled.

"Ruby's been here for at least thirty minutes," Lasadi says. "Wonder what's in there?"

"Whatever it is, it's drawing a ton of power."

"Have you found Aya Marga on that guest list?"

Jay shakes his head. "But this is weird." He swipes a file from his terminal to the desk and she taps it open. It's a person's file, someone named Paul Comadra who apparently retired wealthy after a successful career directing the sorts of sappy relationship comedies Lasadi would shoot herself before watching. His net worth is listed in the file, along with dietary restrictions and medical treatments. "Check out that tab. 'Memory Work.'"

Lasadi opens the Memory Work tab and scans through the notes there. There are tons of biographical details alongside lists of family members, ex-spouses, phobias, places he frequented in childhood.

"Are these all things Lebedevya learned from putting this guy in a dream state?" Lasadi asks.

"Maybe," Jay says. "But this? 'Paul is not receptive to seeds that mother abandoned him as child, but responded to seeds of resentment towards father. Wife has controlling interest in accounts. Seed memory: infidelity?'"

"She wants to get Paul to quote-unquote 'remember' that his wife was unfaithful? Can she do that?"

Jay shrugs. "White flame's a hell of a drug. Doesn't take much to send you on a trip and come back not knowing what's real and what's not."

"Copy those files, then — we can use that."

"There's references to session recordings, but no links. It looks like they've been stored in an external database."

Lasadi sits back, squeezing her eyes closed and trying to think. They came here for Marga and Katriana, but they're not the only two Lebedevya has lured out into the black. Her instinct is to stick to the plan and play it safe, but she can already hear what Raj would say. *We have a chance to make a difference here. We should take it.*

She opens up a new message, to Absolon.

Does the name Paul Comadra mean anything to you?

His response appears on her comm almost immediately.

HIS WIFE IS HERE ON SAPIS. SAYS HE CAME HERE FOR TREATMENT, SHE HASN'T SEEN HIM IN WEEKS. HAVE YOU FOUND HIM? KATRIANA?

RUBY IS WITH HER. STAND BY.

Lasadi drums her fingers, thinking. "This is all incriminating. Maybe the families could use it to get Sapis Co-op to actually do something and get their loved ones back. But it's not quite enough to shut her down. We need more proof."

"What about the session recordings?"

"If they're being stored externally, they're somewhere secure. Close to Lebedevya. We need to find those."

Something else is pricking at her attention. She swipes back to the upper level, zeroing in on Raj's room again, where the room pulses in pale green pulses: *Dreaming.* She turns to Jay. "You said it doesn't take much white flame to send you on a trip. Can you overdose on it?"

"Not at the levels she's using."

"But you could if you upped the dose? How much does she have?"

"With the new shipment, she has enough to take out a small army if she wanted to. Wouldn't be a problem to flood a single room enough to take someone out."

Lasadi gnaws on the inside of her lip. "How quickly would it work? Say, if something went wrong and Lebedevya realized Raj isn't who he says he is."

Jay stares down at the desk, scrubs a hand over his jaw. "Too fast," he finally says. "Good thing there's a problem with the recyclers. Gimme one second."

He flips open a panel, mucking in the wiring until

the entire ventilation system flickers and reboots. One by one the rooms labeled Dreaming blink from green to white, an error message flashing on the screens. A moment later, the woman from the security room across the hallway is pounding on the door. Lasadi throws the cover back over the janitorial cart, pretending to be working on the panel as Jay opens the door.

"What the hell are you all doing in here?"

Lasadi doesn't hear Jay's placating response, because someone gasps in her earpiece, a familiar breath, and Lasadi sits up straighter. Raj's voice comes through coarse and raspy with sleep.

"Captain?"

Thank the olds.

CHAPTER 24
RAJ

Raj wakes up.

For real wakes up.

Feels like the artificial gravity of Sapis Station got turned up a few too many notches while he was sleeping, he has the impression he's sunk so deep in the bed he's about to punch through the mattress. Like his eyelids are lead, his limbs concrete, his head solid iron.

Other than that, he feels fantastic. He drags himself over onto his back and stretches the heaviness from his body, feeling like he finally caught up on three years' worth of sleepless nights.

Maybe what they say about the restorative effect of visiting Bixia Yuanjin is true.

He touches his ear, adjusting the earpiece. "Captain?"

Lasadi's voice comes immediately. "Thank the olds. Are you all right?"

"I'm good. I — " Someone grunts on the other end of the line. "Everything good on your end?"

"Yep, Jay's just tying up a security guard."

A twinge of guilt — they're in the middle of a job and here he is getting his beauty rest. "Sorry. I fell asleep, hard. Guess I needed the sleep."

"I think she drugged you." A faint clip of anger in the captain's tone; Raj doesn't think it's directed at him, but the edges of the world are still a bit blurry. "We found a shipment of hallucinogens, and we think Lebedevya's been using them to make people dream. Like that incense she burned when you and Ruby were with her?"

"Copy that. I definitely smelled something right before I passed out." When Raj reaches back though the groggy haze, he gets snatches of bizarre imagery, fragments that slip between his fingers as soon as he tries to grasp them. "I had some wild dreams."

"Ruby still hasn't checked in," Lasadi says, and any remaining grogginess vanishes.

Raj manages to push himself up to sitting. Manages to swing his feet over the edge of the bed, gets unsteadily to them. His suitcase is still at the foot of the bed. Raj thumbs it open. "Can you track her?"

"She's been communicating via her beacon, flashing a code she and Alex used to use."

"Clever."

"She's found Saint Alixhi, and Katriana. So far she hasn't signaled for help."

"All while I was sleeping on the job." Raj pulls a clean shirt over his head and shrugs on his jacket. Slips on shoes, checks the nerve blade in its calf holster. Catches sight of himself in the mirror and rakes his fingers through his hair, trying to decide if his alias is far enough along in his acting career to go through a deliberately disheveled phase. Decides he might be. "How long was I out?"

"Two hours." Lasadi takes a sharp breath. "Ruby hasn't moved or checked in for almost an hour. And I think we figured out why Lebedevya's bringing in all these drugs."

"Epic party?"

"If that party involves implanting traumatic memories to make people mistrust their families."

"Which is why none of them wanted to leave when Sapis Co-op tried to intervene."

"Exactly."

Raj goes still, a hand on the door to his room. The human memory is less a perfectly recorded vid you can play back at any time, more a sand painting whose lines are constantly being blurred, remixed, nudged. As the years pass you just remember fragments; the coherent storyline you tell yourself later isn't fact, it's your imagination filling in the gaps based on logic and experience and assumptions. It's why two people can remember the exact same event in wildly different ways based on the fragments they retained. It's why if you tell someone something happened enough times, they'll begin to remember it that way, too.

Memory is at the core of human identity; yet how very, very easy it is to manipulate.

"Where's Ruby now?"

"There's a big room in the heart of the lower level. It's not labeled on the schematics."

"Evelyn told us the dream chamber was on the lower level," Raj says. "Near the middle. That's probably where she is."

Lasadi swears. "We're inside," she finally says. "We can be there in a second with guns blazing if that's what you want, but we still haven't found the aya, and we don't have hard evidence on Lebedevya. We got into her system, but we need anything you can find out from other guests."

"Hold off, let me go find someone to charm. Anything I should be keeping an eye out for?"

"We think they've been making recordings of the sessions but we can't find them in the system. We're looking for a secure place to stash data cubes. A safe? A vault? Something like that. And be careful, Raj."

He's not going to read anything into her tone — she's the captain, of course she wants each of them to come back safe. No harm in enjoying the way she said his name, though. No harm at all, except for losing his head by indulging in ridiculous fantasies while on the job. He shoves the warm glow aside.

Raj opens the door and glances down the hall. No one is nearby, though he can make out voices in the distance. They arrived late last night, Sapis time, so if he only slept for a few hours it's still early. Maybe he'll find another night owl out and about he can talk to.

He heads down the hall, glancing in Ruby's open door as he passes. The room is still unoccupied, her suitcase still untouched. She knows what she's doing, he tells himself. And she's found Katriana.

He makes his way back towards the reception desk, guessing that the lounge area with the view of Bixia

Yuanjin is one of the places people gather. And sure enough, he's in luck. One of the low jewel-toned chairs facing the chromothermatic glass windows is occupied by the young woman he'd noticed when he first came in, the one with the suspicious green eyes and choppy brown hair. She's ditched the book she was reading earlier and is simply staring out the window gnawing on a fingernail. She looks away when Raj raises a hand to her, thin shoulders hunched protectively around her tea.

She's taken a vow of silence, Evelyn told him. Still. Her body language screams she's got an interesting story to tell.

Raj pours himself a cup of tea — jasmine and mint — then crosses to the chair beside her. "Is this seat taken?" The answer he gets is a sharp, sideways flick of her head: *No.*

Bixia Yuanjin swirls before them like a polished gemstone, dazzlingly blue and pearly white, set at the center of stacked diamond rings. Raj settles in to enjoy the view in companionable silence.

He'd wanted to travel out to Bixia Yuanjin ever since he was a child — he'd always told himself travel would be one of the consolation prizes of the career military life his father had wanted for him. Turns out it's a nice perk of the freelance grifter life he's chosen for himself. And, bonus, he doesn't have to try to subjugate the citizens of Sapis Station to enjoy the view — instead, he gets to dig for the loose thread that will cause Lebedevya's con artist empire to unravel.

He's definitely more suited to this line of work.

"I'd never get tired of this view." Raj smiles at the

young woman. "I'm Richard. My girlfriend and I got in last night, and I'm not used to the time difference yet — I couldn't sleep."

The young woman relaxed a touch at the mention of his girlfriend, but she still doesn't speak. So she's hearing, and she understands him. She glances towards the reception area, then stares firmly back out at Bixia Yuanjin. Her knuckles are white on her teacup. She's afraid, but he doesn't think it's of him.

Raj winces as though realizing a gaffe. "I'm sorry, is this one of those silent areas? I feel like an idiot." He grins, then mimes zipping his lips shut. It gets the hint of a smile, and this time when she glances at the door to the reception area, her gaze returns to Raj.

"Can I tell you a secret?" he says, leaning in. Her eyes widen. He lifts the cup in his hands. "I really hate tea."

This time she laughs out loud.

"If you guessed my girlfriend was the one who wanted to come here, you'd be right. This isn't really my style — no offense, to each their own." He flashes her an easy grin as if to say it's fine if this is her style. "Olivia — my girl-friend — she seems to love it, and I'm happy when she's happy. And this view's worth having to drink tea for."

"Don't let her stay," the young woman says, her voice barely above a whisper, yet sharp as a razor. She clamps her lips shut again as though surprised by her own outburst.

Raj frowns at her. "We're not going to stay," he says. "We're here for a few weeks and then it's back to Arquelle."

The young woman's made her decision; her gaze flickers to the reception room door again, and she leans in. "Your girlfriend, she has money?"

"That's kind of personal."

"If she does, the Voice of Power will try to get her to stay." Her nostrils flare. "And your girlfriend will do it."

"Why would she?"

"Because she convinced my mother."

"But not you?"

"I'm — " Her jaw clamps shut again. Her hands are shaking so badly tea splashes onto her silk pajama pants. Raj carefully takes it from her hand, sets it on the low table in front of them. "My mother is the only one I have left. I'll pretend to be whatever they want me to if I can stay here with her." She uncoils her legs as if to stand. "I should go."

"What's your name?"

She takes a sharp breath. "Marissa."

"Marissa, if you need help, I can help you."

"What the hell can you do?"

Raj holds up a finger and pulls one of Absolon's privacy spheres from his pocket; the young woman stares suspiciously when he twists it on, then her eyes go wide. She works her jaw as though relieving the sudden pressure in her ears.

"No one can hear us while this is on," Raj says. He leans back in his chair, shifting his body language so it doesn't look like he and Marissa are conspiring; after a moment, she does the same. "I know what Lebedevya is doing. I could help get your mother out." The fear in

Marissa's eyes flickers into something like hope. "But I need your help, first."

That tentative dip of her chin could be a nod.

"They took my friend to the dream chamber. Can you tell me how to get there?"

"Back the way you came, there's a door labeled Sage. It's the stairway to the lower level. Keep going towards the center."

"Thank you." Raj glances at the reception room door, less to check it's still closed, more to let Marissa know he understands the risk she's taking. "One more question. I'm looking for a woman named Marga. She's an aya from the Aymaya Apostles, but I don't know if she would be wearing her robes. She arrived a few days ago."

"She's probably still safe."

"What do you mean, probably?"

"She's not one of the useful ones. The rich ones? Like my mom, like your girlfriend. They're useful, but the others — "

Her lips clamp back together and she's walking almost before Raj hears the door to the reception room sigh open and sees Evelyn appear, perfectly put together despite the hour. Marissa brings her hands together over her heart in greeting to Evelyn, then vanishes down the curving hallway. Raj twists off the privacy sphere and slips it back into his jacket pocket.

"Richard!" Evelyn exclaims. Raj can't tell if she's going for delighted or annoyed to find him up this time of night.

"I couldn't sleep."

"Apparently a lot of people can't tonight." There's a

bite to her tone Raj can't place. "That's natural. I'm sorry about Marissa, she's taken a vow of silence."

"I forgot you mentioned that," Raj says. "Hey, Olivia still isn't in her room. Can you tell me where she is?"

Evelyn gives him a tight smile. "Why don't you come with me and let's talk."

CHAPTER 25
RUBY

THE LIQUID IN LEBEDEVYA'S NEEDLE TRICKLES WARM AND silken through Ruby's bloodstream, more slowly than she would have expected. Time crawls, her heart beating an impossibly elongated cadence as it pumps the drug through her veins, and Ruby can follow the path of every cell and platelet spreading from the crook of her right arm. She can feel individual strands of muscle relaxing, unraveling — or maybe that's the drugs.

The hyperawareness of her body lasts the space of a breath before going wavy along the edges, smudging the border that once existed between everything she knew as *her* — her thoughts, her memories, her very skin — and the rest of the world. She stares at her hand, enchanted as it melts into the surrounding air like a drop of dye in water.

Saints in hell this is fun. She can finally see the appeal.

"Can you hear me, Olivia?"

Lebedevya's voice sounds like it's coming through an air vent, echoey and sharp and distant and false. It's hard to make out individual words, but the tone of Lebedevya's voice is a thread, a tether between the real world and this liminal place where Ruby's currently flickering on the edge of consciousness. Ruby gropes for it. Misses. Gropes for it again.

"We'll start gently today," Lebedevya says. "Picture a place where you have always felt safe."

Ruby-in-consciousness would have picked the Aymaya Apostles convent; Ruby-in-dreaming goes immediately to her first pod.

Ruby-in-consciousness can dissect that later.

The pod was in a part of Artemis City's Bell close enough to the nightlife to party but shitty enough to be affordable. The neighborhood was run by the Aherne gang, and most of her neighbors worked for them. But the gang had largely ignored Ruby and her pod had been her haven. It was the first place she'd found complete privacy, complete autonomy.

It was nothing, but it was hers; she hadn't had to ask anyone else for help paying the rent.

"Where are you?"

"My first apartment." A tiny voice in the back of her mind shouts warning she's supposed to be an heiress to a fancy Artemisian lithium mine, but Ruby hadn't been able to afford a coffee — let alone a pod — in the part of Artemis City "Olivia" would have spent her early years. When she gropes for first-apartment details she could share with Lebedevya, she pictures the garish neon statuary of the Hôtel l'Eza's lobby. She laughs, golden chimes floating from her mouth and drifting into the weightless dark of the dreaming chamber.

"Wrap yourself in the feeling of being safe there. Imagine how that feels."

Thank the saints Lebedevya isn't asking her to describe anything. The part of Ruby's mind that's not relishing the high wonders if she'll be able to keep in character if Lebedevya starts probing. But the real Ruby, the Ruby sitting mellow in her old apartment, wrapped in safety, doesn't care because whatever Lebedevya gave her feels like liquid chocolate, velvety and warm and impenetrable and *right*.

"Are you imagining it?" Lebedevya is asking. "See if you can carry that feeling of safety with you as you walk to the front door."

Ruby-in-dreaming stretches lazily to her feet and pads across the industrial composite floor, worn smooth by a dozen other occupants' feet well before Ruby moved in. The room expands and contracts around her gently in time to her pulse, the walls shimmering like opal.

This door in front of her is not the pod door she expects to see, with its flaking hinges and suspicious, meter-long gouge carved in the metal, but she knows it better than any other door she's walked through in her life. This door is warm blue and twice as tall as the rest of the doors on the block, sweeping up to support a whorl of a stained glass window staring out like an amber eye glowing from within.

Ruby goes still in front of the convent's door, marveling at the brush strokes in the paint, the rivets, the faint scratches. She touches her fingers to it timidly, as though expecting it to vanish. It's solid.

"It's all right, sweetheart," Lebedevya says, but her voice is wrong. She's speaking in a stranger's voice, one that shivers rapid and loose and familiar through Ruby's core.

Ruby turns to see a new woman kneeling beside her. It's not like looking in a mirror, not remotely — but Ruby recognizes her features. That spray of freckles over her nose and cheeks mimics Ruby's own, though Ruby's complexion is darker than her mother's. The same broad nose, the pointed chin, though her mother's hair is shaved to the scalp. She's got a scar on her chin, newly healed.

"Mom?"

Ruby's mother's smile is laced with grief, her dark eyes red-rimmed and bloodshot. Ruby's so focused on those eyes she almost doesn't notice her mother isn't alone. She's clutching a bundle of baby to her chest with the ferocity of a woman who's terrified someone might try to tear him out of her arms. There's a male presence nearby, too, blurred on the edges of her vision.

"Do you remember what to do, sweetheart?"

"I knock on the door and tell them I need help."

Ruby's mother nods once, sharp. Determined. "That's right. The people who live here are very nice. They'll know what to do."

"Where are you going?"

"Away. But for a short while, only."

Ruby's nose itches. One shoe is tied too tight. A dozen petty complaints of a twelve-year-old come tumbling back in the moment, and Ruby tells herself there's no way to know if this is a real memory or just a desperate dream borne from Lebedevya's cocktail of hallucinogens.

"You can handle being without us for a couple of days," Ruby's mom says, and Ruby nods — she can, she has done. She doesn't like it when they leave, but this isn't the first time they've had to have her stay with people they trust.

This is the first time she's had a new responsibility, though: the wriggling, fussy bundle her mother is clutching. Ruby's a big sister now. She's brave and strong and responsible and as fierce as her mother, and if they need her to stay here to protect Alex she'll do it with every ounce of her tiny child's heart.

Her parents may have left her before, but somehow this time feels different. She doesn't know where that scar came from on her mother's chin. She doesn't know why her father's limping — she can see him now that he steps closer, dissolving into the frame with his dark fingers taped and a bruise mottling his left eye.

Saints, he looks like Alex will in a decade, though with a few more pounds and a rangy brawler's stance Ruby hopes Alex never needs to develop.

Her father kneels gingerly to give her a hug. "Be brave, little bug," he says. "Be brave for your brother."

Ruby nods. She can do that. She can be so brave that next time they're in trouble they understand they can take her with them instead of leaving her behind.

Her father plants a kiss on the top of her head and her mother draws Ruby in to clutch her ferociously to her chest beside the baby. She sobs into Ruby's hair, once, harsh, then lets her go. She hands baby Alex to her and sets a knapsack beside the door — Ruby doesn't have to look at it to see it's stamped with the words *Auburn Station*. That knapsack was the only thing from her past life she had at the convent.

And then her mother steels herself, teeth biting her lower lip so sharply Ruby is shocked she doesn't draw blood.

"I love you," her mother says, and touches the back of Ruby's neck. A sharp pinch, and Ruby's eyes flash open in shock and betrayal.

Ruby thrashes away from the vision and her mother and father vanish in slashed ribbons, leaving a lonely, confused twelve-year-old standing in front of the convent door, a blank slate who knew only that if she knocked, the people behind the door would help her.

Ruby stares down at the little girl that was her. The girl looks back, her eyes no longer empty.

"What the hell did she do to you?" Ruby asks.

Her child self cocks an eyebrow at her.

"Olivia?"

The name swims through layers of dreams to finally brush against Ruby's attention.

"Olivia?"

Ruby tears her gaze away from her child self and blinks heavy-lidded eyes open. Lebedevya is watching her with concern.

"Olivia, what happened? You seemed very upset."

Ruby grasps for the thread of what she's supposed to be doing here, attention slipping around the edge of her cover story until it finds purchase. Right. She's here with her boyfriend. Their relationship is on the rocks.

She wants to laugh at how absurd the scenario is, but something else tugs at her memory.

She's here to help Kitty.

"I remembered something about Richard," Ruby says.

"Ah. I suggested we start gently, but sometimes when your mind wants to go to a place, it's best to let it. Close your eyes again. Are you still standing at the door?"

Ruby is, the convent's door looming larger than life above her. Ruby doesn't know if she answers aloud, but Lebedevya is standing beside her now, stroking a hand down her arm like she would a frightened child.

"Go through it. Picture the home you share with Richard."

Ruby has never pushed open the convent door — she's always knocked and it's been opened by whoever was on door duty that day. But when her hand rests on the warm wood it swings open easily, effortlessly, and she's standing in the *Nanshe's* galley. Relief washes through her: *Home.*

Home?

"Picture a time Richard made you feel unsafe," Lebedevya says, and Ruby doesn't have a chance to parse her unexpected reaction to being back on board the *Nanshe* because now Raj is in the galley, dressed ridiculously, like a caricature of the rich boyfriend he's supposed to be playing. He gives her a cheeky grin.

"I don't know," Ruby says to Lebedevya. Raj has never made her feel unsafe. He's gotten her into plenty of scrapes, he's made her furious more times than she can count. But he's always been there for her — same as the captain and Jay and Alex. When she's let them be.

Home.

"Did Richard ever get upset at you for staying out late?" Lebedevya asks, and the Raj in Ruby's fake memory suddenly bares his teeth.

"Where have you been?" he demands, and Ruby takes a shocked step back at the angry, possessive tone in his voice.

This isn't like Raj.

"Because it's not supposed to *be* him," says an impatient child's voice, and she looks down to find her own twelve-year-old self standing at her elbow. Ruby's child self rolls her eyes. "It's your imagination, isn't it. Making a play out of suggestions that awful woman is giving you."

"You're so smart, are you."

The scene's still playing in front of them. "I asked where you've been," says Raj-slash-Richard, and Ruby glares at him.

"Out."

Somewhere in the back of her mind, Lebedevya is still talking quietly; Ruby pays little attention to the words, but she can see them shaping the scene, putting words in her mouth like she's reading a script.

"What else did he say to you? What did he call you? Did he accuse you of cheating on him? That didn't feel fair, did it? That must have pierced you. How many times did you have this fight? This wasn't the first, of course it wasn't. Did you also fight about money? He must have resented your wealth, you must have wondered sometimes if he was using you."

And at every question, new flickers of memory are surfacing, sprouting from the seeds Lebedevya is scattering, nurtured by her leading questions. The memories of Raj feel real, only it's not *Raj*, Raj. It's someone named Richard that Ruby never knew, in an apartment she's never been in.

The feelings of the fights and betrayals are real, of course, but those came from elsewhere. She's had plenty of fights with Kitty over the years to draw from.

Lebedevya is keeping people here by twisting their minds and memories, but Ruby has a superpower none of Lebedevya's other victims has: She knows which parts of her story are already bullshit. Any memory of "Richard" is nonsense. And any memory of her parents . . . Lebedevya hadn't been trying to prompt those.

Ruby looks away from the rabid, angrily gibbering Richard down to the twelve-year-old Ruby who's still standing at her side. "Don't go anywhere, you," she says, and her child self wrinkles her nose.

The transition from dreams to waking is as gentle as Lebedevya brushing her cheek with the backs of her fingertips.

"How do you feel?" Lebedevya asks. Katriana is floating beside her now, smiling down at her.

"How long was I out?" Ruby's not sure how to put into words what she feels.

"Sometimes we uncover troubling memories," Lebedevya says. "If you want to talk about anything you're learning, we have resources to help."

Ruby forces a smile, mind racing. She's done playing this game, especially now that she knows exactly what Lebedevya is doing. She needs to get back to the others and tell them. And she needs to get Kitty out of here before Lebedevya scrambles her memories any more.

Ruby takes Kitty's hand, orienting herself to vertical like the other two women are, blinking her eyes to clear them. She's been drifting as she dreams, and now she's at the far end of the dreaming chamber. Her gaze shifts past Kitty to rest on one of the floating forms behind her.

Her breath catches in her throat.

It's Aya Marga, eyes closed and fluttering, but fast — hand twitching like she's having a nightmare. Ruby pushes off to float to Marga's side, pretending to simply be curious, though her heart is beating in her chest.

"Don't disturb the other dreamers, my dear," Lebedevya says. "Come. Let's have some tea."

Ruby touches Aya Marga's cheek; it's flushed, her lips chapped. In the zero G, in sleep, her face is relaxed and the lines smoothed out. Her gray hair is cut close and practical; Ruby's never seen her without her veil.

How long has she been under? And what drew her here? Was it that same peace Kitty was looking for, the same thirst for self-knowledge? Or had Lebedevya lured her here some other way?

"Come, Olivia," Lebedevya says, more firmly.

Ruby ignores her. No way is she leaving here without Marga.

Ruby squeezes Marga's hand, and the aya stirs, eyes fluttering open. They're watery, red-rimmed, the faux stars in this chamber glittering in Marga's tears as her gaze focuses on Ruby. She smiles, and Ruby suddenly realizes her error.

"Ruby?" Marga says softly. "Oh, Ruby, darling. What are you doing here?"

Ah, shit.

Lebedevya frowns at her. "Ruby?"

"Livvy, is what I think she said." Ruby smiles down at Marga, mind racing. The aya is probably too dazed to catch on if Ruby tries to hint she's here undercover. And she's not mischievous, sly Kitty, ready to follow along with an interesting joke to see where it might lead. Until Aya Marga ran off with all the Aymaya Apostles' funds, Ruby would have sworn she didn't even know how to lie.

Please catch on.

"Call me Olivia," Ruby says to Marga, whose eyebrows draw together. She's been under Lebedevya's dreaming drugs for saints know how long — who knows what muddled memories the aya is trying to sort through in order to get back to reality. A horrible plan hits Ruby like a punch to the gut. She could use Marga's susceptibility. Just to get them both out of here, she tells herself, pushing aside nausea at the idea.

Lebedevya is watching her, gaze flat and cold.

"You're thinking of someone else," Ruby says to Marga, angling her body so Marga can't accidentally glimpse Kitty. If she sees Ruby alongside her ex-girlfriend, Ruby will lose any chance of convincing her. "It's all right, love, you just woke up. Any minute you'll realize your mistake. My name is Olivia."

Marga blinks at her a moment with a faint puzzled

smile. "I'm sorry," she says. "You're right. Don't grow old, sweetheart. Your memory starts to go."

Guilt stabs through Ruby's heart.

"You remind me of such a lovely girl," Marga says, eyes half-closed as though drifting through memory. "I haven't seen her in too long. Not since she came by with . . ."

"It's okay, love," Ruby cuts in. "Why don't you get some rest."

Marga smiles up at her again. "Since you came by with Katriana," she finishes as though not hearing a word Ruby had said.

Lebedevya's nostrils flare, and Ruby's plan A for salvaging the situation goes up in smoke.

Lebedevya points at the door to the antechamber, glaring. "Out, please. You too, Katriana. I think we need to talk." She swipes open a message. "Is Richard with you?" she asks the person on the other end of the line. "We have a situation."

CHAPTER 26
RAJ

Inevitably there's a moment in every job where the mark's trust starts to falter. No matter how well-rehearsed the cover story, no matter how shiny the dazzle of misdirection, eventually something will ping at the edge of a mark's attention: *Wait. Hold on a second. Isn't there something I'm missing?*

Sometimes that moment solves itself. Raj has learned most people want to believe your story. They want to trust you. And if they want the shining golden prize you're offering badly enough, they'll put the blinders back on themselves.

Raj studies Evelyn as she palms the biolock of a door off the lounge, trying to decide if they've come to that moment. Evelyn doesn't seem angry or confused, and she doesn't seem like she's about to call station security and have him arrested. She seems preoccupied, like dealing with Raj is merely one item on a much longer list of minor stresses.

The door opens into a tidy office, decorated in the

same neutral tans and pale golds as the reception area and hallway. This color palette is probably calibrated to be spiritually soothing, but Raj is finding it mind-numbingly boring. A second door is set opposite the door they came in; if Raj's mental map of this level is correct, it must lead to an inner room or corridor.

A large desk is set prominently in the center of the room, with a pair of uncomfortable-looking wooden chairs in front. No circle of cushions or cozy couches here — this is a place where business gets done. Annika Lebedevya's business, by the multiple framed portraits. There's Lebedevya walking hand in hand with a young child through a field of wildflowers. There she is posing with a man in orange robes — a religious leader whose face Raj has definitely seen before. There she is sitting peacefully in meditation on a gorgeous beach.

"The Voice of Power's office?" Raj asks, partly to satisfy his own curiosity, partly to orient Lasadi as she listens in.

"It is," Evelyn says. "We can speak privately here."

Raj turns his attention to the large abstract painting across from the desk. It might be meant to evoke water lilies, but that's not what makes it so interesting. There's a fingerprint lock tastefully hidden in the frame.

"Pretty neat," Raj says, stepping closer. His alter ego would definitely lack the self-awareness not to comment on a cleverly hidden security feature. "Her painting is actually a safe? I need something like that in my office. Biolock and everything," he adds for Lasadi's benefit.

"Good work," Lasadi says in his ear. "That could be

where she's keeping the data cubes of the session recordings. I'll pass it on to Alex."

Evelyn ignores his comments about the safe and takes her place behind the large desk. Raj chooses one of the two seats facing her; the chairs are as uncomfortable as they look. She folds her hands and gives him a sympathetic smile, a faint stitch appearing between her perfect brows.

Raj relaxes. Evelyn's still running her own game; the idea that he and Ruby have been lying to her isn't gnawing away at her confidence yet.

"These types of conversations are always hard," she begins. "But I'm afraid Olivia asked me to deliver a message to you. She needs a bit of space."

So this is how Lebedevya's script goes. They already separated him from Ruby physically, and Lebedevya had been planting seeds to break up their relationship even back in Artemis City. Now they'll drive the wedge.

Raj expected it, but Richard would be blindsided. Raj lets surprise wash over his face.

"Is she all right?"

"She's fine, Richard. But she feels like there are things she wants to explore on her own. I know you haven't been very keen on our work, but we do have some programs that can help you. With anger, for example?"

"Anger?" Raj draws his brows in, confused. "I'd like to hear this from her myself."

"I'm afraid that's not possible at the moment." Evelyn raises her hands to her heart and gives him a slight bow. "Why don't you return to your room for now, and we can discuss this in the morning?"

"I'm perfectly happy talking now," Raj says, but Evelyn's comm chimes softly. She glances absently at her cuff, then gives it a second, harder look. The line of her mouth firms.

Ah.

This is the moment.

And from the angry set of Evelyn's jaw, she's not just starting to catch glimpses of the edge of his mask. His cover has been blown wide open.

"That was Annika," she says. "Apparently you and your friend have been lying to us."

In his ear, Lasadi take a sharp breath. "Copy that, Raj. We're on our way in."

Raj has been in situations before where having your cover blown means everyone in the room draws a small arsenal and starts shooting. So far, Evelyn's been giving him disappointed tutor vibes, and she doesn't carry herself like someone who knows how to fight.

Time to pivot with the truth.

There's an off chance Evelyn isn't actually an accomplice, and she's as under Annika Lebedevya's spell as the rest. Is she a true believer? Or does she have doubts of her own? She's been wearing a flawless mask every other time Raj has seen her, but tonight she seems stressed. Maybe the luster of being the Voice of Power's handler is starting to wear off.

"It's true," Raj says. "I'm not here for your treatments — we're trying to find a friend who went missing."

"If your missing friend is here, it's probably to get away from the influence of people around them like you, who think they know best."

"You know what your boss is doing to people, right? She's isolating them from their families to get their money."

"She's a healer."

"She's a con artist. Evelyn, listen to me."

"No." Evelyn shakes her head. "The work we do here is incredibly important. Skeptics like you are always trying to destroy Annika."

"Think about this. You just got done telling me Olivia didn't want to see me anymore — which I know she didn't say. Did you talk to her yourself? Or was that what Lebedevya told you? How many families have you sat across from in this room and told bald-faced lies to?"

"The work she does is nothing short of miraculous," Evelyn says. "I've experienced it for myself."

"Then she's been brainwashing you, too."

A muscle jumps in Evelyn's jaw, and whatever uncertainty she'd felt vanishes under the weight of new conviction. She's not a grifter like Lebedevya; she's not in on the con. But she's a true believer who's given Lebedevya everything over the past years. She might have caught a glimpse of this house of glass, but she's as invested as Lebedevya in keeping it from shattering.

Lebedevya is offering her the world. The only thing Raj can give her is brutal self-knowledge that she's been living a lie this whole time.

Even if Evelyn suspects Lebedevya isn't being wholly honest with her, she'll put those blinders back on herself in a desperate attempt to keep Raj's version from being true.

"Every great leader makes enemies," Evelyn says.

"You're not the first who's tried to stop her work, and you won't be the last."

Evelyn's hand moves subtly on the desk, and the door on the far wall slides open. A pair of burly security guards enter; they've clearly been standing by, probably used to dealing with problematic families Evelyn has asked into this little office to be told how their loved ones no longer want to see them.

Evelyn waves a hand at Raj. "Please return him to his room until Annika has an opportunity to speak with him."

"Stall them," Lasadi says in his ear. "Don't let her lock you in your room or she could dose you again. We're on our way."

"Hold on a second," Raj says as the guards cross to him. "I'm not angry, I'm not causing problems. I just want to talk to you for a few minutes, and then I'll go."

"I'm done talking." Evelyn folds her hands, face a perfect mask of calm. "Take him."

The guards grab Raj by the arms and haul him out of the chair.

CHAPTER 27
RUBY

BACK OUT IN THE ANTECHAMBER, RUBY STUMBLES UNDER the return of artificial gravity. It shouldn't have been such a hard transition, but whatever drug Lebedevya pumped into her system has made her muscles sluggish.

Kitty is more graceful — maybe she's more used to the drug — but Aya Marga can barely stand.

The aya slides down the wall to rest on a cushion, blinking in the light, frowning up at Ruby as though still puzzling through her presence. She seems to have aged a decade in the year since Ruby saw her last. Her skin is paler than ever, dark thumbprint circles under her watery, red-rimmed blue eyes. She's wearing a simple gray tunic and trousers rather than the blue habit Ruby's accustomed to seeing her in, her salt-and-pepper hair shorn close.

Ruby kneels beside her, taking one of her hands in her own. Marga has always been a solid woman, but she's lost weight and her hand feels thin and frail in Ruby's.

"It's me, Aya," Ruby says quietly. "I came to take you home."

"Ruby?"

"I'm sorry I lied to you in there. I was just trying to get you out."

"I . . ." Marga tilts her head back against the wall. "I don't remember why I'm here."

Ruby squeezes Marga's hand, then gets unsteadily back to her feet. Kitty is now sitting cross-legged on a nearby cushion, still riding a glassy calm by the gleam in her eye and disinterested expression on her face. Lebedevya followed them all out. She closes the door to the dreaming chamber behind her, palm on the biolock until it flashes red.

She's locked the others in, hasn't she. Ruby supposes she doesn't want anyone interrupting their conversation — though no one but the two attendants in the dreaming chamber was coherent enough to come barging out.

Lebedevya's icy calm shatters.

"You do not know what you have done," she snarls at Ruby. "I don't care who you are, but my work here is delicate. Your tainted presence may have unraveled months — even years — of the good work we've done here. You are a poison in this sanctuary."

"Cut the bullshit." There's no point keeping up Olivia Tam's posh Artemisian accent, and what Ruby has to say sounds best in the cadence of gutter-trash Pearls. "You're a healer, love? No. You're a con artist, only, and normally I'd say live and let, but you preyed on the wrong marks, didn't you. Saints help me but I will bring you the fuck down."

"*I* am the con artist?" Lebedevya points a sharp finger at Marga. "This one has been conning me for years."

"Aya Marga's honest as God," Ruby says.

Except she's not, is she? She took the convent funds and fled without a word to anyone about where she was going — not even to Teresa. She'd procured a false identity from saints knew where.

Ruby shakes her head, trying to clear it. None of that is the point.

"Your aya has done nothing but lie to me," Lebedevya says; it's not truth, it's just another layer of lies to keep the hustle going. Only Lebedevya doesn't have to work very hard to tangle up her lies with what Ruby knows to be true. Her incense is doing the heavy lifting. "You know my reverence for the Dreaming Saint. I had a dream to preserve her paintings and relics from unscrupulous collectors, so when I heard that an aya from Artemis City was writing a book about her works, I approached her. I hoped we could work together, but Marga gave me misleading information. She used me to find paintings that came on the market, then told me they were false so she could have someone else bid on them!"

Saints in hell, this woman's gall. Ruby's seen the paintings. They're in Lebedevya's sanctuary, where Ruby was an hour ago at best. The incense, the drugs — this woman's even blurring memories Ruby made earlier today.

Ruby crouches beside Marga again to keep herself

grounded; even looking into Lebedevya's eyes while she speaks is mesmerizing. When she takes Marga's hand, her gaze is drawn by the frailness — and Ruby's heart stops. The long-sleeved tunic falls back slightly to reveal a motley of bruising around Marga's wrist. Two fingernails are broken, like she'd tried to fight back.

Fury flares beneath Ruby's ribcage.

Not for the first time, a vision of slamming her fist into Lebedevya's smug smile whirls through her mind. But she's at the center of a maze of rooms she's not sure she can navigate back — not while shepherding Marga and Kitty in the state they're in. And definitely not if she has to fight her way out. If Lebedevya invested this much into the top-line security systems Ruby can see, she's probably got a bit of muscle hiding around here, too.

Ruby's thrown a punch or two in a bar, but that's not going to get her and Kitty and Marga back to safety.

"Whatever you think the aya owes you, I can pay it," Ruby says. "And then I swear you'll never hear from us again."

"I believe you."

Ruby doesn't like the way Lebedevya is smiling, her fingers dropping away from a control on her cuff. Doesn't like the way her own vision is starting to swim, or the way Marga's blinking harshly as though she's trying to stay awake, or Kitty's dreamy, unfocused gaze. The walls of the room pulse.

Ruby sneezes as clouds of floral incense pump into the room.

"You're so worried about this aya you forgot your-self," Lebedevya is saying, her voice distant and echoing. "You were learning something in the dreaming chamber, weren't you, Ruby? About your mother?"

I'm right here, Ruby Nicole.

Was that her mother's voice? Ruby looks behind her, searching for another glimpse of the woman who shared her features.

"Everything you've been searching for is right here," says Lebedevya, or maybe it really is her mother speaking. "Every secret you want to know is inside your mind."

The smoke swims before her eyes, and when it clears, Ruby's mother is standing where Lebedevya had been, Ruby's child self holding her hand.

"Come," her mother says. "I'll tell you everything."

Beside her, Child Ruby shakes her head. "Think, dummy," Ruby's child self says, rolling her eyes. *"Why isn't the smoke making Lebedevya dream, too?"*

CHAPTER 28
RAJ

Raj would guess these two security guards are more used to escorting angry family members than actually fighting, though they also have an air of disreputability about them that makes him wonder where Lebedevya scraped them up from.

The one on Raj's left has a nasty scar on his nose and an iron grip. From the agonizing way Scar Nose is digging his fingers into the soft part of Raj's triceps, he likes to cause pain and knows how to do it.

The one on Raj's right could've been an action vid star if he wasn't living in the ass end of the Durga System. He's got that handsome rugged jawline and haughty cheekbones, and muscles he's put a lot of time into maintaining. Lifting iron doesn't mean you can throw a good punch, though. Handsome can probably fight, but he's not the dirty brawler Scar Nose probably is.

They haul him down the hallway towards his room, and he doesn't give them any trouble. They're relaxing more with each passing minute, lulled into thinking he's going to make their job easy.

He's not.

Raj waits until he sees the door marked Sage, the one Marissa had told him led to the lower level. Ruby's cover was blown, too, and she's with Katriana. Raj needs to get the hell out of here, but he's not leaving them behind.

Raj drops his weight, pulling both men off-balance and getting his fingers close enough to his calf to slip the nerve blade out of his boot. Scar Nose and Handsome have both lost their grips, so Raj whirls, low, slashing the blade across Handsome's shins. The man yelps in pain, knees buckling as the nerve blade works its muscle-spasming magic.

Scar Nose blocks Raj's next slash with his forearm and aims a punch Raj barely ducks. Handsome uses the distraction to grab at Raj's knife hand, but Raj twists free and slams the butt of the nerve blade back and down into Handsome's thigh. He slashes the blade over Handsome's bicep as he darts back out of range.

Fury and agony tinge Handsome's face beet red.

He yowls and bull-rushes Raj before Raj can step out of the way, slamming him into the wall with his knife hand — and the nerve blade — pinned behind him.

The small of Raj's back tingles at the closeness of the blade — it's millimeters away from touching his skin. A nerve blade on a big muscle like the bicep hurts like hell. Catch one in the spine and you won't be able to walk for hours.

Raj knees Handsome in the thigh, the same spot he

hit him with the butt of the knife, then wrenches himself free.

Scar Nose is waiting with a grin.

He decks Raj across the jaw and lands another heavy blow to Raj's gut — when Raj doubles over wheezing, Scar Nose snaps a kick into Raj's wrist that sends the nerve blade flying.

Raj dives blindly for it, but pain flares up his spine, turning his muscles watery and his blood to fire. It lasts a short second — fucking electric barb, must have been — but it's long enough to knock the air out of Raj's lungs, to dull his response when Scar Nose grabs his shoulders and flips him onto his back. Scar Nose straddles Raj's chest, knees digging into Raj's arms to pin them down.

"Normally Annika likes us not to leave a mess," he says with a wicked grin. "But I don't think she much cares about how the job gets done this time."

Scar Nose jams the electric barb under Raj's chin; the nodes are still warm. Raj's mouth goes dry. A hit to the head won't kill him, but a lot of his wiring won't come out intact on the other side.

Scar Nose grins, all crooked teeth and glee. Raj's eyes squeeze involuntarily closed.

A pulse of energy splits the air.

CHAPTER 29
LASADI

For a horrifying moment Lasadi isn't sure she was fast enough, but then the big man on Raj's chest sways. Slumps to the side with his eyelids fluttering; Lasadi may have her stun pistol set too high, but she doesn't care.

Raj blinks in surprise.

Lasadi runs down the rest of the hallway to reach him, Jay at her heels. She drops to her knees at Raj's side, shoving the big man the rest of the way off his chest. Raj's shirt is torn, but there's no blood; still, he winces as he pushes himself up to sit against the wall. There's a bruise forming on his cheek, blood rimming his nostril.

She'd almost been too late.

She's sweeping that dark hair off his cheek with one hand before she realizes she's going to do it, her fingers tangling in silken strands that glide through her fingers like water. Raj looks confused by the touch, even more so when her lips meet his — *Olds, what am I doing?*

She doesn't stop herself.

For a brief, humiliating second Raj's whole body tenses, his eyes wide. But then his lips soften and part. His eyelids drift closed. His right hand grips her hip, light and careful, and his left palm smooths against her cheek, his fingers firm and steady and warm.

His lips taste every bit as good as she's been imagining they would.

Lasadi finally breaks the kiss, sitting back on her heels with her heart pounding in her chest.

Raj clears his throat. "I — "

"Let me talk a sec, okay?" The words are tumbling out faster than Lasadi can think them through, the rational part of her mind staring on with terror at whatever truths she's about to unleash. "I'm sorry. I was lying to you — and to me — when I said I didn't want you. I was terrified. I still am, but I can't forgive myself if I let fear win. So if you still want to give this a shot — "

"I definitely do."

" — then let's get out of here alive and try it."

Raj laughs, and relief floods through her. "I like that plan."

"Good. Okay." Lasadi's whole world has tilted sideways. She's lost her sure, practical footing and something wild and gleeful is somersaulting through her chest and it's . . . nice. She doesn't know where to put her hands, but she's extremely aware that both of his have slid to her hips, sending waves of heat through her entire body. His right thumb is resting on the ridge of scar tissue on her abdomen. She shifts away from the touch.

"Okay," she says again, more firm. "We need to get to Ruby."

"And Kitty and Marga," Jay says over her shoulder. She glances back, mortified to remember she and Raj are not alone. Jay's been methodically securing the guards.

"I've got a plan," Raj says, which is good because Lasadi's having trouble thinking of anything except the taste of his lips still lingering on hers. "I thought we could go arrest a couple of art forgers. Unless impersonating an Alliance special agent goes against your morals."

Lasadi laughs. "Absolutely not."

"Glad to hear it. Where's Alex?"

"He's busy." Lasadi rocks back on her heels, finding blessed distance from the heat of Raj's body, then holds out a hand to help him to his feet. She gestures at the two unconscious guards. "Which of these guys will give us the least amount of trouble?"

"That one." Raj points to the younger-looking of the two. The pretty boy with the model's jawline, rather than the scarred one who was about to electrify Raj's brains. Good. The scarred asshole can stay out cold.

Lasadi cuts Pretty Boy's restraints and hits him with a stim, patting his cheek to wake him. His eyelids flutter open.

"You all good there, buddy?"

The guard blinks at her and pushes himself up on his elbows. "Who are you?"

"I'm the woman who's about to make you a hero." Las hopes her accent is passably Arquellian. Olds help her, but she's been obsessing over Raj's soft drawl long enough. She jerks a thumb over her shoulder, where Raj is making a show of dusting himself off. "Unless you'd rather be arrested for assaulting an Alliance special agent. Thank your lucky stars my partner isn't injured."

Pretty Boy frowns at Raj, puzzled, and Lasadi snaps her fingers in his face to get his attention once more. His eyes lock on hers, uncertain, but eager to help.

"We need to get to Annika Lebedevya right now. She's in serious danger."

CHAPTER 30
RUBY

I'M RIGHT HERE, RUBY NICOLE.

Two worlds superimpose over each other, two visions fading in and out as Ruby struggles to grasp the one that's real.

She's standing in front of the door to the Aymaya Apostles convent again, the warm blue pulsing slightly with her heartbeat. But when she blinks, the door shifts. It's an airlock door covered in a delicate mandala. Kitty's work, she remembers. Kitty was painting this door when Ruby arrived.

Kitty.

She's here, too. She needs Ruby to keep her head together — as does Aya Marga.

"I'm here," her mother says beside her. "I've always been here with you. Come with me, I have so much to tell you."

If her mother isn't real, then why can Ruby feel her mother's hand in hers? The pressure of her fingers closing around Ruby's?

"Come through the door," Ruby's mother says, squeezing her hand. "Everything you need to know is on the other side of this door."

It's not. It's only more of Lebedevya's lies.

Ruby tears her gaze away from the vision of the door and her mother, searching the room behind her, choking on the thick floral incense Lebedevya is pumping into the room. Marga is still slumped against the wall, her eyes closed and a dreamy expression on her face. Kitty is dancing by herself, a vision with her lithe, long limbs swaying.

She's happy.

Kitty's so happy here — the faint hum of manic energy or sharp depression that always flowed beneath even her happiest days has vanished, and she seems truly at peace for the first time since Ruby met her.

Why would Ruby deny her that?

More lies.

"I wish I could have met her," Ruby's mother says, and Ruby turns back to her.

Ruby knows every line of that face like she knows her own. The freckles, the broad nose and pointed chin, the shorn hair — her mother had loved braiding Ruby's hair with those strong fingers, but she'd never had the patience to maintain her own. "Too much trouble," she'd say. "I have better things to do with my time."

When Ruby had gotten older, she'd started asking what those things were. Why her mother and father needed to leave so often. Why sometimes her mother came back limping and her father came back wincing when Ruby hugged him too tight. Why her father's hands smelled like sulphur and iron. Where her mother had gotten that scar on her chin.

These are stories for when you're older.

By the time she'd gotten older, they were gone.

"Come through the door," Ruby's mother says again, a hand on her arm, insisting. "There's so much more you can remember. Let the Voice of Power help you."

Ah. Right.

The Voice of Power.

That's where Ruby is — she's not standing in front of the convent door, and her mother isn't here. At best, she's a fragment of memory, unlocked after almost two decades by the hallucinogens Lebedevya is feeding her. At worst, she's a figment of Ruby's imagination, manipulated by Lebedevya's suggestions.

Ruby blinks away the vision of her mother and finds Lebedevya standing there instead, holding out her hand to Ruby.

She's breathing the same air as Ruby and Marga and Kitty — yet Lebedevya doesn't seem affected at all by the incense. Something pings at the edge of Ruby's sluggish mind and she reels back through the blurred memories since she arrived on Sapis Station, trying to remember.

Ruby turns to seek out Kitty and Marga again — Kitty's movements are more sluggish; Marga seems to have fallen asleep. How much of this incense can a person take?

"Come through the door," Lebedevya says again, and there it is. When they'd entered this chamber, Lebedevya had taken a pill. For her migraines, she'd said, but it must be some sort of counteracting agent to help her keep functioning despite the hallucinogens in the incense. Where is that vial?

Lebedevya is still waiting, hand held out, and Ruby lets the warm blanket that wants to surround her fall over her shoulders. Lets the smile spread over her face. She takes Lebedevya's hand. "I've missed you," she says. "Mom, I've missed you."

Even through the fog, through the blurring superimposition of Ruby's mother's face over Lebedevya's, Ruby catches the way Lebedevya smiles. Like a woman who knows she's won.

"Come, child," Ruby's mother says, and Ruby lets her draw her forward, towards the door. Lets her pull her close, lets her get distracted with the lock.

And Ruby whirls with an elbow aimed at Lebedevya's sternum.

Her movements are clumsy, but Lebedevya wasn't expecting the attack, and she stumbles backwards with a cry. Ruby fumbles for Lebedevya's pocket, fingers closing around the vial. She rolls easily out of Lebedevya's reach and shakes out two of the pills into her palm. Raises her hand to her mouth, and hears her mother pleading with her.

I have so much to tell you. I can explain everything.

Ruby blinks, lips parted for the pills, heart yearning for answers.

Any answer she can get here is a lie.

She swallows the pills dry, stomach heaving against the cloying incense, slumping down the wall as the fog begins to lift.

Pain flares above Ruby's ear.

She drops the vial, hand pressed to her temple; her fingers come away bloody. *She hit you!*

Ruby's reaction is more instinct than planning, she rolls out of the way as Lebedevya raises her arm again, something clutched in her fist. A flash of glass — part of that awful abstract art installation on the far wall. Lebedevya swings and the glass rod shatters against the wall where Ruby's head had been seconds before. When Lebedevya swipes at her again, the broken edge slashes millimeters from Ruby's cheek.

Ruby ducks and catches Lebedevya's arm. Her muscles are still barely cooperating, but Lebedevya clearly isn't a fighter. Ruby kicks the other woman's feet out from beneath her and rolls with her to the ground, throwing a leg over her to straddle her chest. She jams the sharp edge of the glass against Lebedevya's pale throat, panting for breath.

"Turn off this incense," Ruby says, and Lebedevya touches a button on her cuff, eyes wide. Even though it's no longer giving her visions, it's still tickling her nose, clinging to the inside of her sinuses. Ruby wrinkles her nose, fighting a sneeze.

"Here's what'll happen next," Ruby says. "I'm walking out of here with my friends, and you'll not do a thing to stop us. You'll also not stop anyone else who wants to leave. Do you hear me?"

"You think I'm a fraud?" Lebedevya shakes her head. "Olivia, or Ruby, or whoever you are? You say I'm a fraud, but what did you remember?"

"How can I even tell?" Fury flares through her. "All I've ever wanted was to remember, and now I can't trust a goddamned thing I think I do."

She presses the sharp edge deeper into Lebedevya's pale throat, shocked at how much she enjoys Lebedevya's gasp of pain. She's never hurt anyone before, not on purpose. She's never wanted to, not before now. But that trickle of blood on Lebedevya's neck thrills through her like justice, and the saints might damn her for this, but Lebedevya has caused so many people so much pain. Someone has to bring them justice.

Lebedevya must see the thought on Ruby's face, because her smug expression changes to fear.

Ruby forces herself to sit back, horrified at what she was contemplating, heart pounding. Through the rush of blood in her ears, she can barely make out voices. Footsteps running in the hallway outside.

Lebedevya smiles, cruel, the bead of blood trailing down her pale neck.

"You lost your chance," she says, and the outer doors to the antechamber slide open.

"Put down your weapon!" someone shouts; there's a high-pitched whine of stun carbines warming to the grips of their owners.

Ruby lets the glass rod drop to the ground with a faint thud and a sinking heart. She raises her hands.

CHAPTER 31
LASADI

"PUT DOWN YOUR WEAPON," LASADI YELLS AT RUBY.

Pretty Boy the security guard has led them to what appears to be the antechamber to an airlock, though Pretty Boy nervously explained along the way that it's the Dreaming Chamber, and he's not actually allowed down here. The room is a nightmare of pale purple and fuzzy white and abstract glass art, lavender curtains draped artistically in a way that reminds Lasadi of the saccharine way her sister decorated her room when they were teenagers.

The room would feel serene if not for the chaos of its inhabitants.

Ruby's crouched barefoot and disheveled in the center of the room, blood streaming from a wound at her temple, a vicious scratch down one arm that must have come from a fingernail. She's holding what looks like a piece of the abstract glass sculpture clenched in her hand, knuckles bloodless. Lebedevya's sprawled on the ground in front of her.

Katriana is here, too, and an older woman who must be Aya Marga, though she's lost weight since the images Lasadi saw of her were taken. Katriana and Marga both seem dazed; by the lingering scent of incense in the air, Lasadi can guess why.

She's encountered this scent before, she realizes. This is what was lingering on Lebedevya's robes when Lasadi hid in the closet of her hotel room. Even that small amount had been disorienting; Lasadi tries not to take too deep a breath now.

She swings up her stun carbine as though to cover Ruby — though her attention's on Annika Lebedevya. Ruby seems to have subdued Lebedevya, but if that asshole so much as looks at Ruby wrong, Las will fire first and pretend her aim's off.

"Hands where we can see them," Lasadi orders. Ruby glances back at her, eyes widening in surprise as though finally registering who's speaking to her. She drops the piece of glass, kicking it out of Lebedevya's reach when it hits the ground. "We've been chasing you a long time, but you can't outrun the IASC forever. You and your friends are under arrest for art fraud in eight different jurisdictions." She jerks her chin at Pretty Boy. "Cuff her."

Pretty Boy blinks in surprise at the pair of disposable cuffs Jay tosses him, but he follows Lasadi's orders. He approaches Ruby with caution, and she doesn't struggle as he slaps the disposable cuffs on her wrist. Raj crosses to Katriana, murmuring something in her ear as he slips a pair of cuffs on her wrists, too. She doesn't struggle, but she seems dazed. Can she even follow what's happening?

"Who are you?" Lebedevya asks Lasadi. She turns to the security guard, eyes blazing. "Who are they?"

Pretty Boy frowns at Lasadi in confusion. "IA . . . IA—"

"IASC," Lasadi says. "International Anti-Smuggling Commission." She flashes an ident card on her cuff. "Agent Fayed." She jabs a thumb at Jay. "Agent Liu. And you've already met my colleague Agent Danning — he's been working this case undercover. We'll take this from here. Veronica Wilson and Katriana Chevalier, you're both under arrest for forgery."

Lebedevya glances back and forth between Lasadi and Ruby. "Forgery?"

"That's right," Raj says. "These two have left a trail of forged artifacts in their wake. Agents Fayed and Liu and I have been on their trail for over a year, but the only way to get the evidence we needed was to go undercover. Ms. Lebedevya. Can you show us the artifacts you recently purchased from Wilson and Chevalier?"

Lebedevya shakes her head. "Absolutely not. This is a sacred place, and the Alliance has no jurisdiction in Bixian space."

Lasadi nods seriously. "Which is why we've been — "

An incoming connection request chimes softly on Lebedevya's cuff, and she brushes a finger over it to accept the connection. "Evelyn? I need station security here at once." Lebedevya's fierce glare turns to confusion. "They're already here?"

" — working with Sapis Co-op this whole time,"

Lasadi finishes. "We called them when we realized you were in danger."

Lebedevya frowns at her, worry starting to unravel the edge of her anger. "They're here about art forgery?" she asks Evelyn; it sounds like she's confirming what Evelyn just told her.

"Of course they are." Lasadi smiles bright at Lebedevya. "Listen. I'm really sorry to have disturbed you. Why don't you have them meet us wherever you're keeping the artwork Wilson and Chevalier sold you, ma'am, and then we'll get out of your hair and let you get back to your good work."

Lebedevya's still hesitant, but a glimmer of hope is clearly starting to grow. The tip of her tongue touches her lower lip before Lebedevya schools her expression into something pleasant and accommodating. Her shoulders square. She smiles, even as her hands slide against her thighs to dry her palms.

The promise that Lasadi and the rest of her "IASC agents" will make a speedy exit once they take Katriana's forgeries has calmed Lebedevya down, as Lasadi had hoped it would. It will get them away from the incriminating mess of the Dreaming Chamber, and Lebedevya must be relaxing at the fact that Lasadi hasn't asked any awkward questions about people being detained against their wills.

By the time Lebedevya holds out an arm to usher Lasadi and the others out of this room, she's holding herself like a woman who thinks she's about to get away with something.

"It's right this way," Lebedevya says, then lifts her

cuff to her lips. "Evelyn, please direct the Sapis Cooperative team to the chapel."

Okay. Phase one is working. It just required some flashy footwork and disorienting patter, though — Lasadi can only hope Alex was fast enough for phase two to work, as well.

When they reach the room Lebedevya called a chapel, Lasadi sends Jay back to the ship with Katriana and Marga, then does a round of quick introductions with the Sapis Cooperative security team. The team, a lanky man and stocky woman, have a sharp, no-nonsense vibe Lasadi appreciates. They're not the team sent to break up drunken brawls on the casino levels, they're the ones that get called in to deal with important, high-paying tenants like Lebedevya. They exchange familiar greetings with Pretty Boy, who's taking his assignment of watching over Ruby seriously.

"We were about to seize the forgeries," Lasadi tells the Sapis Co-op team, then holds her arm out for Lebedevya to open the door. "If you don't mind, ma'am."

She wants to refuse, Lasadi can see it in her eyes. Now that the initial confusion is past and her life is no longer in danger, Lebedevya is probably starting to ask questions, at least in her mind. She has a rocky relationship with Sapis Cooperative security, though — if Lasadi hadn't already known about that, she could certainly discern it in the chilly-yet-polite way the team greeted her. Lebedevya must be weighing the value of keeping her mouth shut versus giving the co-op reason to ask any more questions.

Lebedevya opens the door.

Lasadi whistles at the room and trades a look with

Raj, whose smile slips to the side when he meets her gaze.

Olds, what has she done.

She tears her attention back to Lebedevya's vault to stop the heat rising under her collar. It's a circular room with a domed ceiling, the walls hung with artwork. The lights rise slow to illuminate the impressive collection of paintings.

At least, Lasadi assumes it's an impressive collection. She has no way of knowing if the paintings are really Saint Alixhi's or simply excellent forgeries like the ones Katriana did.

She crosses straight to Katriana's sketches and runs a scanner over them, then glances at her cuff as though it told her anything.

"These are them?" she asks Lebedevya, who nods. "Very impressive work. Almost impossible to tell they're fakes to the naked eye, but our lab should clear up the question, no problem. We'll send you a full report, ma'am."

"What about the rest of these?" the Sapis Co-op woman asks.

"We'd be happy to run some tests, ma'am," Lasadi says to Lebedevya, who blanches.

"I had those verified by an expert," Lebedevya says.

"Who's that?"

"The . . ." Lebedevya frowns. "The aya."

Lasadi winces sympathetically. "That's no aya. She's been working with Wilson and Chevalier for years. I hadn't realized how deep they got you in their con. We'll see what the IASC can do to get you restitution."

"Agent Fayed?"

Lasadi turns to where Raj is examining a wooden box in the center of the room. She'd walked right past it to get to the sketches, and she wouldn't have given it a second look except for its prominent place in the center of the room. It's a simple wooden crate. The exact same one she'd ignored in Lebedevya's hotel room, in fact. At a closer look, she can tell it's inlaid with whorls of wire, now polished to gleaming.

"Saint Alixhi's reliquary," Raj says.

"Wow," Lasadi says to Raj. "Just, wow." She turns to Lebedevya with a sad shake of her head. "I've never seen a forgery of Saint Alixhi's reliquary that good."

"It's a really impressive fake." Raj runs a finger over the inlaid pattern. "You remember the one we nabbed in Alusina last year? It was like my kid's craft project. This is incredible craftsmanship."

"It's not a forgery," says Lebedevya, tone clipped. "It's the real thing, legally acquired. I have provenance papers."

"I'm sorry to say it's a fake," Lasadi says. "An incredible fake, but a fake nonetheless."

"It's absolutely not."

"Have you opened it?"

"I — " Lebedevya's mouth snaps shut, and once again her eyes narrow in worry. "I have not," she finally says. "It would be disrespectful."

Lasadi steps back, beckoning Lebedevya and the Sapis Co-op woman forward. "Would you two do the honors?"

Together, Lebedevya and the station security guard carefully lift the lid off the crate. Ruby strains forward against Pretty Boy's grip, craning her neck to see and gnawing her lip in worry. Her eyes go wide as Lebedevya's when the crate's lid is lifted off.

Inside the crate, nestled in silk, is a pile of papers, data sticks, and holo cubes.

The Sapis Co-op woman turns to Lebedevya in surprise. "Now, what's this?"

Lebedevya is staring down at the collection in confusion, so Lasadi plucks up a holo cube labeled Paul Comadra and sets it in the player so conveniently left for her. The bust of a man, eyes closed as though asleep, appears above the holoprojector

Blood drains from Lebedevya's face. She reaches for the holoprojector, but the Sapis Co-op woman stops her.

"Who else makes financial decisions in your family?" Lebedevya's disembodied voice says from the holoprojector.

"My wife," Comadra answers.

"Good, good. Then in today's session, let's talk about her. Tell me about your relationship. What are the points of tension?"

"No tension," Comadra says, dreamy.

"There's always tension," corrects Lebedevya. "You worry, for example, that she's unfaithful."

Comadra shakes his head. "I don't worry that."

"You do," Lebedevya says, firm. And, as though to someone else, "Increase his dose."

Comadra's eyelids flutter, then stay closed. "I do worry that she's unfaithful."

Lebedevya tears the holo cube out of the projector, hand shaking.

The Sapis Co-op security team exchange a look, and the woman pulls another holo cube out of the pile. She shows it to her partner. "Isn't this that girl we just got an alert to watch out for?"

The man nods. "Yeah. Her dad was claiming she'd been brainwashed."

Lebedevya shakes her head. "This is not true. None of this is true." She points a shaking finger at Lasadi. "You. Get out of here."

Lasadi raises her hands, acquiescing. "Absolutely, absolutely. This is definitely not our jurisdiction. Like I said, we'll take the forgeries and get out of your hair."

"We'd actually like to have a word," says the Sapis Co-op woman. "Ms. Lebedevya, if you'll come with us?"

Lebedevya steps back, the fear in her eyes shifting to something calmer. She's already forming her defense, Lasadi thinks, her con artist's mind unfolding her next play.

But then Lebedevya twists her cuff and types in a sequence. There's a faint noise as the vents around them click open, the quiet hiss of air as the ventilation system switches on.

"The work I have done here is too important to be derailed by my enemies like this," Lebedevya says, and she lifts her cuff to her wrist. When she speaks again, her voice echoes out of hidden speakers.

"My children," she says; her voice must be relayed throughout both levels. "In her lifetime, Saint Alixhi was met with enemies and skeptics, her work was torn down by those who did not believe. As the reincarnation of the Dreaming Saint, I, too, am met with enemies and skeptics. I will come again to finish this work, but for now it is time for us all to dream the final dream, as we have prepared to do. Join me. Together we will walk forward as one. Dream well, my children."

She closes her eyes with a peaceful smile.

Ruby gasps in horror as air hisses through the vents around them. "What have you done?"

CHAPTER 32
RAJ

NOTHING HAPPENS.

The hiss of the vents should be accompanied by cloying incense, syrup-thick dreams, tumbling nightmares. And, probably, death. Instead, fresh air flows into the vault. The Sapis Cooperative security team look at each other with confusion. Ruby swears under her breath.

Lasadi's the only one who doesn't react.

Raj studies her profile; he knows that look on her face. In fact, Raj knew that look before he knew Lasadi's name. Back when they scrapped in Parr Sumilang's museum, the very first time they met, he'd thought he had the upper hand. And then he'd seen the tilt of her eyebrow, the quirk of her mouth, the spark of mischief in her eye, and he'd realized she had a blade to his throat.

Lebedevya blinks her eyes open once more, expression of placid acceptance of her martyrdom shifting into confusion. She frowns down at her cuff and types in another sequence; her cuff blinks red with an error sign.

"Oh, sorry," Lasadi says. Lebedevya rounds on her in fury. "Were you expecting that rather large shipment of white flame to aerosolize through the vents? We found your stash and turned it over to the local authorities. Standard IASC procedure."

"It's not illegal!" Lebedevya turns to the Sapis Co-op security team, cheeks pink with anger. "Not out here. Nothing I've done is illegal."

"The drugs aren't illegal on Sapis," the Sapis Co-op woman says brusquely. She nods to her companion, who slaps a pair of cuffs on Lebedevya's wrists before the other woman realizes he's about to. "Attempted mass murder still is, though."

"You'll have to schedule it for another day," Lasadi says to Lebedevya, then turns to the Sapis Cooperative team and indicates the data cubes in the reliquary. "If you don't have enough evidence to arrest her for attempted murder, this ought to help you make the case for unlawful detainment and fraud."

"Thank you, Agent Fayed," says the woman. She nods sharply to Raj. "Agent Danning."

Raj salutes. "Absolutely."

Lebedevya's security guard, the handsome one, is still holding Ruby's arm. He watches as his boss is marched out of the room as though deciding whether or not it's in his contract to stop them.

Must not be.

Raj claps Handsome on the arm; he jumps.

"Sorry about the nerve blade back there," Raj says.

"I didn't want to hurt you for real, but I couldn't blow my cover."

"That's all right," Handsome says carefully.

"Looks like you dodged a bullet today — though I guess you're out of a job. But don't worry. Agent Fayed and I would be happy to act as references when you're interviewing for your next gig."

Handsome straightens his shoulders. "Really?"

Raj grins at him. "Of course." Behind him, Lasadi has already started taking down paintings with care. "I suppose the International Anti-Smuggling Commission will need to seize all of these to determine if they're forgeries. Give us a hand?"

Handsome gestures to Ruby. "But the prisoner?"

"Might as well put her to work, too." Raj slips off Ruby's cuffs. "There's nowhere to run, Wilson," he says sternly. "But if you cooperate, I bet we can work out a deal."

Ruby blows a kiss at him behind Handsome's back, then reaches for one of Katriana's sketches. Her dark fingers caress the frame wistfully, then she takes a deep breath and turns to Handsome.

"Be a love and pull down that curtain so we can wrap these?"

In less than an hour they've cleared out the vault and reconvened on the *Nanshe*. The Sapis Co-op security team hadn't asked too many questions; they've got their hands full with a dozen angry families who began furiously demanding answers as soon as Absolon shared the news.

Raj grabs the final crate from Handsome and thanks him, waves a friendly goodbye from the *Nanshe*'s cargo bay door. They'll have a full flight home with the addition of Katriana and Aya Marga, but right now the cargo level is quiet. Ruby's in the medbay, running Katriana and Marga through the autodoc diagnostics. Absolon, Alex, and Jay are finishing up a last-minute resupply run. That leaves only Lasadi in the cargo bay, securing crates of artwork in the *Nanshe*'s cache.

Raj carries the last crate over and sets it on the pile, then leans a shoulder against the wall, watching her a moment.

He spent most of his time on Sapis Station in dreams he can barely remember: cartwheeling sea stars and dark kelp forests and drowning on the taste of salt. Nowhere in that menagerie of dreams had his mind dared conjure an image of Lasadi Cazinho with her fingers tangled in his hair and her lips searching for his.

Yet it had happened.

Given the past hour's flurry of activity, this is the first time he's managed to catch her alone. He's been running this moment through his mind nonstop, and he can't tell if the tremor in his stomach is anticipation or anxiety. Probably a bit of both.

Raj clears his throat. "Can I have a word, Captain?"

Lasadi straightens from tightening a strap, then turns slowly to meet his gaze. She's not smiling, but her expression isn't cold. She's tense, but not wary. She's emanating quiet, steady calm, but Raj can make out her pulse fluttering in the hollow of her throat.

For a brief, soul-searing moment he thinks she'll take it all back. Tell him she got carried away by the heat of the moment, and he'll say, *That white flame's a wild drug, yeah?* and —

The corner of Lasadi's mouth slips into a smile. Her gaze trails down his body and back up, setting every nerve on fire. She takes a step closer, almost close enough to touch.

"Yes, Raj?"

He swallows, hard, trying to remember how to talk.

"I had a question for you," Raj says, but before he can ask it, she's shifted forward to close the gap between them, lifting her chin. Her body a handsbreadth from his; he can feel the warmth radiating from her skin. It's an invitation. One he'll gladly take.

Her lips are soft and sweet and warm, and her scent ignites him: vetiver laced with caramel and a hint of smoke. Is it her shampoo? A perfume? He's dying to explore every inch of her, but he doesn't touch her, not yet. He's still not convinced she won't vanish the moment he does — and if this is a dream, he wants to let it last as long as possible. His body blazes with heat when her teeth catch his lower lip, and for a moment he doesn't remember how to breathe.

She breaks the kiss, but doesn't step back. Raj lets his fingertips rest gently on her waist, careful to avoid the place where she flinched away from his touch earlier. He'd felt what seemed like the ridge of an old scar, maybe, and he wonders if it's still painful to touch or if she's self-conscious. Gods willing, there will be plenty of time to indulge that curiosity later. He lowers his lips to kiss her cheek, then her neck, breathing deep and memorizing every detail: the mole beneath her ear, the tempo of her pulse, the wisps of her escaped hair tickling his cheek.

"I meant every word I said earlier," Lasadi says; her breath across his ear is electric and Raj straightens to meet her gaze. "Does that answer your question?"

"Almost." Raj tucks a strand of hair back behind her ear. "Are you still scared?"

She searches his gaze a moment as though trying to find the answer, and there's not just banked embers in her smoky brown eyes anymore. There's fire.

"No," she finally says. "I've never felt more right about something in my life."

He kisses her again, more chastely than he wants to, but there will be time for more later. For now, he can hear Ruby's boot on the floor above, hear Katriana's laugh. Lasadi's comm is chiming and he catches the message flash on her cuff. Jay and the rest will be here in five.

Lasadi takes a deep breath with her eyes closed, and she looks so peaceful. Gods but he'll do anything to make sure she always looks that content.

"Time to get this show on the road," she says when she opens her eyes, and Raj can't help but grin. Wherever the *Nanshe*'s headed next, he and Lasadi are going there together.

CHAPTER 33
RUBY

Ruby doesn't relax until the ambient noise of the *Nanshe* has become a comfortable background hum around her and Sapis Station is a mote of dust in the distance against the brilliant swirling glow of Bixia Yuanjin. Not until she's gathered with the rest of the crew and Aya Marga in the cargo hold and the celebratory whiskey is flowing.

Something about the ship dynamic has fundamentally shifted in the short amount of time since she left it to enter Annika Lebedevya's labyrinth of dreams. Raj and the captain have finally gotten over themselves, haven't they — and if they're trying to hide it they're doing a shit job. Raj's fingers linger flagrantly on Lasadi's when he passes her a drink, and when Lasadi laughs now she sounds like she's dropped a decade of worries. Ruby catches Jay's attention with a raised eyebrow and tilt of her head towards the lovebirds. He rolls his eyes in answer. She can't wait to badger the story out of Raj later.

But it's not just the drop in tension between those two. Nor is it the added presence of Kitty and Marga and Absolon.

Stepping back on board the *Nanshe* felt like coming home. The people gathered here in the cargo bay around the crates of stolen paintings feel like family. For the first time since Ruby left the convent as a young woman, she's not anxiously wondering what happens next — because whatever it is, she'll be after it with this crew at her back.

"Does everyone have a drink?" Lasadi asks, and assent comes from around the group. Las lifts her bulb. "Then let's toast to a boring flight back to Artemis City. And welcome aboard the *Nanshe*, Aya."

When the cheers die down, Marga lifts a hand. She's been gaining color since Lebedevya's drugs have washed out of her system, and the autodoc seems to think she's fine beyond mild dehydration and a few bumps and bruises. Same with Kitty, though Kitty's got a faint tremor to her hands that Ruby doesn't like. The autodoc has her on a regimen of recovery stims that should help even her out while she comes down from the white flame and whatever else Lebedevya gave her, and Ruby and Absolon have already agreed to tag-team keeping an eye on her. He's with her in the medbay while she sleeps right now.

"I suppose I owe you all an apology," says Marga.

"A story, maybe," Raj says. "But we don't need an apology. Lebedevya was one hell of a con artist."

Marga gives him a sad smile, but doesn't argue. She takes a sip of her tea, then cups it in her hands. "I'm the one that reached out to Annika Lebedevya," she says.

"Years ago, I read a profile on her interest in Saint Alixhi. From what I read — and from our conversations — I thought we had a shared interest in making sure the saint's artwork was respectfully preserved."

Marga looks down at her hands. "Annika said she loved my vision of starting a museum of Saint Alixhi's works at the convent. It would have saved our finances, but we couldn't have afforded to buy any real paintings on our own."

Ruby can guess where this con is headed. "And Lebedevya said she would help."

Marga nods. "She asked for my advice in navigating all the fakes that came up for auction. She told me she would buy pieces and donate them to the convent, but she kept being outbid."

"You believed her?" Lasadi asks.

"The antiquities trade is competitive. And opaque; it can be impossible to find out who purchased a given piece. So, yes. I believed that Annika had been outbid — but she'd been buying them for herself all along. And then the reliquary — "

Marga takes a deep breath. Ruby strokes her back, as gentle as Marga had done for her when she was a child.

"When I saw the reliquary come up for auction, I was as certain as I could be without seeing it myself that it was real. This time, Annika said we had to go in together to avoid being outbid. She told me a horror story about the collector who was planning on buying it, and I agreed to help. I pulled the convent's funds."

"Why didn't you talk to anyone?" Ruby asks.

"Annika convinced me that the reason people were able to outbid her was that someone at the convent was sharing our information. I didn't believe her at first, but after I spoke with her in person, I even started to remember things — I thought it might have been Julio. He wouldn't have meant it maliciously, but he does love to talk."

"She planted those memories."

Marga nods sadly. "Once I gave her the money to bid on the reliquary, she stopped responding to my messages. I went myself to find out what had happened, but by the time I realized she'd cheated me — that she'd been cheating me the whole time — she was about to leave Artemis City. I was so ashamed of what I'd done, I wanted to make it right. I decided to follow her to Sapis."

"Well." Lasadi slides open one of the crates and begins to carefully extract the paintings within. "We'll at least make sure Lebedevya honors her original agreement with you. Sapis Co-op let us take anything we wanted to check for forgeries."

"I couldn't take these."

"Lebedevya never would have known to buy them without you," Ruby points out. "And she told you she'd donate them. The paintings should stay in Artemis City to help the convent."

Marga is quiet as they carefully unwrap the rest of the paintings, setting them adrift in the cargo bay like a pop-up art installation. "I hadn't seen any of these in person," she finally says, reverence in her gaze. "They're beautiful."

Alex touches one with a fingertip, spinning it gently to face Marga. "Is this one of her alien ones?" The painting is a haunting nightscape, deep reds and charcoals of iron-rich soil silvered by snow and moonlight.

"One of her human ancestry series," Marga says. "From the old solar system." She frowns as her attention falls on one of Kitty's sketches. She takes it carefully in hand to study it. "This one's a forgery. Very talented, but a forgery nonetheless."

Ruby laughs. "Good thing you weren't around to advise Lebedevya when we sold her that batch, then. That's Kitty's work."

"Ruby Nicole Quiñones!" Marga gives her a look of complete shock. "You scammed Annika?"

"It was for the greater good," Ruby says quickly, but Marga's disapproval doesn't diminish. "And we refilled the convent's coffers with the profits. We already gave it back."

"Does the ayalasi know you got the money through lying and forgery?"

Ruby winces. "She didn't ask. Teresa knows, though."

Marga's shoulders slump. "Teresa will never forgive me."

"Of course she will, Aya." Ruby pulls the older woman into a hug, holding her until the tension eases from her shoulders, then giving her one last squeeze before letting her go.

Marga strokes a finger down the frame the sketch is caught in. "This is very good, but I can't accept it for the collection."

"It'll look nice in the *Nanshe*," Lasadi says; she's returning from the *Nanshe*'s cache with another bundle, which she begins to unwrap. "We could use some artwork to brighten the place up. Ah, yes. Here we go."

Lasadi peels aside the rest of the wrapping to reveal the reliquary crate: unassuming dark wood inlaid with wire scrolls. Ruby's heart sinks. Another forgery, Lasadi had called it when they were in the vault with the Sapis Co-op security team. Ruby hadn't believed her at first — she'd *felt* Saint Alixhi's presence when she knelt beside Lebedevya. She'd felt how holy it was in her very being. But then Lebedevya had opened the lid to reveal that the reliquary was empty. Even if this crate had once held Saint Alixhi's relics, the saint herself is still lost to history.

Aya Marga stares at the crate, gutted. "I was so certain," she murmurs. "I threw so much away, all for a fake."

"I'm honestly surprised Lebedevya never opened it," Ruby says.

"She was a true believer in her own way," Marga says. "She lied enough about her devotion to everyone else that I think she even believed it herself."

Lasadi's watching them both with that same playful gleam in her eye as when Lebedevya tried and failed to gas them all. Alex is grinning like a fox. Jay takes a nonchalant sip of whiskey that doesn't quite hide his smile.

"What are you all about?" Ruby demands.

Lasadi holds out a hand to Marga. "If you'd do the honors, Aya?"

Marga looks puzzled, but she reaches for the lid of the crate, easing it open. And she gasps. Ruby's skin blazes hot, then cold, the fine hairs on the back of her neck and her arms standing at attention. The pile of data sticks and holo cubes is gone, and in their place is a yellowed skull, crossed arm bones, finger bones strung on gold wire and curled gently as though in rest, ribs laid in neat rows, pelvis, femurs, feet. All lovingly nestled in protective blue silk that has faded with age.

Ruby doesn't even hear the curse that comes out of her mouth, she only catches Aya Marga's bemusement. "Sorry, Aya. But you said this was a fake? And this is — isn't this . . . ?"

"This is the work of someone who's the master of his craft," Alex says smugly.

"You made these relics?" Ruby asks.

"I *stole* them. C'mon."

Aya Marga bursts out laughing, her eyes glistening with tears. "Of course you did."

"Cap had me running all over the place," Alex says. "'Alex, go break into the safe behind the painting in Lebedevya's office.' 'Alex, go disconnect that pile of drugs so we don't all get murdered.' 'Alex, go steal a cursed saint's skeleton and leave some incriminating evidence in its place.' — Sorry, Saint Alixhi," he says to the bones. "No offense."

"We couldn't have done it without you," Lasadi says, and Alex shrugs like it's nothing, though the tips of his ears flush a shade darker, his shoulders stand a touch straighter.

"Thanks, little brother," Ruby says. He winks, and she turns to lift the cover gently back over the Dreaming Saint. *We'll take you home,* Ruby promises silently, fingers drifting over the smooth wood surface.

Saint Alixhi's empty eye sockets stare back as the lid settles into place.

"So," Raj says. "Success?"

Ruby sighs. "Mostly. I'm still worried about Kitty. Lebedevya was very skilled at implanting suggested memories. It'll take us some time to help her sort through what she was 'remembering' there." She turns to Marga with a frown. "Can you speak with her?"

"Of course. I'll see what I can do for her." Marga looks back down at the crate with Saint Alixhi's bones. "I'm going to get some rest for now. I think some real sleep will do me good."

The crew works in silence to repack the paintings as Marga leaves; when the work is done, Lasadi pours them all another round. Her expression is serious.

"We've heard how Kitty and Marga are," Lasadi says to Ruby. "How about you? Did she put you under?"

Ruby glances around the ring of expectant faces. Her instinct is to say no and change the subject — after all, it's hardly a big deal. Lebedevya tried to skew her memories of Richard, a person who never existed, so her brain isn't having any trouble sorting true from false. But the other memories? The ones about her parents?

Is none of their business, Ruby thinks. But that doesn't mean she can't ask them for help.

She takes a deep breath and locks eyes with Alex; she owes him this, at least. "I thought I remembered some things about our parents," she says. "Flashes, only. Like, being on a ship with them that was taking fire. And right before they left us at the convent door,

Mom told me they'd be back soon and then she . . . *did* something to me to make me forget." Ruby touches the back of her neck, where she'd felt the sharp pinch in her memory. "Or at least that's what Lebedevya made me remember. Impossible to say if it's true, but I thought I saw their faces."

Alex gnaws on his lower lip a moment, then reaches for his comm. Flips open a file and floats his comm over to her. "Did they look like this?"

It's a pair of ident cards: a man and a woman whose genes could certainly have combined to create Ruby and Alex. The man has Alex's high cheekbones and angular jaw; Ruby would bet money the same contagious, broad smile splits his face. He's not smiling in the ident photo, though, his expression is grave. The woman is the same one who's been haunting Ruby's memories, with Ruby's full lips and spray of freckles across her nose and cheeks — though her head is shaved and her face is more angular, a set to her jaw that warns people not to cross her.

"Where the hell did you get this?"

"The identity fixer," Alex says. "I was going to show you, once we finished this job."

"You've had this for a week?" Ruby stares at him, shocked. "And you didn't tell me?"

Alex snatches back his comm, glaring. "Oh, are we working together to find our parents now? Because you haven't shared a single thing you learned at Auburn Station with me."

"Because I didn't learn much."

"Well, maybe I didn't learn much, either," Alex shoots back, and Ruby holds up a hand.

"I'm sorry, you're right." She sighs. "Alex, will you help me?"

Her little brother's fierce glare fades, which is good. Anger doesn't suit him, and it was breaking Ruby's heart to be the source of it. She holds out an arm and he finally relents, hauling her into a bear hug. Ruby laughs, caught off-guard.

"Saints in hell, when did you get so strong?"

"Muscles are built with effort, not excuses." Alex nods solemnly to Jay. "Isn't that right."

"You got it," Jay laughs. And his expression softens, kind. "Alex and I have been talking, and we've got some ideas of where to start searching for answers. We're all here to help, Ruby. If that's what you want."

"I do." It's not even a question, not anymore. She needs to know what happened to her parents, but more than that, she needs Alex and Raj and Lasadi and Jay to be there when she does.

"Maybe Vash and Gracie will have some ideas," says Raj. "They've been running the Traveler's Emporium longer than any of us have been alive. And we still need to give them that totem I picked up for them — "

"I think you mean the totem *I* picked up," says Lasadi.

Raj grins. "Sorry, the totem *Las* picked up. And Vash said she had a quick job for us when we do. A simple pick-up and delivery."

Ruby lifts an eyebrow. "Is it something Vash made? Because some of those explode."

"If it explodes, I'm out," Lasadi says. "I like this ship too much."

"Vash's inventions only explode on purpose," Raj

says quickly. "And we don't have to worry about that. This job should be pretty straightforward."

"Good, then," Ruby says. "After this one, I could use an easy job."

Ruby grins at Alex and raises her bulb of whiskey in toast. The kid she remembers, the one who made up codes and leapt off balconies and drove the ayas crazy? He's not gone. He's just grown whip-smart and goofy and clever and so, so much stronger than she thought he was.

She can't wait to take on the world with him.

CHAPTER 34
LASADI

LASADI CAN'T SLEEP, WHICH SHE'S BEEN GETTING USED TO, but tonight is different. Instead of anxiety over decisions she doesn't know how to make, her mind is racing on the buzz of a job well done — and well toasted to.

It's been little more than a month since she decided to go back and save the charmer with the Arquellian accent, but it feels like yesterday. Feels like yesterday when Ruby and Alex first set foot on the ship, since those awkward initial dinners where each of them was trying to suss the others out to find out who they could trust.

Trust had come slowly, but it had always, inevitably, felt like the correct decision, every time Lasadi made it. And tonight, with every one of her crew home safe and sharing a drink in the cargo hold, it had felt right. For the first time in three years, Lasadi feels like she's home. Like she's among family.

She and Raj had stayed up talking long after the

others went to bed, not about anything particular or profound, just telling each other stories.

He spins yarns so vividly it's like she's there with him. Reliving the aftermath of a practical joke while a student at the Mar-Alif officer's academy. Tasting every morsel of a delicious seafood feast, laughing together at the cousin who'd been caught out after curfew even as Raj made it home free, taking in the sunset on a southern Arquellian beach, the warm wind caressing her cheek and sand between her toes. She'd never wanted to visit Arquelle before, but as the bottle of whiskey emptied, she found herself making plans with Raj. *When we go to this town, when we travel to that beach, when we explore this place.*

She'd shared her own tales, the simple act of talking bringing back people from the dead — CLA colleagues and old friends. They didn't talk about the war, not specifically. But he'd asked about the crew of Mercury Squadron, and sharing with him had felt like an honor to their memories.

It also had felt like a safer topic than her family. Raj had probed in that direction, too, but Lasadi isn't ready. She can't talk about her grandmother without explaining that her family thinks she's dead, she can't talk about her siblings without explaining that Evvi Faye is writing letters to Lasadi's ghost — letters that Lasadi hasn't known how to answer.

Lasadi also hadn't been ready to act on the implied invitation in his eyes when the bottle of whiskey ran dry. She'd been comfortable and confident and *happy* over the — olds, it had been *three hours* they'd been talking. She'd wanted to go to bed with that glow; she's not ready to navigate whatever horror or pity she'll see on his face when he gets his first glimpse of her scars.

So she'd gone to her cabin and he to his.

She thought she'd fall right to sleep, but the whiskey has made her mind a whirl of thoughts: snippets of remembered conversation and story from the evening, Raj's voice in her ear, little turns of phrase and teasing jokes, and, most loudly, something he didn't actually say, because she hadn't actually brought up Evvi Faye's letters.

Seriously, Las, she can hear Raj saying. *What's the harm in writing her back?*

Lasadi isn't falling asleep, and she doesn't have a good answer for that question no matter how her mind races to find one. Lasadi takes a deep, shaking breath, pulls out her tablet, and opens a new message to Evvi.

✳

The adventure continues in the next book.

Want more of Raj and Lasadi's story? Don't miss the free Nanshe Chronicles prequel novella, *Artemis City Shuffle.*

Head to jessiekwak.com/nanshe for more.

ABOUT JESSIE KWAK

Jessie Kwak has always lived in imaginary lands, from Arrakis and Ankh-Morpork to Earthsea, Tatooine, and now Portland, Oregon. As a writer, she sends readers on their own journeys to immersive worlds filled with fascinating characters, gunfights, explosions, and dinner parties.

When she's not raving about her latest favorite sci-fi series to her friends, she can be found sewing, mountain biking, or out exploring new worlds both at home and abroad.

(Author photo by Robert Kittilson.)

Connect with me:
www.jessiekwak.com
jessie@jessiekwak.com

facebook.com/JessieKwak

twitter.com/jkwak

instagram.com/kwakjessie

THE BULARI SAGA

With stakes this high, humanity doesn't need a hero. They need someone who can win.

Complete 5-book series + 3 prequel novellas + bonus short stories = over 500,000 words of adventure.

Willem Jaantzen didn't ask to be a hero. He just wants to keep his family safe in the shifting sands of Bulari's underground — and to get the city's upper crust to acknowledge just how far he's come since his days as an orphaned street kid. With his businesses thriving and his dark past swept into the annals of history, it looks like he has everything he could ever ask for. Until, that is, his oldest rival turns up murdered and the blame — and champagne — begins to flow.

It turns out Thala Coeur died as she lived: sowing chaos. And when a mysterious package bearing her call sign shows up on Jaantzen's doorstep, he and his family are quickly swallowed up in a web of lies, betrayals, and interplanetary politics. It'll only take one stray spark to start another civil war in the underworld, and Jaantzen's going to have to pull out every play from his notorious past if he wants to keep his city from going up in flames.

Jaantzen never wanted to be a hero, but that might just be a good thing. Because a hero could never stop the trouble that's heading humanity's way.

The Bulari Saga is a five-book series featuring gunfights, dinner parties, explosions, motorcycle chases, underworld intrigue, and a fiercely plucky found family who have each other's backs at every step. Perfect for fans of The Expanse, Firefly, and The Godfather.

Start the adventure today at jessiekwak.com/bulari-saga

DID YOU LIKE THE BOOK?

As a reader, I rely on book recommendations to help me pick what to read next.

As a writer, book recommendations are the most powerful way for me to get the word out to new readers.

If you liked this book, please leave a review on the platform of your choice — or tell a friend! It's the easiest way to help authors you enjoy keep producing great work.

Cheers!

Jessie